FATED HEARTS

SHADOW CITY: SILVER MATE

JEN L. GREY

THE COOL DECEMBER night air blew past me, and the half-moon shone down, igniting the moon magic in my blood and speeding up the healing of the fresh bullet wound in my calf. But even that didn't comfort me.

The negative energy from the man standing before us swirled with the tension from PawPaw, Mom, and Nana as our group faced down the enemy wolf pack. Annie and Cyrus flanked the three of them, and Cyrus's hand inched toward the pistol holstered at his waist.

Adding to the tense atmosphere, the sounds of nocturnal creatures, such as raccoons and flying squirrels, were missing. The woods and the wolves surrounding us were quiet, unnaturally so. The animals sensed the danger.

Griffin slowly moved around Eliza, positioning himself behind Cyrus as Sterlyn bent her knees, readying to grab the knife hidden at her ankle under her jeans.

Looking over her shoulder, Eliza focused her forest green eyes on Circe and Aspen, the two witches in front of Killian and me. She ran a hand over her light caramel hair, which was pulled into a bun, and when her hand was fully behind her head, she pointed at the sky. She had to be communicating something to the other witches.

My gaze kept going back to Mom's ex. I wasn't sure what to call him. *Boyfriend* didn't seem like a strong enough word because Mom had almost mated with him, but *mate* didn't fit either because Dad had been her fated. The one word that might fit made me want to vomit—*lover*.

I'd just stick with ex.

He was attractive for a man old enough to be my father, but his ice-gray eyes held no warmth, and his spiked, light blond hair probably mirrored whatever he had chained around his heart. This man...this alpha...seemed dead set on harming Mom and everyone she cared about.

The fifty or so wolves who had appeared from behind the red cedars and oaks were hunkered down, awaiting a command. And this wasn't even all of them. The number of scents in the air indicated there was double that number in the area.

The ex's—er, *Tom's* words repeated in my head. *Turn around and head back inside.*

He wanted us to return to the secret government building from which we'd just rescued PawPaw's pack. The very location where humans had run blood tests and forced wolves to shift so they could learn about our kind's genetics for gods knew what reasons.

Mom stood straighter and stepped in front of the group. Though she was a normal wolf without extra power from the moon, she wanted to keep his attention on herself. Her long hair hung limply, appearing a murky dark brown without any of its normal cinnamon highlights. I didn't have to see her cognac eyes to know they were glowing from her wolf surging forward as she stared at him.

Chest heaving, Killian moved closer to me. His dark

chocolate brown eyes flicked to mine as our arms brushed and our fated-mate connection buzzed to life. His short cappuccino hair was messier than usual, and despite our dire situation, I couldn't help but admire his full lips and strong cheekbones. His closeness and his delicious sandalwood scent were keeping me grounded.

The others will be here in a few minutes, Jewel, he linked, using our new mate connection.

We both knew getting help was likely futile. Though most of our wolf shifter allies who'd arrived earlier today were heading our way, we were at a huge disadvantage. The two hundred members of PawPaw's pack, Mom, and Chad, who we'd barely rescued, had been drugged for over a week and weren't in fighting condition. That left us with Sierra, Luna, Lowe, Scott, April, and Collin from our pack, the two angels—Rosemary and Eleanor—the three demons—Levi, Bune, and Zagan—the vampire royals Ronnie and Alex, Darrell from the silver wolf pack, and the witches—Herne, Aurora, and Cordelia.

Our only blessing was that the witches, angels, demons, and silver wolves gave us a strategic edge over Tom and his pack, but sometimes, quantity *did* matter when there were tons of the enemy against one of us, and they'd caught us by surprise. We'd expected to fight the humans guarding the building, not supernaturals who had betrayed us.

"Tom, I understand that I hurt you—" Mom started.

"Hurt me?" He laughed harshly and narrowed his gaze. "How about obliterated me and took away the future we had planned alongside your *father*?"

My heart constricted, and I cringed. I didn't like him saying that to Mom. The only person she should've ever had future plans with was Dad.

"Now wait just a minute." PawPaw puffed out his

chest. His body was frail from lack of movement, but hopefully, anyone who wasn't around him often wouldn't notice. He turned slightly, and I could see his warm brown eyes stare down our threat. A streak of gray stubble grew down his cheek from his ear, visible against his black hair. Before his capture, he hadn't had any gray in his beard. It added wisdom to his look but also aged him compared to the much younger man in front of him. "She found her *fated mate*. You can't blame her for that."

"At one time, I would've listened to you." Tom wrinkled his nose. "But now I understand why *she* did what she did. She was raised by a weak-minded man who thought a fated connection trumped promises made to others."

"But it *does*." Nana threw up her hands, her oily, silver-streaked chestnut hair barely moving as it clung to her face. The moonlight gave her already pale olive complexion a more ghoulish tone.

The humans hadn't only kept the captured pack asleep the entire time—they also hadn't given them access to sunlight or nature. Their wolves were weakened just as much as, if not more than, their human selves.

"Are you implying that because you were supposed to choose each other that night, she was already committed to you?" Nana pressed, trying to drive her point home.

I had a sinking suspicion he wouldn't get it, mainly because he didn't *want* to.

"That's exactly what I'm saying." Tom stepped forward, his feet rustling through dead leaves. He wasn't even attempting to stay quiet, and it was a domination tactic, as if he could make all the noise he wanted and remain safe. "She pledged herself to me."

Something inside me snapped, and with the rage, the buzz of Killian's touch, and the moon surging through me,

I couldn't remain quiet. "If that were the case, she would've never been able to complete the bond with *my father*."

Tom's hands clenched at his sides as he turned his wrath to me.

Sterlyn's iridescent lavender eyes cut toward me as her long silver hair whipped around her face. Her skin glowed faintly in the moonlight, another trait of the silver wolves' true alpha. The fuller the moon, the more radiant her skin became.

Though I'd become part of Killian's pack only a few hours ago when we'd completed our bond, this was the first time I was relieved she could no longer link with me—until I felt Killian's immense displeasure and concern slam into me, making my lungs struggle to work.

Jewel, what the hell are you doing? Killian linked as his jaw twitched in a way I'd never seen before.

"You're the *spawn* that resulted from their union?" Tom's chest heaved as he searched the group. "If you're here, where is *he*?"

My heart squeezed. He had no idea Dad was dead. The pain of losing my father was just as overwhelming today as it had been the day Mom and I had felt Dad's link extinguish within our chests.

I wouldn't give the jerk the satisfaction of knowing he was dead. "He's here with us and will give me strength to protect us from your vile ass."

Better for this man to spew his hate at me than at Mom. I hadn't been there to protect her a few weeks ago, during the silver wolf pack's battles with the demon wolves and the demons, but I was here and able to now. Besides, she was a normal wolf, whereas I was a silver. It made sense for Tom to channel his anger at me.

Are you trying to make him focus on you? Killian linked, then went still. *Of course that's what you're doing.*

I'd expected him to understand now that he'd put together my plan, but when fear and anger coursed through our connection, adding to the weight in my chest, I was certain that knowing had only increased his frustration. *She's weak from being asleep for so long and can't handle the burden. I need to protect her.*

Killian growled, and Griffin's shoulders shook with laughter. The top of Sterlyn's mate's slightly longer honey-brown hair fell into his face as he glanced at me. His hazel eyes lightened with mirth before darkening again.

Killian linked with the rest of the pack that was heading back to the farmhouse with the rescued captives: *Where are you?*

Sierra replied immediately. *April stayed with Aurora at the farmhouse to keep an eye on the shifters. The rest of us, including the freed shifters, are halfway to the house from the facility, but we're moving a little slower since Herne and Cordelia are with us. Maybe five minutes tops. Darrell and Alex, with their silver wolf and vampire speed, are a few minutes ahead. Has the fight started? Do we need to carry the witches or leave them behind to catch up?*

It would be hard for Killian's wolves to carry the witches because they weren't larger like the silver wolves and Annie. Since the moon was half full, both the silver wolves and Annie, the lone demon wolf, were larger and stronger than the regular wolves.

Don't leave them, Killian commanded. *I don't know how many wolf shifters our enemy brought, but we don't want the witches to get into trouble and have no way to contact us. Just stay back and take out the enemy pack from behind if possible.*

Maybe that plan would work. Tom's pack might not expect some of us to circle back and attack. Tom seemed focused solely on his hatred of those of us standing before him.

"If it's any help, I'm Bart's nephew," Cyrus rasped from his place at the front, closest to Tom. Though he was Sterlyn's twin and an alpha heir in his own right, he wasn't the pack's true alpha, so his skin didn't glow as much, and his silver hair was several shades darker than his sister's. His irises were the same shade of silver as Sterlyn's, but there was no purple in his eyes. He and Killian were the same height in human form, giving him an inch or two over Tom. He continued, "And I can see why she picked him over you."

I wanted to chastise him, but my words would still have the most impact on them all. I was the product of Mom and Dad's love and represented everything Tom hated. I would bear the brunt of his anger and protect my former pack, my current pack, and everyone I loved.

"That will make it all the sweeter." Tom lowered his head as if he was about to charge. "To know I am the reason his *mate*, *daughter*, and *family* are being tortured and experimented on."

Four shadow forms floated down from the sky, two of them landing behind Tom while the other two moved into the trees. They must have been getting a headcount of Tom's pack. One of the shadows behind Tom had mocha eyes, and the other had icy black eyes, informing me they were Levi and Zagan.

If the demons were here, that meant the angels likely were, too. They'd been back at the government site, fighting the armed humans so we could escape into the woods. They must have been heading to the farmhouse when they heard what was going on below.

Good. The fight was about to take place. We were poking at Tom, hoping to provoke a reckless reaction from him.

That was our safest bet.

"You may have more people on your side, *boy*," Eliza spat, "but you should know that a group of people may be stronger than they appear."

Tom threw his head back and laughed so hard, his belly contracted. After a few seconds, he stopped and glared at the older witch. "And you have *no* idea what my pack and I are capable of."

There was no way to delay the fight. We had burned as much time as possible, and the surrounding wolves were growing restless. The one closest to me pawed at the ground and bared its teeth.

There was no question I would be his first target.

Fine. I'd accept his challenge. Little did he know what kind of wolf I was.

Annie lifted her chin, her honey-brown eyes wide. "We just helped over two hundred pack members escape a locked-down facility. You don't think we can take you?" She tilted her head, examining him, her light golden brown hair spilling over her shoulders.

"You escaped from humans, and you're about to see what a pack can do with a *true alpha* leading them." He raised his hands toward us as his irises turned almost white. The negative essence of his soul increased as he tapped into his wolf's power.

Low growls grew louder and morphed into snarls as Tom's pack moved forward.

Shift! Killian commanded, though I could still feel his displeasure and worry.

He didn't want these wolves to know I was a silver wolf, but we didn't have a choice. We'd waited as long as possible. If we'd changed into our animal forms already, the communication would've stopped sooner.

My skin tingled as my fur sprouted, but the enemy wolves had no intention of waiting for us to change for a fair fight.

They were out for blood.

As I attempted to spin around and shift, the wolf closest to me lunged.

CHAPTER TWO

FOR THOSE FEW SECONDS, while my body transitioned from two legs to four, my attacker flew toward me.

My calf screamed from the injury it had sustained while I was human. Shifting while injured was never ideal, but the wound wasn't fatal, and I'd have a better chance of defending myself on four legs. Luckily, the bullet had only grazed me; if it had lodged inside me, shifting would have made the damage worse.

Not that it mattered. As soon as I could move, he'd be on me.

My clothes ripped and fell in shreds at my feet, and the wolf's murky eyes locked on my injured leg as he soared toward me, his teeth bared. That was my salvation: he only wanted to injure me so I could be a lab rat when the attack was over.

Jewel! Killian linked, and his panic combined with mine. He was shifting as well, and there wasn't a damn thing he could do.

Bracing for the inevitable pain from the wolf's teeth, I

closed my eyes. Then a *whoosh* passed me, blowing a faint rose-peony scent in my face.

Rosemary.

A body thudded to the ground as I opened my eyes to find one of the most beautiful women I'd ever seen standing beside the wolf. Her huge charcoal wings expanded, and her purple-tinged burgundy hair fell down her back between them.

All my life, I'd been taught to keep my existence secret from supernaturals, but in the short amount of time I'd spent with Sterlyn and our allies, I'd learned how much stronger our group of mixed supernatural races was *together*.

I'm okay, I assured Killian as he finished his shift. His panic still mixed with mine. *Rosemary protected me.*

Thank gods. He looked my way just as another wolf lunged at Rosemary.

Flipping her feathers over, Rosemary used her left wing to shield her body. These wolves had no clue what they were up against. Most supernaturals didn't know much about angels because the angels had been confined inside Shadow City for over one thousand years.

I focused my attention on my mate and our allies. Another angel, Eleanor, was beside Killian, protecting him. Eleanor's blonde hair looked more golden in the moonlight, and her beige wings looked white next to Killian's dark brown fur. She stood at his side as she faced three wolves heading toward him.

I'm going to help PawPaw, Mom, and Nana. Under most circumstances, I'd have allowed my alpha to instruct me on what to do in battle, but this time, there was no question about where I needed to be. The four of us were Tom's ultimate targets.

As I moved forward, Circe raised her hands in front of her, her warm beige skin shadowed by the night. Her rich brown irises lightened as she chanted, *"Evoca ventum!"* The breeze picked up and swirled around her, lifting her midnight hair. Her black shirt flapped.

Aspen, her mate, stood next to her, following her lead. He chanted the same words but turned around, raising his hands in the opposite direction. His jet-black hair whipped into his face, and his ivory skin looked vampire pale.

I'm going with you, Killian linked, and I could hear his paws pounding the ground just a few steps behind me.

My fur ruffled as I ran between the two witches. Thankfully, it was too short to get in my eyes, unlike my long auburn hair in human form.

I scanned the area for immediate threats. Sterlyn, Annie, Cyrus, and Griffin were in wolf form, but Nana, PawPaw, and Mom were still human. Sterlyn and Annie flanked Nana, while Griffin and Cyrus flanked PawPaw.

Cold realization unfurled in my belly, and I stumbled. Their magic was too weak to allow them to shift. There was no telling what drugs the humans had pumped into their systems while they'd been held captive.

Several of the enemy wolves noticed that I was moving toward them, but that didn't matter. I had to get to my family.

Levi and Zagan stayed still, waiting for the perfect time to cause chaos.

The enemy wolves descended, five of them focused on Mom, Nana, and PawPaw. My heart raced as I realized I wouldn't reach my family in time.

Circe's whirlwind pushed past me and slammed into the enemy wolves, throwing them several feet away onto their backs, giving us more time.

As I picked up speed, a wolf howled a battle cry in the distance.

Backup was arriving.

I rushed past Eliza and watched her lift her hands out to her sides. She rasped, *"Evoca ventum!"* as I inched between Mom and Nana. Luckily, I was now out of the path of the wind.

The air whirled around us, preventing any of Tom's pack from reaching us as we prepared to fight. The witches had bought us time to get acclimated and shift before our opponents launched a direct attack.

I hunkered down, glaring at Tom and the cream wolf by his side, who was standing in front of Annie, and the tan one in front of PawPaw.

Is everyone okay? Killian linked with all his nearby pack members. *I heard a howl of warning.* He edged between PawPaw and Cyrus.

Chest expanding, I couldn't believe he'd found a way to make me love him more. He was as determined as I was to protect my family while also caring for his pack.

We're a mile out. That had to be Darrell and Alex catching up, Lowe replied. *But don't worry. We're coming.*

Be careful, Killian replied. *We don't know how many wolves are on their side.*

That was terrifying, but the only way out of this situation was to fight. *There are at least fifty here, so I'd guess they'd have double that to catch us off guard.* That was what I would do if I were in charge. I would want my strongest wolves around me to force us to retreat while the rest acted as lookouts for anyone the main pack couldn't see. *I bet they're tracking the shifters we rescued back to the farmhouse.* If Tom had an agreement with the humans to guarantee his pack's safety, they would need to get as many of us into the government building as they could.

Shit. Killian growled next to me as he hunkered lower. *You're right. We need to get through these assholes, and fast.*

The link in my chest tied to April shrank and hardened with fear. She linked, *The enemy is coming here? I'll tell the others so they can prepare to fight.*

That was the problem. Most of the rescued shifters were too weak to protect themselves. Chad had gotten away before Tom cut us off, and since he was a silver wolf, he should bounce back more quickly. *Is Chad with you all?* I asked.

He left a few minutes ago to join you, April answered as her panic increased.

Tom's hateful gaze locked on me. He tilted his head back as he examined my fur. He had to suspect there was something different about me, though I doubted he realized what I was since silver wolves had been in hiding for so long. Either way, Tom seemed like the entitled type. The realization that not only had Mom chosen another man over him but one who was stronger—as was their offspring— couldn't be sitting well with him.

"Hurt them just shy of *death,* and make sure you capture the angels and witches, too," Tom commanded, and his nostrils flared. "Make sure their hearts are beating when we drag them back to our *allies.*"

Lovely.

Sterlyn told Chad to circle back to you, April. He's on his way, Killian linked.

Some of April's tension eased, and I could only hope that the moon was recharging Chad quickly.

The wind petered out, and I glanced behind me to see

all three witches' faces lined with fatigue. They had drained what little magic they'd had left after the escape.

Rosemary and Eleanor stepped behind the witches with their wings extended. A wolf lay dead at Rosemary's feet, and blood splattered her cheek.

That angel was damn scary.

Now that there was no magic at play, the five wolves climbed to their feet as a gray wolf ran toward PawPaw. Killian and Cyrus moved to protect him, and more wolves charged from all sides at once, several targeting Eleanor and Rosemary.

They were attacking PawPaw as a distraction—not that they needed it. Only six of our wolves could fight.

Six of *their* wolves focused on me, and my pulse pounded in my ears. I'd only been in two real battles to date, and they'd occurred within the past two weeks. There were two things on my side—a lifetime of training and being a silver wolf. Due to the current phase of the moon, I was almost double their size.

I bared my teeth and surveyed each one. I wanted them to know I was on to their strategy. One wolf kept darting its gaze from me to Killian, giving me pause. It might be planning on attacking him as well and was trying to throw me off.

The wolf would soon learn I wasn't so easily fooled.

The wolves surged forward at once, testing to see if the witches would attempt another spell, but we had a different surprise up our sleeves that should give us a huge advantage.

Several wolves each attacked Annie, Cyrus, and Sterlyn. They were attempting to take out our largest wolves, though I doubted they understood what Annie was. Demon wolves hadn't even been known to silver wolves until recently. Annie's magic was at its height during a new moon, while the silver wolves were strongest during a full moon.

The remaining three wolves rushed Killian and Griffin as the six charged at me. Each of the five wolves who had been tossed onto their backs charged behind the rest, but my attackers soon blocked my view.

I'm coming to help as soon as I can, Killian linked as fear took root inside him.

I'm fine. Just focus on your fight. If you don't, you'll get injured, and I'll lose my mind.

Taking my own advice, I centered myself as the six wolves soared toward me. I crouched and rolled to the left, and three of the six hit the ground where I'd been standing a second ago. The two wolves closest to that side reached me first, and the smaller gray wolf opened her mouth and went for my left shoulder. I waited until she almost hit, then shifted my weight to my right. Her mouth missed my shoulder, and I bit into her neck.

The metallic scent and taste of blood overwhelmed my senses as my teeth thrashed through fur and skin. The amount of blood spilling from her neck couldn't be normal... I must have severed an artery.

Overwhelming guilt surged through me, nearly stealing my breath. I hadn't meant to hurt her that grievously; I'd just followed my natural instincts. But now wasn't the time to let my emotions get the best of me.

As if Fate were confirming that thought, a sharp pain seared into my side. My wolf took over again, and I jerked my head, ripping out the gray wolf's throat, and turned to find a red male wolf with blood coating his paw. He bared his teeth, drool dripping from his mouth, and a black wolf came around my other side.

The red wolf could've hurt me worse. Swatting me to get my attention had been an odd strategy, but I imagined his type of wolf enjoyed seeing the fear in his victim's eyes before he killed them.

Too bad. I wasn't scared, and I *definitely* wasn't a victim.

A whimper of pain gave my heart pause. When Sterlyn and Annie didn't react and I didn't feel any pain from Killian, I assumed the injured wolf was not on our side.

I snarled and made my move.

I lowered my head as if I were planning to bulldoze the black wolf. The red wolf would buy it, thinking I was scared of him. I needed him to feel confident. My side ached with each move, but I gritted through the pain.

You're hurt, Killian linked, his fear and panic strobing inside me like a beacon.

It's just a scratch, I replied, and began to play Mozart's *Eine kleine Nachtmusik* in my mind. During training, I'd discovered that certain classical songs could help a person endure pain, and this particular masterpiece helped me do that better. I channeled the song and gave myself over to my wolf, needing to make it out of this alive. If I didn't, I was fairly certain Killian wouldn't, either.

Another yelp sounded from the direction of Sterlyn and Annie, and my stomach churned. *What the hell is going on?*

The demons are attacking, and some of the wolves are freaking out, Killian replied. *Some are getting more determined.*

That must have been why the cries hadn't sounded quite pained. They were afraid.

Focusing on my task and on the music in my head, I

countered the black wolf's advances and steamrolled him onto his side. The red wolf leaped toward me and did exactly what I'd expected: he aimed for my back leg.

Once he'd committed his momentum, I kicked my back legs up like a rodeo bull. The red wolf tried to correct himself by pushing his legs in front of him, but I slammed my back paws into his head, letting my claws dig into his skull.

He went down with a *thunk*. That sickening feeling overtook me again, but I concentrated on the piece of music playing in my head, distracting my human side. Though I was a silver wolf, I wasn't sure my human counterpart was cut out for battle, considering the agony swirling around me.

The wolf lay still, and my stomach churned. I'd never experienced anything like this before. Training had taught me skills, but actually hurting and killing people was something I wasn't prepared for.

Not like this.

However, it was us or them, and we hadn't started this war. We hadn't turned our backs on the supernaturals to save our hides. In fact, Killian had made himself a target to protect us all.

The other three wolves were on me, and I pushed down harder on the red wolf's head as I jumped off. I needed to ensure he stayed knocked out for a while. I didn't want to kill a man or animal when they were that injured. It just didn't feel right.

The black wolf turned toward me, his dark eyes wide with rage. He went for my neck, no longer bothering with the illusion of not trying to wound me fatally. I stood on my back legs and swiped at his snout with my claws.

He stumbled back and pawed at his injured nose. He'd be miserable for a while.

As I turned to face the other three, I heard Mom's strangled cry.

CHAPTER THREE

MY HEAD JERKED in my mother's direction as uncomfortable tingles spread through me.

What I found was worse than I'd imagined. Three wolves were sneaking up on Killian as he engaged in battle with two, and Mom was running to protect him. Despite being weakened and in human form, she was trying to save my mate. Not only might I lose one of them, but I could lose both.

I *had* to get to them.

Killian! Watch out! I desperately warned. *Three are sneaking up behind you!*

As I ran forward, the light brown wolf targeting me sank her teeth into my shoulder, but adrenaline and fear made the pain almost unnoticeable. It felt like a bee sting, though it would hurt like hell later.

My wolf surged forward, taking the lead, just as desperate as I was to reach our mate. I turned my head, nipping into the side of the wolf's face. I thrashed her skin, wanting to cause as much damage as possible before she could obliterate my shoulder.

She whimpered and jerked back, releasing her hold.

Jewel, stay engaged. Your Mom and I are fine, Killian linked. *I'll be with you shortly. Just don't get hurt.*

As I was about to argue, one of the wolves who had been sneaking up behind Killian flew through the air and smacked into a large oak tree eight feet from me. My attention flicked back to Killian, and I saw a shadow form aiding him and Mom.

A demon had seen they were in trouble. I smirked. With their fellow pack members being tossed around by an invisible force, the wolves focused on Killian didn't seem so sure of themselves.

The other two wolves rushing me reached my sides. The cream one circled left as the dark gray one moved right. The light brown one I'd bitten had blood pouring down her face, but she still positioned herself in front of me as the black one moved in from behind. Luckily, the red wolf was still unconscious, or I'd have had five wolves to contend with.

My best bet was to injure them before they could take me down. I relinquished control to my wolf so my human side wouldn't be overcome with intense guilt.

I focused on the melody in my head, along with the whimpers and cries of the enemy wolves around us. The demons were our greatest asset since none of the regular wolves could see them. Thankfully, PawPaw and Nana had heard about them from Mom, and they'd seen them in the facility when we'd helped them escape, or they would've been petrified, too.

The four wolves circled me. My wolf threw her head back and howled at the moon, ready to prove herself, and the others stumbled back uneasily.

The red wolf pawed at the ground, likely to intimidate me. He was in charge, so I'd handle him first.

Another wolf flew by as if it weighed nothing, and Eliza dodged it just in time as she continued to cast weakening spells at the single wolf attacking her. The wolves around me were startled, and I took my chance.

I jumped at the red wolf, and his attention shot back to me. My teeth nabbed the side of his neck, and he swiped at me with his claws. They sliced into my chest near my already injured shoulder, but I clamped my jaws tighter. I needed to wound him as deeply as possible. Pain burned into me, but I forced my lungs to work so I wouldn't grow lightheaded. I sensed the three other wolves coming up from behind.

Reluctantly, I opened my jaws and took a few hurried steps away. The red wolf hadn't expected that, and he lost his balance without my chest there to hold him up. As he stumbled forward, I jumped onto his back and bit into his neck. Blood slicked my mouth and his fur, and he bucked and twisted, trying to throw me off.

The other three wolves paused. They'd have to ensure they struck me and not their friend.

My shoulder and chest screamed from my injuries, the pain in my calf now a mere annoyance.

When the red wolf dropped onto all fours, I braced myself for his next move.

His weight shifted sideways, and I released my hold on his neck. As he rolled over, I pushed off him, landing on all fours. The pain in my shoulder exploded, and the edges of my vision blackened.

I'm on my way, Killian linked, his concern almost frantic.

I blinked, focusing on the music on repeat in my head.

The pain began to recede, but the three wolves were already here.

"Don't you dare touch her!" Mom screamed as loud as a banshee, getting closer.

The wolves didn't pay any attention to Mom, but when I glanced at her, my heart leaped into my throat. She held a gun, pointing it at the dark gray wolf's head. The sight of her with a firearm was foreign, as was the steadiness of her hands. She aimed as if she was fully comfortable with the weapon. Her finger pulled the trigger, and the wolf's head jerked forward. He swayed on his feet.

The other two rushed in from both sides. I hunkered close to the ground, my injuries aching. My eyes blurred, and I shook my head, trying to force the tears to either fall or dry.

As the dark gray wolf crumpled, the light brown wolf and the cream wolf engaged.

I couldn't fight off both, so I would have to jump over them. With no better option, I stood on my back legs. Inhaling, I jumped as if I were still in human form, tapping into the moon magic surging through my veins. As I soared a few feet into the air, the wolves countered my move, lunging for my hind legs.

I'd hoped they wouldn't realize I was jumping until it was too late.

Something dark flashed past me, and the momentum of the cream wolf on my left changed. He fell away as a shadowy figure caught the corner of my eye.

A demon.

Thank gods for friends and allies.

As I landed, I shifted my hips away from the light brown wolf. He was too close for me to avoid him without injury, but his teeth only nipped my hind leg.

A prick of discomfort shot up my limb, but it wasn't anything near what it could've been and more like hitting a sharp rock or branch while running for pleasure. The wolf tumbled face-first into the ground.

My shoulder and chest smarted, and I tried to push away the agony as I faced him on all fours.

Mom glanced at me and back at Nana and PawPaw, torn between where to go and who to protect. I wished I could communicate with her and tell her I was fine, but since we weren't pack mates anymore, it wasn't possible.

I nodded in my grandparents' direction, hoping she got the message. Though I was injured, I had only one wolf left to fight. All the others were engaged in battle, and the chaos the witches, angels, and demons had created made Tom's pack numbers less devastating than they would have been.

The light brown wolf growled as he climbed to his feet, a dead leaf stuck to the side of his face. He snarled, oblivious to how ridiculous he looked.

It was time to end this so I could help the others.

He stood on his hind legs, his claws extended as he maneuvered to get on my back, similar to how I had attacked the red wolf. This was one tactic I'd trained for.

As he struck at my face, I ducked my head to go under his leg and dodge the blow. I rose quickly and used my faster speed to sink my teeth into his neck and jerk back, ripping out his throat. I moved quickly so the blood didn't soak me and instead poured onto the ground.

His eyes widened, then glazed over as he dropped.

I'd killed way too many people for one day. The bile that had been churning deep inside my stomach inched upward.

Forcing my gaze away from the light brown wolf, I scanned my surroundings. Tom had disappeared, and thirty of his wolves lay still. I tried to tune out the sounds of battle, needing a moment to find some peace within.

Sterlyn, Cyrus, Griffin, and Annie were helping the witches, and Rosemary and Eleanor stood back to back, dead wolves forming a circle around them. The demons floated close to my grandparents and Mom, protecting them.

Killian rushed to me, blood coating his dark fur. *You're hurt worse than you let on*, he linked, nuzzling me gently. He examined my chest and shoulder and snarled. *I will kill them all for what they've done.*

Just having him close soothed my wolf. He was okay and next to me, the two most important things in the world.

The wolves who hurt me are dead. Vomit burned my throat. I wished no one had died, but those wolves had forced our hands. I rubbed my head against his neck, the stench of blood causing the bile to finally come up. I swallowed it, not wanting to spill my guts and look weak in front of everyone. *You're injured, too.*

It's not my blood, he assured me. *Griffin and I worked together, and the demons helped us as well. I should've gotten to you sooner and protected you.*

His words both warmed my heart and had my blood pumping faster in annoyance and uncertainty. I took a deep breath, trying to remain calm like Dad would've done in this situation. He never let his temper get the best of him, unlike Mom and me. *I was trying to reach you as well for the same reason, but you need to remember I'm a silver wolf, and I've trained for this, just like you have.* When the silver wolves had hidden away all those centuries ago, his pack had taken on the role of protectors of Shadow City. Then the angels had deemed the silver wolves abominations and killed five of the original seven. The angel creator of the silver wolf line, Rosemary's uncle Ophaniel, who was the Guardian Angel of the Moon, had helped the last two escape slaughter. Then he'd been executed for his efforts.

That doesn't mean I want you to be in danger. He whimpered as he glared at my wounds. *That should've been me, not you.*

This time, I couldn't hold my words back. *Because I'm a woman?*

He flinched. *No, of course not. Because I love you.*

My anger fizzled, and I hung my head. I should've known he wouldn't think like an ordinary guy.

Before I could apologize, panic soared through the pack link bonds. *Guys!* Sierra linked to us. *If you can, we could really use your help. We still haven't made it back to the farmhouse, and we're surrounded. A group of enemy wolves peeled off and are heading to the farmhouse. We can't stop them.*

My blood turned cold. Realization weighed heavily on me, making me want to sink to the ground. We were more outnumbered than any of us had guessed.

CHAPTER FOUR

WE HAD TO MOVE QUICKLY. I focused on my supernatural hearing for any hints of enemies approaching, but all I heard were growls, snarls, and other signs of war.

Killian took a step back and stared me in the eyes. *Stay with Eliza, Circe, and Aspen, and keep an eye on them while the rest of us head off to help the others.*

Something inside me shriveled at his dismissal, but between Killian's attention and Sierra's call for help, I'd forgotten about some of the devastation around us. When I tore my attention away from him and glanced back at the witches, I saw Mom fire her gun again, shooting the enemy wolf attacking Sterlyn right in the heart.

The ease with how she wielded it made my stomach drop. Though I knew Cyrus had started training the silver wolves with firearms, seeing them with guns made it real. Yet another way I was behind and letting my friends and family down again.

I shouldn't have stayed away for so long.

Sterlyn's iridescent lavender eyes glowed with gratitude as she nodded at Mom. She had to be linking with Mom, and I wished I were still part of the pack so I could join that conversation.

Mom's face was lined with stress as she lowered the gun. "Rosemary. Eleanor." Her gaze darted around, searching for something or someone...most likely the demons. "And the guys, if they're here."

Mom was the designated spokesperson since she was the only one in human form who could communicate with Sterlyn, Cyrus, Annie, Chad, and Darrell as part of the silver wolf pack. My heart panged with a sense of loss. Yesterday, I would've known what they were saying on their side, but at least now I could communicate with Killian and his—er, my pack.

Sterlyn must have been instructing Mom where to look because she glanced left and right where the demons had been hovering moments before getting closer to her. She cringed and shook her head slightly, as if she felt strange, then turned her attention back to the angels. "The others need you. They're outnumbered, and—"

Before she could finish, Rosemary flapped her wings, elevating herself skyward. "We'll go now."

Eleanor rolled her eyes as if she didn't like Rosemary speaking on her behalf, but her feet lifted off the ground, and she followed Rosemary's lead.

Both demons floated into the sky, trailing the angels. Levi would follow Rosemary anywhere, and with the little time I'd spent around Zagan, I was certain he liked Eleanor, much as he tried to hide it. He seemed to protest too much about all the reasons she was here.

"Wait!" Circe exclaimed, and fisted her hands.

Rosemary paused, her large wings flapping, holding her in place.

"I hate to ask this of you, Rosemary." Eliza grimaced but

held the angel's gaze. "But Aurora told us you healed her magic fatigue when you all fought against the demon wolf pack and Annie and the others were escaping. Is there any chance you could recharge us before you go?"

I stilled, my attention caught. That fight had happened after Mom's anger had spewed out of control, and she'd wound up getting herself, Chad, Theo, Theo's mate—Rudie—and Cyrus captured by the demon wolves.

Rosemary halted her ascent as Eleanor's eyes bulged. The blonde angel gasped, "You *healed* someone?"

A lump lodged in my throat. Rosemary had healed Killian and me, too, but that was best left unsaid...not that I could speak in wolf form, anyway.

"It was either that or let everyone *die*." Rosemary glowered as she landed. "Similar to now. So you can judge all you want while I try to ensure that our friends survive."

I wasn't sure how long healing the witches would take, but one thing was certain: we had to get to the others. There was no telling the state they were in now. Some pain wafted through the bonds from their connections, but I couldn't tell the level since I wasn't as strongly connected to them as I was to Killian. *Let's head to Lowe and the others while Rosemary heals the witches.*

Shaking his head, Killian stomped. *No, you're hurt. You should stay back—*

I'm not asking for permission to fight, Killian. Even though he was my alpha and mate, there were certain things I couldn't give in on. *I'm a silver wolf. Fate bestowed that honor on me, and I will defend our packs. I missed too many battles while I was with my grandparents, and I won't abandon everyone again.*

He huffed, and his frustrated displeasure washed over me, making my stomach sink. I wasn't trying to be difficult, but I had to stand for what I believed in. Dad would never have stayed behind when his pack was in danger, and I wanted to follow his example.

As Rosemary's hands glowed white from her healing power, her charcoal wings caught my eye. A shadowlike mist wafted from them that hadn't been there the other times I'd seen her heal. It was as if she had a faint trace of demon magic.

She had to be using her fated-mate bond with Levi to draw more power.

Interesting.

Sterlyn, Cyrus, Griffin, and Annie took off toward our pack. Not wanting to be left behind, I linked with Killian, *Are you coming?*

He was still as a statue until he exhaled. His dread weighed down my bones. *Let's go.*

Though he'd relented, the satisfaction of winning never came. I almost wanted to cave in to him since he'd listened instead of fighting me, but I couldn't. I meant everything I'd said.

"Go with the wolves," Rosemary said through clenched teeth. "I'll carry the witches once I'm done and catch up with you."

"You can't drain your magic and carry three people," Eleanor grumbled, and landed in front of Eliza. Eleanor's hands glowed, but not as brightly as Rosemary's. "I'll help recharge them and carry one as well."

Rosemary's purple, starry eyes squinted, but all she did was nod.

It appeared I wasn't the only one trying to compromise.

Not wanting to waste time, I took off behind Sterlyn and the others. I tapped into my moon magic to heal myself so it didn't hurt as badly to run. Each quick movement stretched the muscles inside my chest, intensifying the pain, and every roll of my injured shoulder opened the wound more. I tried to lock down the agony so it wouldn't waft into Killian, but considering how tensely he ran beside me, I was sure I wasn't succeeding.

The demons soared overhead, rushing to the battle. I'd always thought the silver wolves ran as fast as the wind, but seeing how quickly the demons and angels could get to places put that logic to the test.

Dad had cautioned us that if silver wolves weren't careful, we could grow arrogant, especially while we'd been hiding from the world. I'd dismissed his concern, but now I understood. It wasn't that we thought we were stronger than the entire world—we just thought our abilities made us more invulnerable than we were.

Are you sure you're okay? Killian linked. The emotions swirling off him confused me. A dread-like coldness wafted through our connection but also an eagerness that helped me push my legs harder, despite the discomfort.

I wouldn't lie to him. I was hurt, but I couldn't sit idly by while we were greatly outnumbered. If people died while I watched or hid, I wouldn't get over that. The more I fought, the more I regretted not being there when my pack and friends had needed me most. I'd stayed with my grandparents to mourn my father so that the rage I tried so hard to control wouldn't control me. I didn't want to be like Mom and blast it everywhere, so I'd taken time away to heal. Little had I known until it was too late that my pack had been under constant threat and battling for their lives while I'd stayed safe at PawPaw and Nana's.

I'm not trying to upset you. I wanted him to *know* that without a doubt. *And I understand why you asked what you did. But Kill, I can't—*

A loud cry rang out, and a spot in my chest began to cool.

No.

Scott was hurt badly enough for the bond to cool and for me to feel pain, which meant the worst thing possible.

Death was imminent.

Though we'd been pack mates for not even a day, the bond was forged. This hurt just as badly as when I'd felt Dad and all the other silver wolves die along the way.

I threw back my head and howled, letting out my hurt, anger, and frustration. Those wolves needed to know we were coming, and we were *all* going to fight.

Killian and I ran faster. Soon, we caught up with Sterlyn, Annie, Cyrus, and Griffin.

The musky smell of the enemy wolf pack grew stronger. The scents were just as overwhelming. There had to be at least forty of the other wolves, which was more than I'd thought but less than we'd just fought. Our group was tired, but we had more people to offset the burden.

We slowed, the cool night air ruffling my fur. The half moon was bright, and the world silent.

As we ran between two ginormous red cedars, my lungs stopped moving.

Though I'd estimated forty wolves, it was another thing to see it. Tom was still missing, which made me think he was part of the group heading to the farmhouse. Of course, he'd want to be there to claim that he led the charge in locating PawPaw's pack members while using it as an excuse to not be near the actual war. But we'd get there soon enough.

We had to.

Herne stood in front of an ash-brown wolf who lay crumpled on the ground, blood pooling underneath its head and neck. *Scott.* Herne's long ruby hair blew behind her, and her onyx eyes locked on the wolves in front of her. She held up her hands, ready to cast a spell.

Sierra's sandy-blonde wolf stood by Scott's left side, and Luna's wheat-colored wolf kept watch on his right. The person behind Scott was Cordelia, though I could only see her back. Her curly midnight hair blended in with the night sky, and hints of her golden brown complexion picked up a silhouetted glow in the moonlight.

The witches were protecting our injured. At first, I'd found it strange that the silver wolves had integrated with a mixed supernatural crowd, but now I realized how much the members of our group had in common. We all wanted good things for everyone, including humans. Not many supernaturals strove for that, and many had a what's-in-it-for-me mentality.

Lowe stood a few feet in front of Herne and Luna, his pecan-colored fur spiked around his neck. He lunged at the closest enemy wolf. His friend Collin's sizable wolf raced toward him from the edge of the woods, aiming for three enemy wolves who were attempting to take advantage of Lowe's distraction.

Fifteen enemy wolves circled the vampire king, Alex, who was several feet away from everyone else. His pale skin appeared almost the same shade as the moon, making his piercing blue eyes stand out. His golden brown hair was unusually messy, but his tall, athletic body held a regal poise even in battle. Ronnie, his demon-vampire queen and Annie's foster sister, hovered close by in her shadow form, her emerald eyes locked on the wolves surrounding her mate. Whenever more than one attacked, she stepped in to help, and the wolves frantically searched for her invisible-to-them form.

They must have peeled off from our group to lure more of our enemies away from Scott, but about twenty-five more adversaries were circling the others.

Sterlyn raced toward Herne and Lowe. The rest of us followed, growling and snarling to pull their attention away from our injured friend.

Several wolves charged toward us. Two focused on me, possibly realizing I was injured and thinking I would be easy to pick off. They must not have realized what my size and silver fur meant, or they might have been more hesitant.

Please stay close to me, Killian linked from beside me.

That was one request I'd happily oblige. *Promise.*

Some of the tension from our connection eased, and my lungs moved more freely. At least I could ease his mind a little.

The two wolves ran at me in sync.

Killian stepped in front of me, blocking me from the wolves, but before I could pivot around him, one attacked him while the other lunged for my injuries.

Snarling, Killian stood on his back legs and attacked the brown wolf.

Needing to focus on my own battle, I spun and used all the strength in my back legs to kick the red one.

My claws sliced skin, and the wolf yelped. Gritting my teeth, I whirled around, trying to stay focused. Between the almost cold bond in my chest and my injuries, my head was swimming.

I glanced at Scott to find Zagan and Levi joining the group around him. Once Rosemary, Eleanor, and the other three witches arrived, things would lean in our favor.

The red wolf swatted at me, and I stumbled back a few steps, barely avoiding her claws. I had to stay in the game.

I jumped toward her, ready to end this battle. She didn't

budge. I stared at her neck, wanting her to think I was going for a kill shot. She tracked my gaze and lowered her head. My tactic had worked.

I hoped to injure her and get her to run away. I pretended to go for her neck, but at the last second, I dropped my body and sank my teeth into her upper leg.

She whimpered as I thrashed her skin. I wanted her injury to be bad enough that she couldn't put weight on the leg.

Paying attention to how her body moved, I relaxed when she tried to jerk back. Her natural reaction was flight instead of fight.

Jerking my head, I dug deep, and she whimpered and tumbled to the ground. She tried to stand, but she fell back onto her stomach.

Something weird is going on, Collin linked with our pack. *They're retreating.*

Checking on Killian, I watched as he ripped out the throat of the brown wolf, eliminating his opponent.

My attention flicked back to the wolf I'd injured. She'd managed to get back onto her feet but was slowly limping away after her comrades.

I agree, Killian replied. *What are we missing?*

I glanced around to find the demons tossing some of the shifters around while others backed away. We were getting the edge here like we had before, but the enemy wolves kept glancing in the opposite direction to the farmhouse.

When I followed their gazes, my stomach dropped.

More wolves were coming.

CHAPTER FIVE

I COULDN'T BELIEVE how many damn wolves Tom had brought. How *big* was his pack? Surely he hadn't brought every single wolf here? We were already fighting around one hundred, and the pack racing toward us was easily another fifty.

How the *hell* were we supposed to survive if they kept coming? Scott's bond was almost like ice. Death was moments away, and we couldn't do a damn thing to help him while engaged in battle.

Locked on the retreating red wolf, Killian took a step after her, his anger thrumming through our bond.

The pain from Scott's fading connection and the agony of my physical wounds collided. My injuries were deep, and the continuous fighting wasn't allowing me time to heal.

Killian, Collin linked with all of us. *We have incomers.*

Killian stopped in his tracks.

Wow, Sierra shot back from where she crouched by Scott, staring at the newcomers. *Stating the obvious much? Might as well have said the moon is in the sky or that men always notice the special twinkle in my eyes.*

Before Sierra, I'd never met anyone whose default was smartassery, even in a dire situation.

If the twinkle is the first thing they notice about you, you're doing something wrong, Luna shot back from her spot beside Scott. *Boobs and ass are what you use to get what you want.*

Yeah, because that worked so well for you with Griffin, Sierra snapped. *At least I'm memorable.*

I did an internal double-take. Luna'd had a thing for Griffin? He and Sterlyn were fated mates, and I couldn't imagine another wolf ever thinking they had a chance with him.

If you two are staying focused, banter all you want, but leave the rest of us out of it, Killian linked. *Not everyone can stay engaged through your sniping.*

I exhaled. I'd never considered that snark was Sierra's coping mechanism. Maybe it wasn't just a cry for attention and served a deeper purpose, like my internal music player. Killian probably already understood that about her, and as the alpha's mate, I needed to learn the intricacies of the pack as well.

Killian moved closer to me, his side brushing mine. My wolf stirred, loving being next to our mate in our wolf form. The buzz of our bond came alive and dulled some of my aches.

Alex blurred toward Sterlyn, who was standing beside Sierra, staring down the new wolves as they arrived. Ronnie followed him and flickered from shadow into her natural form.

Flinching, Sierra snarled at Ronnie and linked, *I love that girl like a sister, but these demons appearing out of nowhere is damn disconcerting.*

Tell me about it. We need the witches to spell us so we

can see them like they did during the demon war, Luna replied, though her attention was locked on the wolves charging toward us.

"Herne and Cordelia, how are you on magic?" Ronnie asked as she pushed her long copper hair over her shoulders. Her emerald eyes weren't as bright in human form since her skin was fair and didn't provide as much of a contrast as the darkness of her shadow form. "Because we have a fresh group approaching."

Both witches were in the same spots: Herne at Scott's feet and Cordelia at his head. They turned in unison, sweat coating their faces. Licking her lips, Cordelia straightened her shoulders. "Low, but I'll manage. We need to finish this—the warmth of his presence is fading." She nodded toward Scott.

"And I'll manage as well, but if these wolves keep coming..." Herne trailed off. "We need to get to the farmhouse to help Aurora and everyone there."

Bune, Zagan, and Levi soared to Ronnie. Still in shadow form, Levi said, "Rosemary and Eleanor are on their way with the witches. They replenished most of their magic, but they can't keep doing it. Rosemary was already low on her power, and Eleanor took a hit by helping."

"The fact that Eliza, Circe, and Aspen aren't drained is a relief, though." Herne rolled her shoulders. "Especially since these wolves look fresh and unharmed. We'll figure it out."

Everyone circle around Scott, Killian commanded. *Protecting him for as long as he breathes is our main priority. We're hoping Rosemary will arrive in time to save him.*

My chest expanded as hope surged through me, but then Levi's words replayed in my mind. Rosemary was already drained. Maybe she wouldn't be able to save Scott.

The weight of the world crashed onto my shoulders, but I kept my thoughts to myself. I didn't want to dampen anyone's hopes, especially when hope fueled our survival.

Following instructions, our group surrounded Scott. Killian moved toward Luna, and I followed dutifully behind him.

The wolves we'd been fighting were gone, and a shiver ran down my spine. They must have left for the farmhouse since their backup had arrived. The new wolves drew closer and would be upon us at any second.

Jewel, for the love of the gods, please stay in the back, Killian linked to only me. *You're injured, and it's not getting better. I can feel your pain.*

My wolf growled internally. She didn't like Killian treating us as if we were weak. At least he hadn't broadcast it over the pack link. *My place is beside you. When you cemented the bond with me, you agreed to that as well.*

White-hot anger mixed with too many emotions to sort through exploded through our bond and soared into my blood. *Your place is beside me, but not on the battlefield when you're injured. My job is to protect you.*

Rage and hurt boiled through me, but I bit my tongue, the way I always did. If I reacted in anger, I would say and do things I'd regret. Instead, I trotted behind him, trying like hell to ignore the pain. The wolves were now within range, and when I recognized the ash-brown fur and aqua eyes, I didn't feel disgust or anger for once.

It was Ruby.

Herne lifted her hands and chanted, "*Vocamus ventum!*"

I had no clue what that was, but that didn't matter. What I *did* know was she was spelling wolves who might have actually come to help our side.

Adrenaline pumped through my veins, dulling the pain, and I ran toward them. I needed to communicate with the witches to stop the spell before they hurt innocent wolves, but every single one of us was in animal form, and there was no way to communicate unless it was with April. *It's Ruby! Get them to stop!* I linked with the others as I raced forward.

If anyone was going to get caught up in the spell, it might as well be me. Thank gods Mom and my grandparents weren't here yet to see.

Damn it! Killian linked, and I heard his paws pounding behind me.

The negative energy swirling from him made no sense to me. I wasn't sure what emotion emanated from him, but he wasn't happy. If Ruby had brought people to help us, the last thing I wanted was to hurt them. I could protect them in a way I hadn't been able to with my own pack.

The wind picked up, informing me that a tornado was forthcoming.

"Herne! Stop the spell before Jewel and Killian get hurt!" Cordelia shouted from behind us.

My feet lifted off the ground as the wind swirled around me. My body spun, reminding me of the times when Dad had taken me to a local carnival and we'd ridden the tilt-a-whirl. We'd laughed as we'd sat next to one another, leaning to make the cart spin faster and faster as we'd held on to the bar for dear life.

This wasn't fun, and there definitely wasn't anything to clutch for safety.

As my body rotated, the pain in my chest and shoulder intensified. My body twisted in whatever way the wind blew...literally.

The wolves stopped in front of us...or I thought they did. I saw only glimpses of the world around me as my body rotated in the funnel cloud. My eyes blurred with unshed tears, and I couldn't make sense of anything.

Get ready, Killian linked as black fur flashed in the corner of my eye. His fear constricted my chest.

Don't do anything foolish, I replied, not wanting him harmed in the crossfire.

My body slowed marginally, but then a beating sound lodged into my ear. I thought my heart was calming, but clearly, it wasn't if I could still hear it. Something hard slammed into me, and arms of steel wrapped around my torso, dislodging me from the tornado. Agony exploded in my chest, and a scream stuck in my throat, but I couldn't relinquish it in animal form; all I could do was whimper.

When the strong wind vanished, Rosemary's scent filled my nose.

The beating had been her wings, not my heart.

She landed gently, barely jostling me, and placed me on all fours.

Thank gods, Killian linked. He ran around the clearing I'd been swirling in and nuzzled my side, tingles surging between us.

Breathing became easier now that I was back by his side.

"Jewel!" Mom screamed. She, the witches, and my grandparents were here with the angels.

"Mila, wait!" PawPaw yelled as bones *cracked* behind me.

I glanced around to find Ruby shifting. Though most wolf shifters didn't have issues with nudity, the level of acceptance changed when someone found their fated mate. That bond was sacred, and even before it was truly formed, the two halves of one soul recognized it in each other. Once that happened, you never wanted your mate or yourself to see anyone else unclothed. It wasn't jealousy so much as the two of you being completely devoted to each other.

Killian nuzzled me again and connected, *I feel your pain. You have to rest. April has been in touch, and Aurora is holding off Tom's wolves. We might not need you.*

I didn't hide my annoyance. I understood he was concerned, but I couldn't walk away from this. We'd already had this conversation, and I refused to waste any energy while the farmhouse was under siege. *We have to tell them Ruby's pack isn't the enemy.*

"Now!" Cordelia shouted, then both she and Herne said, "*Ventus—*"

"We're here to help!" Ruby bellowed, half-shifted. Her face was caught between its animal and human forms. "Don't attack."

"That's Ruby," Rosemary interjected. "She's no threat, just a nuisance who was attempting to woo Killian."

Whoa. You had someone trying to woo you here like you always do back at home? Sierra linked and laughed in her animal form, which sounded more like coughing. *Leave it to Rosemary to call this girl out.*

"*That's* why Jewel ran in front of the spell." Cordelia exhaled behind me. "She recognized them."

I held back a snarl. Ruby stood in human form, her silky blonde hair cascading over her shoulders, but it wasn't long enough to cover her breasts, which were on full display. "That wasn't the best impression I've ever made." She winced. "Birch heard your battle cries and convinced Father that we couldn't sit back while wolves were in danger. He agreed with Birch and me that it was only right to help fight, so here we are. Forty-eight of our strongest are at your side. Father stayed behind in case something happened to the pack there."

The other wolf in front had ash-brown fur that matched Ruby's wolf, but his eyes were emerald green. Birch—her brother.

"Thank the goddess," Eliza murmured.

I glanced to find her, Aspen, and Circe standing next to Eleanor. Though the witches looked refreshed, Eleanor and Rosemary had dark circles under their eyes.

They were drained, but we needed their help with Scott.

The last bit of warmth from Scott's pack link vanished. Killian left my side in a flash, rushing to Scott.

Collin and Sierra threw their heads back and howled heartbreakingly as Killian's pain wafted to my own. This was far worse than the physical pain I was enduring.

Laying her head onto Scott's chest, Luna whimpered. The sound of his heart faded to nothing.

"His soul is vanishing!" Herne exclaimed as she spun toward the dying shifter. "Rosemary, can you heal him?"

Eleanor scoffed. "Of course she won't—"

"I'll try," Rosemary said as she flew the short distance to him and kneeled. Her hands glowed faintly, more dimly than I'd seen before. She placed them on Scott's chest.

"*What?*" Eleanor snapped in disbelief as she hurried to Rosemary.

A shadow figure dropped in front of Eleanor, cutting her off. Zagan's black-ice irises narrowed at her, and he rasped, "What do you think you're doing?"

Levi and Bune inched over to Rosemary to stand guard. The urge to join them nearly overwhelmed me, but the self-restraint I'd developed over years took hold. Getting involved in an angel–demon conflict wouldn't bode well for me. Clearly, Sterlyn and Griffin felt the same, because they were staying put as well.

Undeterred, Eleanor spread her wings. "She can't heal him. He's a *wolf*. It's bad enough that we helped the witches!"

"Why *can't* she?" Zagan's voice hardened. Even in his shadow form, I could see his hands go round, as if he'd formed them into fists. "She has the ability. Why shouldn't she use it?"

"Because we're *angels*," she gritted out, chest heaving. "We don't help—"

"Anyone outside your special supernatural race." He barked a humorless laugh. "Rosemary *was* right about you. You're just as arrogant as the others."

Her chest deflated.

Scott's bond was ripped completely from my chest, and pain radiated internally.

He was gone.

Tears burned my eyes as the loss took hold. The other wolves closed in around us, understanding what was going on. We all experienced the same thing when we lost one of our own.

The wolves from the other packs lowered their heads in respect, and Rosemary removed her hands from his chest as she sat back. Her face contorted as she murmured, "I'm sorry."

Levi touched her shoulder. "You have *nothing* to apologize for. I hate that I was too weak to help you more."

We were all spent emotionally, physically, and magically. Everyone here had been fighting, giving it our all.

"If anyone should be sorry, it's me." Circe rubbed her hands together. "If she hadn't replenished us—"

"Everyone needs to stop," Alex said. He stood tall and lifted his chin, portraying the confidence we needed. "We did what we thought we needed to do. This is *no one's* fault but our enemy's."

Ronnie changed into her human form and stood next to Alex, and Ruby's pack jolted back a few feet. They weren't used to being around demons. They must not have realized who had been talking earlier when Zagan and Levi had spoken.

"I warned you they had demon allies who could do that," Ruby said, still in all her naked glory.

The girl needed to shift back to four legs. The battle wasn't over. I linked with Killian, *We need to get to the farmhouse to help the others.*

He stepped closer to me as he linked with our pack. *Let's go help April and Aurora, and when it's over, we'll bury Scott.* Even in wolf form, his head hung noticeably low. *We will not let his death be in vain, and we'll bring Tom and his pack to their knees.* His hurt and anger swirled together, blending into one strong emotion.

The all-too-familiar sting of loss poured over me. It was a grief no one could ever get used to. I stood tall, needing to be strong for my mate. I couldn't fall apart, just like Killian couldn't, but that didn't mean we couldn't mourn his death.

A spark of light shot into the sky. It resembled fireworks on the Fourth of July.

A lump formed in my throat. No one would make a spectacle like that unless there was trouble. They wouldn't risk nearby humans noticing unless it was an emergency.

Killian, we need you. Aurora can't hold them off any longer, and Chad is struggling to get to us, April linked to everyone. *Aurora's drained, and the enemy is taking over the farm.*

CHAPTER SIX

WITH THE ANGUISH, my frantically beating heart from April's words, and the dimming light of the flare, the world seemed more chaotic. After everything we'd done to rescue my grandparents, Mom, and Chad, their recapture would make all the pain, sacrifice, and death in vain.

Circe's hands shook. "Aurora needs us. That flare was her signal that she's dangerously low on power."

Which meant she'd used more power to light up the sky.

"Let's go, then," Ruby rasped as fur sprouted all over her body.

Under normal circumstances, I'd have been relieved that she was shifting into her animal form, but her nudity was suddenly unimportant in the face of our danger.

Cyrus, Annie, Sterlyn, and Darrell ran to the witches and crouched in front of them. Though I was no longer part of their pack, I knew they were offering to carry the witches. Even with the extra weight on their backs, the silver and demon wolves would get the witches there more quickly than if they ran on foot.

"I'll carry Aspen," Rosemary said, but she swayed on her feet.

Levi hissed, "You don't have the strength. You're completely drained."

"Jewel's injured." Rosemary gestured to me. "And you and the other demons can't carry anyone in your shadow forms."

I stepped forward. Rosemary had sacrificed enough for us. Carrying one of the witches was the least I could do.

Don't you dare, Killian linked. His displeasure weighed me down more than my emotions. *I'll carry one of them.*

You can't, I replied. He didn't understand that this was something I had to do. *The reason Sterlyn and the others offered is that they're extra powerful. They're trying to get the witches there faster, not slower.*

He flinched as if I'd smacked him.

I hung my head. *I didn't mean—*

"I'll carry someone." Eleanor spread her wings behind her. "I'm not as drained as Rosemary."

"Are you sure you want to help?" Zagan asked haughtily.

Mom had mentioned the tension between angels and demons, but I hadn't seen any until now. *Most* members of this group were the exception to the rule.

Lip curling, Eleanor glared. "Who am I carrying?"

"Me," Circe said eagerly. "You can get there before the others, right?"

Nodding, Eleanor stood straighter. "Flying takes less time."

"Then it's settled," Circe said as she rushed to Eleanor. "Guys, pick a wolf, and let's go."

Aspen climbed on Cyrus's back, Eliza mounted Annie, and Herne jumped on Sterlyn, leaving Cordelia with

Darrell. They took off, and Ronnie flickered back into her demon form.

Sierra, Luna, Collin, and Lowe, follow Jewel's family. We'll come back for Scott when this is over, Killian commanded, then linked with only to me, *Let's take the lead. We'll need to keep an eye out for Tom's pack.*

Since completing our fated-mate bond, he'd emanated love, fear, or anger toward me. Now the indifference with which he'd addressed me and the lack of emotions flowing through our connection gave me pause. A deep ache splintered my heart. At least when he was angry, it was because he cared. Indifference was a different story.

We hadn't been mated for twenty-four hours, but already, his feelings for me had changed. Dad had said that despite their faults, he and Mom had fallen more in love every day and their different strengths had balanced each other's weaknesses.

My heart panged. Maybe my relationship with Killian wasn't as strong as my parents' bond had been.

Killian and I followed the silver wolf pack with Mom, Nana, and PawPaw behind us. Sterlyn must have linked with Mom to tell her the plan. Griffin and the rest of the wolves took the back, and I gritted my teeth as I tapped into my moon magic to help me run.

The flapping of wings had me looking up. Rosemary flew just above the trees, flanked by the four demons.

Alex blurred past me. His sweet scent filled my nose as he raced after his mate. He wouldn't want to be far from Ronnie.

With each step I took, my injuries burned as if my muscles were being pulled apart. If only I could stop and rest, I'd be in much better shape than I was now, but there wasn't a damn thing I could do about it.

Killian glanced at me now and then, making the fact that I couldn't hide my pain from him obvious. I'd never had such a close connection with anyone before, and I hadn't figured out how to hide what I was feeling. Part of the fated-mate bond was not being able to hide from each other, though over time, each mate could tamp down the connection. He must have already known how to do it since he'd been alpha for a while.

Needing to focus on something else, I linked with Killian, *I'm sorry for what I said. I didn't mean that you're weak. It's just—*

I know, he cut me off. *Silver wolves are stronger and faster. You don't have to remind me.*

His words hit me like a gut punch. They were true, but I hadn't meant to make him feel inferior. He wasn't. *You're strong. It's not like that.*

He didn't even glance at me as he replied, *Let's focus on the threat in front of us.*

My throat burned, and my wolf whimpered inside me. I wanted to make things right between us, especially since we were facing another fight. I didn't want to die with tension between us, but every time I tried to make things right, the opposite happened. Yet I *refused* to grovel.

The trees blurred past, and I focused on keeping my breathing slow and steady. I played Ravel's *Sonatine* in my head to drown out my physical and emotional pain. With Killian treating me with such indifference, I wanted to curl into a ball.

But that wasn't an option.

I glanced back, keeping an eye on Mom and my grandparents. Sweat dripped down their faces, but despite being weak from captivity, they were moving at a good pace.

Grunts, growls, and shaky screams grew louder. The sounds of torment urged me to move faster.

Is there a plan? Lowe linked with the entire pack. *We're marching toward who knows how many enemy wolves, and we're all worn down.*

Stomach souring, I resisted the urge to snap at him. The last thing we needed was for the pack to feel less confident. Mentality and hope were *just* as important as strength and skill.

Ruby and Birch's pack aren't, so we have that. Also, we won't have a plan until we get there, Killian replied, and his annoyance with the situation fluttered through our connection. *We've been in worse situations and come out on top. Remember the demon wolf and demon battles? We weren't expected to win in either situation, but we worked together and came through with an outcome in our favor.*

He'd chosen to say *in our favor* instead of *we won.* In moments like these, his wisdom and leadership revealed themselves. In this instance, he reminded me of Dad, who had said there were no true winners in any fight or disagreement.

April said there were at least fifty but likely more, Killian continued. *Do you have any further insight?*

Some of the tension eased from my body. Maybe he wasn't indifferent but rather distracted and worried about April...though that didn't explain why I couldn't feel his emotions.

There are around seventy-five, April replied as her fear pulsed through the bond. *They've already pushed ten into the woods toward that facility.*

Just stay strong. Killian sent calmness and determination through the pack links. *Eleanor should be there with*

Circe any second, and Rosemary. I think the demons are with her.

They are, I confirmed. I'd forgotten I was the only one in Killian's and my pack who could see them, and I wanted April to know that help was coming.

A strained howl rang through the woods.

They're here, April replied, and her relief unknotted some of the stress in my chest.

I hadn't noticed how much her tension had affected me until now. I'd never experienced that sort of increased sensation before, though it wasn't as intense as when I sensed Killian—or how I'd sensed him until the last little while.

Sounds of fighting ensued, and our group pushed on to reach the others.

The trees soon began to thin, and the ten wolf shifters in human form stumbled into view. Some of Tom's wolf shifters were chasing them, and I noticed they were all men. They were likely sacrificing themselves to protect their mates, other females, and children.

The silver wolf pack ran toward them, not altering their path. Two dark wolves ran around the men to the front so they could charge at us. These two wolves seemed fresh, as if they had yet to fight. They must have been part of the group that had split off originally to hunt down the captives.

Eliza lifted a hand toward the wolf on the right and shouted, *"Audite me vites!"*

Vines shot up through the dead leaves on the ground and caught the wolf's back paw.

I blinked. I'd never seen anything like that. Every time I opened my eyes again, another vine had caught a paw. The vines crawled up the wolf's legs and wrapped around his body.

"*Audite me vites*," Aspen repeated, and lifted his hand toward the second wolf.

More vines broke through the ground, and though they weren't as thick as the ones Eliza had conjured, they got the job done. He continued to chant the words as Cyrus reached the first enemy wolf.

The men's eyes widened as they took in the restrained enemy wolves who had surrounded them. Like me, they hadn't been around witches before.

"Head back to the farmhouse," Herne shouted to the ten men, her hair flowing wildly behind her.

They spun on their heels, obeying the witch, no doubt desperate to get to their pack, and moved to one side so we could run past them.

Wolves were faster in their animal form.

Soon, the white siding of the farmhouse came into view. The situation was worse than I'd expected. Enemy wolves had pinned down a few men, their teeth inches from their necks, trying to force them into submission—not to join their pack but so the men would have to obey them. In a corner where a section of the house jutted out, a group of women huddled in front of the children so no wolves could ambush them from behind. April and Aurora flanked the group as the women blocked the horrific scene from the children's view.

Chad lunged in human form onto the back of a wolf running toward the women and children.

With Circe in her arms, Eleanor hovered in the center of the large field that had once grown crops. Circe cast spell after spell, her lips continually moving. The wind she'd called only hit a few people at a time, so the rest of the enemy wolves were free to attack.

The demons each fought a wolf as other nearby wolves

fled, looking fearful, including the ones we were protecting. I couldn't blame them, but I wished they'd stop panicking and making it harder for the demons to engage the enemy wolves.

As expected, Rosemary darted from the sky, fighting a wolf of her own. Her moves weren't as steady as they usually were, proving how strong she was to continue battling.

The rest of our group and I followed Killian onto the ten-acre field, and I zeroed in on the three wolves who had turned to watch us enter. Their gazes landed on Mom and my grandparents.

Tom must have made them a priority. He wanted them captured to make them pay for their betrayal. Little did he know that despite Dad not being here, that wouldn't happen.

I hunkered in front of them, wishing I could communicate. PawPaw's attention was locked on his pack at the expense of his own safety, like any good alpha's would be. He ran toward his betas while Mom and Nana stayed close to each other.

Can you cover—? I started to ask Killian, but he was already moving after my grandfather.

Seeing Killian protect PawPaw should've comforted me, but terror constricted my chest. They were running into the thick of the battle.

Ruby and Birch's pack charged onto the field, and they all ran toward the wolves attacking humans. That was the only way they could differentiate friend from foe. It wasn't long before I realized Ruby's pack wasn't adequately trained. Within seconds, a few of them were injured.

The three wolves whose attention was locked on us

hurried toward Mom, Nana, and me, and my lungs quit working.

I crouched, ignoring the stabbing sensations in my shoulder and chest. This time tomorrow, things would be better, whether it was due to my supernatural healing or death. Either way, this would be the worst of it, or so I hoped.

"Jewel, run!" Mom shouted from behind me, her voice breaking in sheer terror. "You're hurt. You need to get out of here."

I growled. She was drawing attention to my injuries—not that they were hard to see. We were trained *not* to point out weaknesses, and Mom was letting her emotions overrule her judgment.

The wolves were on us, and the caramel-brown wolf in the center glanced at my uninjured side. A few seconds later, the chestnut wolf on the left and the sandy-furred wolf on the right followed her line of sight.

One lunged at my left shoulder as the other two charged my sides. I had nowhere to go. If I stumbled backward, I'd knock down Mom and Nana. I was surrounded.

My wolf surged forward, taking control, and I jumped higher than I ever had before. The chestnut wolf and the sand-colored wolf collided, but the caramel wolf had been watching my every move and dug her paws into the ground, stopping.

As soon as I landed on top of the two wolves, she lunged. I was balanced steadily enough to swat at her with my left paw. She nipped my shoulder but not deeply.

The two wolves underneath me began to stand, and I jumped off before I tumbled over.

When I landed, my body jolted, and sharp, blinding agony surged through me.

Tires rumbled as multiple vehicles barreled down the farmhouse's gravel road. It was likely more of Tom's backup.

Jewel! I'm coming, Killian linked, his fear slamming into me.

I could feel him again, but the onslaught of his emotions added to my torment and damn near doubled me over.

The caramel wolf snarled and leaped at me. I growled deeply and rushed forward. I was tired of dodging and running. If I was going to die, I might as well inflict some damage on my way out.

Pulse pounding, I lowered my head and moved to the right, hoping not to get bitten anywhere that would cause significant damage. I didn't have a death wish, but I'd do whatever it took to protect those around me.

As I slammed into the caramel wolf's chest, sharp teeth sank into my neck. I pushed through the pain as I ran hard to the right. Eventually, we would run into a tree; I only hoped it was before she severed my artery.

A loud roar sounded, and she jerked, causing me to lurch forward. The metallic stench of fresh blood assaulted me, and the wolf's hold went slack.

When the caramel wolf was tossed away from me, Killian's dark fur came into view.

His chest heaved as he ran beside me, but his attention went to the driveway where seven large SUVs had lurched to a stop.

The fight paused. Everyone stared as the newcomers climbed out of their vehicles.

Thirty people lined up on one side of the house, their hands extended in front of them. A woman stood in front of the group, her scarlet-streaked black hair a stark contrast to her pale features. Her long, bloodred fingernails were easy to see even from this distance. She wore a black dress that left very little to the imagination.

Holy shit! No way! Luna linked, her shock wafting through the entire pack link. *I must be on the brink of death. There's no way in hell that Erin and her coven came to help.*

CHAPTER SEVEN

THE NAME *ERIN* rolled through my head, sounding familiar, but I couldn't place it.

Who says she's here to help? Sierra shot back. *The mighty priestess of Shadow City is* not *one to side with us.*

The information clicked into place, but the pounding of my head and the agony racing through my side made staying upright a struggle. I had to get my bearings before someone else attacked.

Stay focused, Killian said, standing protectively beside me. *Continue the course, or you'll be injured worse.* He tensed, and I followed his gaze to see what threat he'd found.

A low snarl came from a light-blond wolf with ice-gray irises fixated on Mom. There was no doubt in my mind who it was.

Tom.

He raced past Griffin, who was engaged in his own battle, and flew toward us.

Erin, the woman with the scarlet and black hair,

shouted, "*Fac qui impetum somno!*" The witches behind her joined the chant.

The wider battle resumed with growls and yelps. Sterlyn fought beside her mate and next to Eliza. The older lady chanted, not pausing. She didn't seem worried about the new arrivals, giving me hope.

Mom stood beside me and stared down her ex-boyfriend. "Jewel, get behind us. You're injured, and this is all happening because of me."

I snarled at the absurdity, communicating with her the only way I knew how since we couldn't link anymore. I would *not* stand down when people I cared about were under attack. Though PawPaw's pack wasn't mine, I knew each and every pack member. Not only that, but Tom was threatening *my family*.

As Tom neared, the world around me slowed. The enemy's movements became more sluggish, and Tom's face was strained, as if he were trying to maintain his speed.

Maybe I had lost too much blood and everything was catching up to me.

Fear gripped my chest, squeezing it hard. I wanted to call out for Killian, but that would be selfish. He needed to concentrate.

The Shadow City witches chanted louder, and something akin to sludge coated my fur. I glanced down, but all I saw was crimson, which was mostly my blood.

Am I insane, or did my opponent just fall asleep? Collin linked. *Is this a trick?*

I tore my attention away from Tom and surveyed the area. The enemy wolves' movements had slowed, and now that I was paying attention, I realized the wolves on our side were moving at normal speed.

It had to be a spell.

When Tom was ten feet away, his eyelids drooped, and he slowed to a stumble.

Maybe we would make it out of this after all.

One by one, the enemy wolves fell unconscious. PawPaw's pack members frantically glanced around, their faces paler and their fear more prominent than when the wolves were attacking us.

Aurora stepped away from the women and children she was protecting. She pushed back her dark bronze hair and tugged down the hem of her black shirt. Her chestnut brown eyes were warm and calm. "Don't be scared. The witches spelled the enemy to fall asleep."

One of the young girls from PawPaw's pack, Dominique, stepped forward, her gigantic sea green eyes wide. Her darkly tanned skin glistened under the descending moon as she wrapped her arms around her waist. "Will we fall asleep, too?"

She was one of the sweetest kids in the pack. When the other six-year-old acted like a brat, Dominique became even kinder.

"Oh, no, sweetie," Aurora said as she bent down and touched the girl's arm. "They're only spelling the wolves attacking us."

"Which makes me wonder *why*," Eliza bit out as she stood straight.

Tom was the last enemy wolf to fall asleep. I allowed myself a deep breath when he finally dropped. Now that we weren't under immediate threat, most of us relaxed, but Sterlyn, Griffin, Alex, and Rosemary seemed tenser than they had been during the battle.

"Diana," Erin said as she glanced to the right, "continue the spell. I'll be back in a few minutes to reinforce it."

The younger woman, who was close to my age, nodded,

causing her maroon hair to bounce behind her. Her dark, soulless eyes darkened as she took the spot where Erin had stood and led the other witches.

As Erin sashayed toward us, her tight, short skirt made her legs appear as if they went on for miles. The woman was as old as Mom, and she had a confidence I would have admired if the negative essence floating from her soul hadn't been so vile.

"There's no reason to be upset." Erin smiled, but it fell flat. There wasn't any kindness to it. "A council meeting was called yesterday, and Pahaliah, Yelahiah, and Gwen informed us of the *terrible* travesty you were handling." The council members' names were familiar, and I knew Pahaliah and Yelahiah were Rosemary's parents. I hadn't met any of them, though. "We thought you might need assistance. It's a good thing we came, or you would've been overrun."

Even if Mom hadn't told me stories about this woman, I would've disliked her. She was condescending, and everything inside me screamed not to trust her. I stepped closer to Killian, needing to feel his presence.

Ronnie flickered into her human form in front of Erin, arms already crossed. The corners of her eyes tightened as she examined the priestess. "How did you find us?"

"A location spell, of course." Erin batted her lashes. "Are you actually upset we came to help?"

That was a loaded question, but I was glad they were here. I wasn't sure we would've survived without them, and we'd already lost one good wolf tonight. I linked with Killian, *Has she ever helped you before?* I didn't want to ask everyone to avoid adding more drama to the already volatile situation.

She only helps when she's getting something out of it, Killian replied as he turned his attention to my neck and shoulder. *But I don't give a shit what her ulterior motive is tonight. You're injured, and now you can heal.* His concern washed over me, and my chest tightened.

Alex blurred to his wife. "We both know there isn't a good answer to that question," he said to Erin. "Will you warn us before you release them from their slumber, or are you hoping to catch us off guard?"

Erin stuck out her bottom lip in an exaggerated pout. "You've known me for so long. Do you think *I* would do that to fellow Shadow City residents?"

"Does the wind blow through feathers?" Rosemary asked as she landed beside Ronnie. "Because the answer works for either question."

Tilting her head back, Erin chuckled. "That's the closest thing to a joke I've *ever* heard from Rosemary. The *demon* must be influencing you, and I must say, I approve."

"Your approval isn't needed." Rosemary fluffed her feathers, making her wings appear twice their size. "And Levi is a better person than you'll *ever* be. He's always been on the side of good."

Sterlyn and Griffin trotted over and stopped next to Alex. All the Shadow City council members from our group were backing one another.

"Look, I get that we haven't always seen eye to eye." Erin shrugged and leaned back, her high heels digging into the grass. "But after the demon war and Killian *exposing* us, I figured we're all on the same team, especially since supernaturals have been captured and experimented on."

Killian's sense of guilt crashed through me, making it hard to breathe.

I growled, not liking how the witch was making him feel. *It's not your fault.*

It is, he replied, hanging his head slightly. *And you*

thought it was my fault, too, until the mate bond changed your mind.

My chest heaved like the wind had been knocked out of me. *Is that what you think?* I hated that he assumed our bond was why my opinion had changed. Even if we hadn't been mates, I would've changed my mind after getting to know him. He hadn't been seeking attention or approval, and after learning that someone else had planned to reveal our existence to the world, it made sense that he'd wanted to control the message.

It is *my fault. You* should *still be upset with me*, Killian replied, and I wanted to smack him.

Now wasn't the time to push the issue. I went to take a deep breath, but my chest felt as if it might rip open. Shallow breathing was my best option, but it didn't help me calm down. *This conversation isn't over.*

"We figured you'd need help, so we performed the spell and luckily got here in time." Erin spread her arms, emphasizing the entire field. "Otherwise, things might have gone differently for you, even with the help of those unfamiliar *wolves.*"

My attention turned to Ruby and her pack. A few had blood spotting their fur, but they'd remained on the field, determined to help as promised. The fighting was done...for now.

We should shift back, Killian linked with us all, *so we can talk and strategize with everyone.*

Good plan. Though I wouldn't say much, it would be nice to be able to ask questions and communicate with the others outside our pack.

But when I took a step forward, I whimpered and almost toppled over from the pain.

"Wait, Jewel," Mom said, and squatted next to me. "You need to heal more before you shift."

She was right. Though my injuries weren't fatal, I could die if I shifted; the wounds were deep, and I'd lost so much blood. If I shifted, it would stretch the wounds and make everything worse.

Ronnie's head snapped in my direction, and she blurred to my side. She kneeled beside me, examining my wounds.

I hadn't been around vampires often, but I knew they didn't crave supernatural blood, so I wasn't in danger. Killian also didn't seem worried, and I tried not to let anxiety grip me.

Her sweet cookie smell filled my nose and made my stomach churn worse, reminding me of a bakery shop. Delicious when healthy, but not when vomit roiled in your stomach.

Her teeth elongated, and she bit into her wrist and held it out to me. "Here."

She wants you to drink her blood. It'll heal your wounds, Killian linked. The connection between Killian and me flared warmly with hope and relief. *And you won't be in pain anymore.*

The thought of drinking vampire blood didn't sit right with me. That wasn't something I'd heard of a wolf shifter doing. *Are you sure it's safe?*

Yes. They've given their blood to shifters before. Nothing bad ever happened. I promise. If I had any doubts, I wouldn't be encouraging you to do it, Killian replied, and stepped closer to me.

Needing his comfort at this time, my body leaned toward him.

"You only need a few drops," Ronnie said again as she

stepped forward and squatted so her wrist was under my nose.

PawPaw hurried toward us, and most of his pack was watching me. Though I wasn't truly part of their pack, they treated me as if I were. Right now, I was acting scared and uncertain, putting everyone on edge.

Stomach gurgling, I lowered my snout to her wrist and licked.

"Wait—" PawPaw stopped when he realized I'd taken some of the blood and frowned.

The blood tasted like chocolate and cooled my mouth. As it slid down my throat, a chill went through me, but it wasn't uncomfortable. Rather, it was as if an ice pack had been placed on a wound to ease the pain.

Ronnie stood and licked her wrist. The two incision marks closed, and her skin appeared flawless.

Amazing.

As the blood reached my stomach, my body flushed as if I'd drunk wolfsbane. The pain receded.

PawPaw's eyes widened, and he gasped, "Her skin is healing right before my eyes."

His and Ruby's packs watched in bewilderment, and I took a step backward toward the tree line, uncomfortable with everyone's attention locked on me. The only people who weren't watching were Erin and her coven.

I ran into something, and Nana rasped, "Be careful, Jewel. I'm right behind you."

In my discomfort, I'd backed into her. I linked with Killian, *I'm going to go back to the house so I can shift.* Anything to get me out of being the center of attention.

When I took my first step forward, I braced for the pain, but only mild discomfort greeted me. My lungs filled completely for the first time since I'd been injured. Relief swirled inside me like a ravaging tornado. Eyes burning, I blinked back tears, unprepared for the emotional onslaught.

When Ronnie made it to Alex's side, he turned to Erin. "How long do you plan to stay here and help?"

"We will keep these shifters asleep while you get everyone out of here." Erin glanced over her shoulder at the witches still casting the spell. "I figured the numbers would be great, which is why I brought so many of my coven. We should be able to keep them asleep for the next couple of hours."

My body became heavy once more.

We hadn't even considered where we would take all the pack members. Their homes had been destroyed, and they were too weak to shift.

Rosemary's wings lowered behind her back. "That will be interesting since we haven't planned where to take them from here."

She had to be reading my mind.

"Why don't all the wolf shifters transition back to human form so we can discuss it? The rest of us will keep an eye on the Shadow City coven," Circe suggested, and lifted her head. "We'll alert you if we need anything."

Though they were all tired, we needed to be able to communicate.

Everyone, grab your things and shift, Killian commanded. *We can meet outside once everything is settled.*

That was all I needed. I moved forward again and almost forgot I'd been hurt. Though my shoulder still felt a little weak, that was the worst of it. It was as if I'd trained too hard and needed a few hours to recover.

Are you still in pain? Killian asked as we trotted toward the farmhouse's back door. His body brushed mine, and the buzz between us sprang to life.

April opened the door again, and Sierra, Luna, April, Lowe, and Collin filed in behind us with Annie, Cyrus, Darrell, and Chad bringing up the rear as if they were keeping an eye on things.

I'm not. I couldn't believe how a little of Ronnie's blood had healed me. It was similar to Rosemary healing me the night PawPaw's cabins had burned down.

In the living room, Savannah—the human we'd captured back in PawPaw's neighborhood when his pack's houses had been burned down—sat on the coral loveseat perpendicular to the matching couch in front of the double windows. A television hung on the opposite wall. Savannah's dark eyes were wide, and her ghostly pale skin made her golden hair seem brown. She'd been watching the attack and had seen things no human had ever seen. She was in shock, and when her gaze landed on me, she drew her knees up and wrapped her arms around them.

Sterlyn and Griffin appeared, dressed in jeans and T-shirts. Sterlyn said, "There are two bedrooms and full baths that way if you want to split up and shift. We're heading back out there to see what we can glean from Erin."

We have our room, Killian linked.

Our room. I wasn't sure how much longer he'd consider it that.

We hurried down the hallway and entered the room where we'd shared several hours of incredible sex not too long ago. Killian shut the door with his head.

I hurried to the small closet and pulled my magic back inside me. For a second, my wolf resisted, still feeling threatened, but I was in control, not the other way around.

My wolf finally listened just as Killian's bones broke and he shifted back to human. I soon found myself on two legs. Killian was slipping his jeans on, and I hurried to get dressed so he didn't have to wait for me. I knew time was short.

I slipped on my hunter green shirt and then turned and found Killian watching me. His milk chocolate eyes, surrounded by dark, thick lashes, were not as warm as usual. He crossed his arms, making his biceps bulge, and I stepped forward, needing to touch him.

"I know we don't have time for this." My body warmed at his gruff tone. "But what in the *hell* were you doing out there?"

His words were the equivalent of a cold shower, and I gritted my teeth as frustration and hurt boiled through my blood.

CHAPTER EIGHT

HANDS CLENCHING AT MY SIDES, I forced my lips to remain still. He was upset and acting out of concern; he wasn't trying to be difficult.

I replayed all the things Dad would tell me when Mom got upset. He hadn't excused her actions but had noted that when someone loved and cared as much as Mom did, it was both a blessing and, at times, a curse. He'd pointed out that all of us had flaws and we had to love people despite them, love them for their strengths.

Those talks meant so much to me and proved I didn't want to be a person who reacted in anger.

Taking a moment to figure out how to respond, I stared at the white popcorn ceiling, then let my gaze drift around the room. I ran my hands over the bed's paisley comforter. I still didn't understand why the owners had picked this comforter to go with the peach walls, but that wasn't my burden to carry.

"Are you going to answer me?" Killian asked as he marched around the bed toward me. His shirt conformed to his chest, emphasizing his athletic build, and his musky sandalwood scent swirled around me. I swayed toward him, forgetting that I was angry.

When he towered over me with his nostrils flaring, I snapped back into the present.

I'd never liked people who tried to intimidate me, and I wouldn't have a fated mate who used those tactics on me, either. I lifted my chin, refusing to back down while trying to remain calm. In other words, I was going insane. "I'm not sure what you're *referring* to. I fought alongside you and the others."

"*Fought?*" He laughed harshly. "More like acted *suicidal.*"

I'd never heard him speak this way to anyone, including me, and it did not sit well. "I'm a trained sil—"

"Yes, I *know.* You're a big, strong silver wolf, and I'm not." Killian ran his hands through his hair as his jaw twitched. "You made that clear."

My body tensed to lean back, but I stopped myself. My instinct was to submit, especially to my alpha, but this was different. Killian wasn't only my alpha; he was my mate, and I refused to be in a relationship where both sides didn't respect each other. I scowled, trying to release my frustration in some other way besides words. "Kill, I don't know what I did to upset you, but that wasn't my intention."

"You ran into danger headfirst, continuing to do so even when you were severely injured." Killian bared his teeth. "*Then* you refused to sit out, as if you were hoping to get killed!"

My heart fluttered erratically as my anger took hold. "I was protecting my pack, family, and friends. For gods' sake, Killian, Scott *died.* If I were him, you wouldn't be having this conversation with me."

"You're *right,* because you'd be *dead.*" He lifted his

hands to his side. "And I'm extremely grateful you *aren't* right beside him."

I went still. He was afraid of losing me. That's what this was about. "Is that why you shut down the bond between us? Because you were hurt and worried? You were just as likely to die out there, so maybe I should be asking you what *you* were doing!"

"Yes, I didn't want you distracted while you were fighting. I held back because you were already hurt. Besides, if I died, it would be *justice*. But not if you did," he murmured, and cupped my cheek. "This world needs you."

Any hope of remaining rational flew out the window. I'd bet my last fuck was flying higher than Rosemary ever could. "Sounds like I'm not the suicidal one."

"What?" His brows furrowed. "No, that's not what I meant. I'm just saying this all happened because of me."

"And now you sound egotistical." I rolled my eyes and raised my voice. "You volunteered to be the spokesperson. Someone had to do it, and everyone decided on *you*. That was a *group* decision to expose us and not something you can take the blame for. You also did it because you were trying to control the message before someone who didn't care spoke for everyone. I was wrong to blame you—I didn't have the whole picture." He didn't get to change the story of how he felt. That wasn't how this worked.

"My job is to protect you, the pack, and my friends." Killian dropped his hand from my cheek and pounded his chest. "That's *my* job. And you keep putting yourself in harm's way."

He was being an ass, but with the amount of fear and guilt surging through our bond, there was no question about what was driving him. "And I was created to protect those in need. You don't think I can do it, but I will." There was no way I would slack on that job again. I'd make sure of it.

"I don't care if you're a silver wolf or the weakest person in the entire world." He snarled and touched my shoulders. "You are *mine* to protect. I can't allow something bad to happen to you."

Things were escalating instead of getting better, and I didn't know how to fix it. I couldn't say he was right, because he wasn't, but I also understood that finding your fated mate was scary as hell. While fighting, I'd been worried about him, too, but there was nothing I could do to allay whatever was going around inside of him.

Going with my gut, I stepped into him so our chests were touching and kissed him. If words wouldn't work, maybe actions would. I *loved* him, even when he was being unreasonable.

His arm circled my shoulder, and he grabbed a fistful of my long auburn hair. He didn't pull, but the pressure was perfect.

Our lips crashed together, and his tongue swept into my mouth, filling it with his sweet citrus taste. There was nothing better than his touch, smell, and taste, even when I wanted to slap him.

Damn it, Jewel. He groaned as he deepened our kiss, and his other hand grabbed my ass. *I wasn't sure I'd ever get to do this with you again.*

My hands slipped under his shirt, tracing the curves of his hard abs. His skin was smooth, and the buzz between us quashed some of the raging storm inside.

His stomach quivered, empowering me. He still wanted me. He still loved me, and in this moment, I knew we'd get through everything as long as we were together. All sense of time fled as my senses were consumed by him.

A loud knock pounded on the door, and Darrell said, "I want to check on Jewel."

The voice of the man who was like a second father to me warmed my heart. Even though I was no longer part of the silver wolf pack, he was still concerned.

Always with the interruptions, Killian complained as he pulled away. *But I'm not about to get upset when someone wants to check on your well-being.* The turmoil inside Killian eased.

We're not done talking about this. I arched a brow and kissed him lightly one last time. *You threw a lot out there at one time.*

He hung his head and nodded.

Untangling from him, I hurried to the door and opened it. Darrell's blood orange eyes homed in on my neck, chest, and shoulder immediately.

The pain of the injuries was a memory now. "I'm fine. I promise."

"Thank gods," he murmured, and pulled me into a hug. "When I saw how badly you were injured...I should've known. Since Bart's gone, I'm supposed to look out for you as if you're one of my own." He barked out a hard laugh. "What am I saying? You've always been family."

The tears I'd held back outside flooded into my eyes, blurring his face. "You couldn't have known. We aren't pack anymore, and I couldn't tell you." Not that I would've anyway, but that was better left unsaid. "I would've been worse off if it hadn't been for your and Dad's training."

All those times I'd begrudgingly gone to training, I wished I'd run there eagerly. Maybe I could've been a better fighter and prevented Scott from dying.

Killian placed his hands on my shoulders. "At least she's better and alive."

I didn't want to ruin the moment, but there were two hundred weakened shifters outside that needed to get out of here. In reality, *all* of us needed to get out of here. Who was to say that Tom's pack was the only one working with the humans against us? Fear gripped my throat.

Killian's hands tensed on my shoulders. "What's wrong?"

"None of us may be alive in a couple of hours if we don't leave." We'd already wasted too much time and energy disagreeing with one another.

Huffing, Darrell yanked the door open. "You're right. We need to figure a way out of this mess, and everyone else is already outside."

Even though the last thing I wanted was to step away from Killian's touch, I forced my legs forward. If I wanted the luxury of him touching me more later, we had to find our way out of this hell.

Killian followed me. As I entered the hallway, he linked, *I'm sorry I was an ass.*

In fairness, I probably came off like a jerk, too, though it wasn't my intention. When I'd mentioned that the silver wolves were stronger and faster, I'd made him feel weak and not very alpha-like. I'd never had to worry about that until I'd joined a pack that wasn't made up of mostly wolves like me. *And I'm sorry. I didn't handle that situation well.*

He didn't respond, informing me that he agreed. At least we'd been asses together.

As I stepped into the living room, I found Savannah standing at the double windows that overlooked the open field. She rubbed her hands together as a line formed between her brows.

"Are you okay?" As soon as I asked, I cringed. Of course

she wasn't *okay*. She'd been our prisoner for over a week and was scared for her life.

Darrell and Killian flanked me as if danger were all around us. In a way, I supposed it was.

"All those people. The children—" Her voice cracked, and she sucked in air. "I knew we captured a pack, but I was in the woods watching the perimeter. I...I didn't see..."

She hadn't *seen* the people she had been essentially leading to the slaughter. Her essence had never felt negative, indicating she was a good person. Fear could lead even the best person to do something they never would have done willingly.

"After being around your friends, and seeing these people..." A tear rolled down her cheek. "You guys aren't *much* different. Well, beyond the obvious, but you have feelings and care. None of this should've happened to you."

"It might very well still happen if we don't get everyone out of here," Killian said as he took my hand and tugged me toward the back door. "They're too weak to shift, and we didn't expect another pack to be involved." His words hardened at the end in accusation.

Maybe she had known. I hadn't thought of that.

"I didn't, either. Only the higher-ups know the whole story in case of capture." She bit her bottom lip. "If I'd known, I would've warned you."

The air didn't reek of sulfur, meaning she wasn't lying. She and Eliza had forged a sort of kinship, despite Savannah being a prisoner. Our decent treatment had probably made things easier on her.

Darrell tucked a strand of midnight-brown hair behind his ear. "It doesn't matter. Right now, we need a plan. It's early morning, and not many places will be open, especially anywhere that might have transportation to move everyone out of here."

Are you two ever going to come out? Sierra linked with the pack. *Please tell me you aren't getting it on while the rest of us debate how to get out of here alive. I mean...I understand desperate sex—*

Do you? Luna shot back. *I'm not sure I believe you.*

Oh, dear gods, Collin complained. *Will you two stop? Killian and Jewel, if you love us, come outside so we don't have to listen to them anymore. Why can't the two of you be more like April?*

April was by far the quietest pack member...at least here. My gaze flicked outside to where she stood beside a woman with a toddler held tight in her arms.

Both Luna and Collin need to be quiet, Sierra sniped. *Like I was saying before I was so rudely interrupted, get your asses out here before I come in. We need everyone's brain on this.*

She was right. "They're trying to decide what to do out there. We should join—"

"Wait!" Savannah snapped her fingers, her face lighting up. "School's out, and my family lives in Knoxville. They could get here in forty-five minutes."

I failed to see how that was relevant, but her face was so animated that I waited to hear her idea. I didn't want to discount her, especially when she was warming up to our kind.

"You'll be home soon," Killian responded. "We'll make sure you get out of here unharmed."

"That's not what I'm getting at." Savannah bounced on her heels. "My brother owns a fleet of school buses that aren't in use right now. He subleases them during the school year to various bus drivers, but during breaks, they're kept on his lot. He could rent them to you."

My heart skipped a beat. "How many does he own?"

"Four." She beamed. "I could call him, and he and a few friends could drive them down. You probably don't even need all of them."

Darrell bit his bottom lip as if he wasn't certain, and Killian's and Darrell's irises glowed faintly as they used the pack links. They had to be talking to the silver wolves.

After a moment, Darrell removed his cell phone from his back pocket and held it out to Savannah. "Don't make us regret this," he said gruffly.

We're taking her up on the offer? I asked only Killian. I didn't want the rest of the pack members to hear what was going on. It was Killian's place to inform them, not mine.

We don't have a better choice. Killian's jaw twitched as he stared out the window.

All two hundred of PawPaw's pack members were severely malnourished. Their skin was pale. Their hair was greasy from not bathing in over a week, and their bodies were frail from malnourishment. The humans had no idea how many calories shifters needed every day and had probably given them the same amount they would have given any human, not realizing we metabolized food four times faster than an active human while just sleeping. To get back to normal, the pack needed rest and food, which we couldn't provide them right now.

Savannah snatched the phone from Darrell and stumbled back a few steps. Though she might not want us harmed, she still wasn't comfortable around us. She dialed, hands shaking, and placed the phone to her ear. I tapped into my hearing, wanting to know whatever was said on the other end.

It rang twice. Then a groggy, deep voice answered, "Hello?"

"Greg!" Savannah exclaimed as she gripped the phone tighter. "It's me."

"Savannah." His voice grew alert, losing all traces of sleep. "Where the hell are you? We've been worried sick. You went on that job and vanished. We thought—" His breathing quickened. "We were waiting for someone to show up at our door and tell us you were dead."

I hadn't considered what her family might be thinking, and I despised that we'd put them through that.

"I'm fine. I...I couldn't call you. The assignment took longer than expected." She twirled a piece of hair around her finger. "But I have friends who need your help."

"What? Are you all okay? Is it your whole unit?"

"It's classified, but we need to relocate some people." She paused. "A lot of people. I was hoping we could borrow three of your buses."

"Are you in trouble?" His tone hardened.

"No, but they are, and it's partly my fault." Her words broke. "Can you please help?"

"I'd do anything for you, sis." He groaned. "Even at four in the morning. I'll call Rick—"

"Not Rick or any of your police buddies," she said quickly, then winced. "I mean—"

Police buddies. My stomach dropped. *This might not be a good idea.* I'd been hesitant enough when it had been her brother, but now he had close friends on the human police force? I doubted they were tied to what was going on at the facility, but they were government nonetheless.

"And you aren't in trouble," he deadpanned. "Sure. Just text me the address. I'll be there as soon as I can."

"Okay." She hung up and handed Killian the phone.

Should we allow her to give him our address? That could invite trouble.

If he has police connections, they could track down the GPS signal anyway. If we're screwed, we're screwed. We can only pray we haven't made a horrible choice, Killian replied as he typed in the address. *Let's prepare the others in case we make it out of this alive.*

CHAPTER NINE

AS I STEPPED OUTSIDE with Killian, Mom and my grandparents rushed toward us. Mom threw her arms around me and murmured, "I was about to storm in there and check on you, but I figured you needed a moment with your...mate."

For a minute, things felt right in the world. Killian and my family were here with me. My family was safe and sound, even if it was only for a little while.

Someone cleared his throat, and I glanced up to find Sean, Heather's brother, standing between his parents. Sean's shaggy, buttery-blond hair was plastered to his face, and his olive eyes had dark circles underneath. He asked, "Where's Heather?"

My mouth dried, and grief slammed into me all over again. I didn't want to have to tell them the news, but they deserved to know.

I can do it, Killian linked, but I shook my head.

This was my responsibility. Heather and I had gone through so much together, and I owed this to her. "She's..."

The words cut off, and I took in a shaky breath, steeling myself to finish the sentence.

"Gods, no." Her mother clutched her chest. Gail's honey-blonde hair fell across her face as she closed her emerald eyes. "My baby girl." Her legs almost gave out, but Sean wrapped an arm around her waist, preventing her from falling.

Heather's father's head snapped back as if he'd been slapped. "How? How did it happen?" he asked, his cobalt irises turning navy.

"A human shot a tranq at her when she was in wolf form." I had to hold myself together.

Placing a hand on the center of my back, Killian lent me strength—strength only he could provide, and something I very much needed.

My voice cracked, unable to hide the pain. "She stood on her hind legs, and the tranq's needle was so long that it lodged into her heart."

A tear trailed down her father's cheek, and her mom turned to Sean, burying her face in his chest.

Killian lifted his chin, his face twisted in agony. "Though I didn't know Heather for long, it was easy to tell she was a strong and intelligent woman with a determination to save her family and pack. My life is better for having met her, and she will not be forgotten."

"Thank you," Sean said as he turned to guide his parents away. "But we need a moment." They moved to a part of the huge farmhouse lawn, away from everyone else.

PawPaw growled, "They're going to pay."

And they would...but we had to get the rest of the people out of here first.

THE NEXT HOUR FLEW BY, each second seeming worse than the last. After informing PawPaw and an already broken pack that their homes had been destroyed, delivering the news about Heather to her family, and trying to comfort all the run-down shifters, we were exhausted and on edge.

People were looking to Sterlyn, Griffin, Killian, Rosemary, Alex, Ronnie, and Levi for answers, and I relished not being in charge. I'd rather support my leaders and be in the background than always have someone breathing down my neck.

Any second now, Savannah's brother, Greg, would be here, and we still hadn't reached a resolution. Chad and Darrell were down at the end of the drive, waiting for the buses to arrive and to ensure nothing was amiss.

"What about my childhood pack home?" Sterlyn suggested. She paced in front of Erin's coven as they continued the sleep spell. "You could all stay there, and you'd be far enough removed from Shadow City that you should be safe. We have around one hundred homes, so you may need to double up for a while, but we have a secondary location with forty-eight homes we could finish building, which would make plenty of room for both packs."

Birch flinched. "You're suggesting we leave our *homes*?"

Griffin moved next to his mate, his hazel eyes glowing as his wolf surged forward. He wrapped one sizable, muscular arm around Sterlyn's small waist. "You said you wanted us to protect your pack in case more supernaturals came here and followed your scents to your neighborhood. Well, this is our solution. We can't stay here, so you need to come with us until the threat is eliminated."

"But—" Birch started.

"If you want our protection, we have provided you with

an option." Rosemary regarded Birch and Ruby. "It's truly that simple."

PawPaw looked at Nana, then turned to Sterlyn and cleared his throat. "We accept your generous offer, though we will do everything in our power not to take advantage and to relocate as quickly as possible."

Though he was a proud man, he was also a good leader. Turning up his nose at Sterlyn's offer would be foolish, and unlike Birch and Ruby's people, his pack didn't have anywhere else to go. They had no home or belongings, whereas Birch would be asking his pack to leave their lives behind, even if it was temporary.

A tender smile crossed Annie's face, making the honey shade in her eyes stand out. "No one lives there now that the silver wolf pack has relocated to Shadow Ridge to live among Killian's pack. There would be no rush for you to leave, and it would be nice to have more family around." She laid her head on Cyrus's shoulder, her warm brown hair enhanced against Cyrus's dark silver. She was small for a shifter, about the height of an average human woman.

Cyrus chuckled, his silver irises shining. "More babysitters that way."

"Family?" Nana asked.

"One thing you'll learn about us is that if you're Jewel and Mila's family, you're our family, too." Ronnie waved a finger around their core group. "But *I* am the main babysitter. Let's get that clear right here and now."

Alex strolled over to Ronnie and leaned forward to address Annie. "Until we have one of our own. Once that happens, *our* child will be her priority."

"Wait your turn, vampire," Levi hissed beside Ronnie. His long espresso hair was in complete disarray. "Rosemary and I are going to get pregnant first."

"Gods," Sierra snorted. "Why do men always say *we're* going to get pregnant? Will a baby be growing and stretching your stomach out and then popping out through a small hole? No? Then the woman is the one who gets pregnant. There is no *we*."

"If Rosemary gets pregnant all on her lonesome, I won't say *we*." Levi waggled his eyebrows. "And I'm all for watching her try."

Mouth dropping open, Sierra resembled a fish out of water.

Bune slid his fingers into his coffee-brown hair and massaged his temples as his shoulders shook with quiet laughter. His eyes twinkled with mirth. "That's stuff you normally don't say around people, son. Especially your father."

"He's never been one to keep his mouth shut. He's similar to Sierra that way." Zagan shook his head, his raven hair falling into his eyes, emphasizing his tan clay-colored skin.

The only person who appeared unamused was Eleanor, who stood to one side, away from everyone else. She and Zagan exchanged a long glare. As far as I knew, they hadn't spoken since she'd refused to attempt to save Scott.

Don't worry, Killian linked, and intertwined his fingers with mine. *I would never talk about you that way.*

I had no concern whatsoever that he would. Killian was a gentleman, whereas Levi was not. Still, Levi was obviously smitten with Rosemary and would do anything for her. He was almost the polar opposite of the serious angel, but his words didn't seem to faze her.

Rosemary fluffed her wings. "I don't understand why mortals are so uptight about sexual acts. None of it is something to be ashamed of."

Air rushed from my lungs. I hadn't expected *that* from her.

Killian's humor floated through our bond. *She's a free spirit when it comes to sexuality.*

My blood ran cold. *And how do you know that?* The thought of him being intimate with anyone else made me want to vomit. In fact, I was more nauseated now than when I'd been in severe pain. I wasn't foolish; there was no question he'd been with other girls, given how amazing he was at sex, but that didn't mean I wanted to hear him talk about it.

His head snapped toward me, and he tugged me close. *No, it's not like that. She and I were never intimate. She just makes those kinds of comments often.*

Between the buzz from our touch and his words, my heart started beating again.

"As moving as this moment is, do you know how much longer it'll be before you leave?" Erin moved in front of the coven, perspiration dotting her forehead despite the cold December night air.

I snapped out of my panic and pulled away from Killian, scanning the other witches and noting they were in a similar state. The first signs of strain were upon them.

A phone dinged. Savannah removed Darrell's phone from her back pocket and grinned. "Greg is almost here."

Killian linked with the pack, *Sterlyn just got word from Darrell and Chad. They can hear the rumbling of engines.*

Sweat pooled under my armpits. Savannah's brother was suspicious, and there was no telling if he was bringing buses or an army. Though Savannah hadn't said anything to give him insight about the threat surrounding us, he would be cautious.

PawPaw's pack stirred like they were coming back to

life. Most of them had been sitting on the ground or leaning against the farmhouse in a daze.

Birch stepped toward the trees. "I linked with Dad, and the pack back at the neighborhood is loading up their vehicles now. The rest of us will head back to grab some things."

"What's your phone number?" Sterlyn unlocked her phone. "I'll text you the coordinates so you can meet us there."

Ruby rattled off her number, and their pack disappeared from sight.

I'm so ready to get home, Lowe linked. *Who's going to be driving the buses, and when are we going to bury Scott's body?*

That was something we hadn't addressed yet.

Rosemary said she and Levi will carry his body, Killian answered. *And the plan is for you, Collin, and Darrell to drive the buses. Alex will mess with their minds so her brother believes they have the appropriate licenses.*

Loud engines revved closer. There had to be at least three buses, as promised, but relief didn't fill me. It could be a ruse.

"They're almost here," Sterlyn said out loud. "So not much longer, Erin. Can you hold on for a little while until we get the shifters away and figure out what to do with them?"

Erin lowered her hand. "We can handle it. All of you look exhausted."

"But we have to do something about Tom's pack," Griffin said as his nose wrinkled.

The meaning of his words suffocated me—we had to kill them. The thought felt wrong, especially when they were lying unconscious at our feet, but if we didn't, they would hunt us down or have the humans target another pack to save their own skin. It was one of those situations with no good answer.

Aurora stood from her spot between Eliza and Circe on the bench swing at the side of the house. "Maybe Alex can erase their memories."

Vampires could manipulate minds, so that was a better alternative than killing them.

Alex shook his head and tugged Ronnie to him. "They're supernatural, so it won't work. Only those without magic or who have completely suppressed magic can have their memory altered."

"Then we suppress it," PawPaw interjected, looking worse since escaping the government building. His and his pack's metabolisms had sped up since waking, and we didn't have much food to go around. They were getting more run down.

"It would have to be permanently suppressed, which is impossible since they've all connected with their wolves." Annie tapped her fingers on her thighs. "Believe me, I know. Alex manipulated my mind to forget certain things, but as soon as my wolf began to break free, the spell fractured, and I had nightmares. When I got strong enough, the illusion shattered and left me feeling angry, confused, and betrayed."

"Three emotions we don't want to add to whatever they're already feeling toward us," Cyrus said, and rubbed Annie's back. "And we already have enough eyes on Shadow City and the surrounding areas where my pack and children are located."

Eleanor huffed. "You guys are acting like imbeciles. There's no question about what has to be done. If you want to survive, they have to die."

One of the younger girls from PawPaw's pack began to cry.

We didn't need to discuss this in front of everyone. Killian had explained to me that Erin had been working against everything Sterlyn and the others stood for.

The engines grew louder as the buses came closer. They'd be here in a few minutes. We needed a plan.

"Eleanor," Rosemary chastised, and lifted her chin. "Watch what you say. There are *children* around."

I swallowed a laugh. Rosemary was fine talking about sexual things around children, but to bring up killing was a whole different story.

"And I thought you couldn't annoy me more than you did when we were younger." Eleanor crossed her arms, and her feathers ruffled. "Clearly, I was wrong."

"We were both wrong about many things," Zagan shot back, and she flinched.

"I understand that you are all *sensitive* about what Eleanor suggested, which is the exact reason why my coven and I will handle this." Erin flipped her wrist. "We will be sure to *handle* the top few in charge and give the others a chance to make the right decision. I promise you that. Now, the buses are almost here, so focus on the evacuation before my coven can't continue to hold the spell. All this chatter is wasting time and fraying everyone's nerves."

Licking her lips, Sterlyn glanced around the area. Her eyes tightened as she processed Erin's insinuation—they would kill Tom and his top-ranking pack members.

This was another time I was glad I wasn't an alpha. These types of decisions were ones that no one wanted to make, and I wasn't sure I'd be capable of it.

Griffin's jaw twitched. "You'll spare as many as possible?"

"I may be a witch, but I don't enjoy killing for the sport of it." Erin lifted her chin, the sweat beading even more. "I only do what is required to get the job done."

Killian's guilt and terror added to mine. I took his hand, wanting to be there for him like he'd been there for me so many times.

Griffin, Sterlyn, and Killian glanced at one another, their eyes glowing as they communicated.

"We can't hold it much longer," Erin pressed.

"Fine," Sterlyn said, her voice breaking. "Just the bare minimum, and quick and easy. No dragging it out."

Eliza nodded as if she could somehow pack link with them as well.

Can the witches link with Sterlyn? I didn't think that was possible, but I'd never been around witches before.

Killian shook his head and squeezed my hand comfortingly. *She's been part of this group for a while, and we've all forged a bond. There are times we can read each other without words.*

Though I felt like part of the group, I was the newest member and wasn't in sync with all of them. If I'd stayed with the silver wolf pack, I'd have been acclimated like the others and would have met Killian months ago.

My heart constricted, and my chest ached as if my wounds were still there. Not only had I not fought beside my pack when they'd needed me, but I'd lost precious time with Killian and this group.

My guilt and regret kept growing stronger, and I wished I could turn back time and do things differently. I'd thought fighting beside them now and getting to know everyone would make things better. Instead, I was seeing how much I'd missed out on by running away to mourn Dad, but that was also something I'd had to do.

This was a situation where there was no clear right answer.

Hey, what's wrong? Killian asked as he shifted toward me. *Are you upset about what I said?*

Great, now I was making him paranoid. *Nothing like that. Just struggling with having been gone for so long.*

Well, you're here now, he assured me, and kissed the top of my head.

The buses turned down the long driveway.

"Please, Erin, handle the situation as delicately as possible." Sterlyn arched her brow.

"Of course." Erin gestured behind her. "I will do whatever it takes to protect Shadow City and my coven."

Levi squinted at her as if trying to read her mind.

"What's the plan?" Ronnie scanned the tree line.

"I'll do a flyover to make sure nothing appears out of the ordinary." Rosemary spread her wings, ready to take to the sky. "I'll link with Levi if anything is out of sorts." She shot up as fast as a bullet. Her black wings blended in with the dark sky. Within seconds, she wasn't visible, even to my supernatural eyes.

Circe wiped her forehead with the back of her hand. "I hope this plan works. We're all exhausted, and these shifters need a place to recover."

"My brother won't let me down." Savannah tugged on her black jacket, wrapping it around herself.

That was the problem. She could've given him a code word without any of us realizing it. He knew she was in trouble, and he could have brought reinforcements, especially if he had cop friends. Her directive not to bring the cops could have been the code to let him know she needed help while making us think she was acting honestly.

Lovely. I was talking in circles.

She bounced on her feet. "He knows you have a lot of people to transport, but if he saw them, it would only make him more suspicious. Let me go out there with one or two of you so we can get the keys and get everyone on the bus."

PawPaw's pack looked worse for wear, and that might cause Greg to ask questions we didn't want to answer.

When Sterlyn's eyes glowed and her face fell, my gut told me everything I needed to know. Chad and Darrell must have seen something that gave them pause.

CHAPTER TEN

THOUGH I'D LOCKED my attention on Sterlyn, desperate to know what Chad and Darrell had reported, Levi was the first to speak. "There are two cars trailing the buses."

Two.

I hadn't considered the possibility of an extra vehicle being part of the mix, but one made sense. The bus drivers needed a way home. But two could signal a problem.

Everyone tensed, and the only sound for a moment was the sound of the engines and the branches swaying in the cool breeze.

"I'll call him," Savannah offered, and removed Darrell's phone again.

"Don't." I hated speaking up during times like these, wanting to leave commands to the true leaders, but in a way, I was one of them now as Killian's mate. "That will make him suspicious about how we know. You can't say anything to him."

One of the mothers clutched her young child closer to her chest, her mousy hair lying over the child's face.

We were adding to their trauma. They'd done so well, sitting out here even with the enemy wolves asleep at their feet, and I didn't want to rip away what little comfort they had. But I couldn't link with the human to stop her from calling her brother.

"Jewel's right," Killian said as he straightened next to me. "A few of us should go with Savannah and get a sense of the situation. There could be an explanation."

Alex kissed Ronnie on the lips and then released his hold on her and stepped toward the driveway. "I'll go so I can *handle* matters."

He was going to mess with their minds. *What will he make them remember?* I asked Killian.

I'm guessing as little as possible—just enough for things to make sense, Killian answered. *He'll need to create a believable story for why Savannah was away for so long.*

The thought of manipulating someone's mind made me shudder, but this was for our safety. The more Savannah remembered about us, the more at risk we'd all be, including her for helping.

Herne, Cordelia, and Aspen moved around Erin's coven and came into view. They'd been spread out behind the coven, each watching a section of the yard. I hadn't been around either coven long, but I knew there was history between them. Each group stared at the other with suspicion and hate. The snide comments made it clear their feelings went beyond distrust.

Annie pushed a piece of hair from her face. "I'll go, too. That way, I can link with Sterlyn, Cyrus, Darrell, and Chad if something goes wrong."

Annie had an uncanny way of connecting with people. When we'd been trying to calm the captive shifters, she'd been the most effective among us, especially with the mothers and children. She was even better than PawPaw, although that made sense, given his current state of mind.

Frowning, Cyrus remained quiet. He wasn't thrilled about his mate leaving. At least Killian and I weren't the only ones struggling with that issue.

"Just be careful." Ronnie exhaled loudly. "If anything were to happen—"

"It won't." Annie winked and looped her arm through Alex's. "And if your husband gets threatened, I'll protect his honor."

"I may be a *king*, but I do a fine job of fighting and protecting my people." Alex puffed out his chest, reminding me of a rooster.

Eleanor laughed, then covered her mouth with her hands. Her brows furrowed. "I'll never get used to that weird sensation."

What weird sensation? Sometimes, I felt as if the angels spoke a different language.

Laughing, Killian answered. Angels only recently regained their emotions, and many are struggling with the sensations.

"What's so funny?" Zagan glared. "Did you stomp on a rabbit?"

"Of course not." She placed her hands on her hips. "They are cute and innocent. However, Alex would've lost all his feathers with the way Gwen kicked his ass—"

Crimson bled into Alex's irises, and he interjected, "That was over two hundred years ago, and nothing that needs to be repeated."

"Babe, she's just giving you a hard time," Ronnie said as she placed a hand on his chest. "We're all on edge. Let's just calm down so we can get out of here. And later, you're going to tell me that story."

Eleanor had a way of upsetting others, but from what I could tell, she did it on purpose, almost as if she were afraid to get close to people and pushed them away.

Alex's breathing steadied at Ronnie's touch, and he nodded. "I won't be long," he said, and began walking down the driveway.

"Come on, Savannah." Annie waited for her.

The three of them soon were out of sight.

Mom clutched my arm, forcing me to turn toward her. "Honey, if something happens, you need to get out of here. That place was horrible, and you don't—"

"*None* of us are going there. We got you out, and no one needs to contemplate going back." I closed my mouth, not having meant to snap at her. Mom had been through a lot, too, and she didn't deserve to be the target of my frustration. She was concerned the same way Killian was.

"She's right, Mila." Nana wagged a finger. "None of that thinking. Everyone here risked a lot to get us out. We'll be just fine."

Action will make her feel better, Killian linked, and clapped his hands. "All right, we have three buses. Let's split into three groups so when the humans leave, we'll be ready to load up and take you all to a safe place."

The downtrodden wolf shifters became more animated. Now that we weren't talking about threats, they all seemed to buzz with excitement and energy.

PawPaw walked into the center of them and began talking with individuals, splitting them into groups. I noticed he was keeping families and close friends together, anything to offer as much comfort as possible.

As the minutes passed, I tried to hide my anxiety. I could only hope no news was good news.

"Guys," Ronnie said loudly, and beamed. "It's time.

Savannah and the other humans have gone, and Alex adjusted their memories so they won't recall anything odd."

The weight on my shoulders disappeared, and for the first time since we'd stumbled upon Tom, I believed we would be okay.

I hated that I hadn't gotten a chance to say goodbye to Savannah, but it was probably for the best.

"Now get out of here," Erin said, her face pink from exhaustion.

PawPaw and Nana led the pack around the house while the rest of us waited for the pathway to clear.

"Is Rosemary waiting for us at the Navigator?" Sterlyn asked as she tilted her head upward, searching the sky.

"She just linked with me. I'm meeting her at Scott's body so we can fly back together." Levi flickered into his shadow form. "We'll meet you at the first silver wolf pack neighborhood."

Bune lifted a hand. "I can go with you."

"Stay with them." Levi gestured to the driveway, his body tense. "If something goes awry, they may need backup. We can't get too comfortable—we both learned that in Hell."

When his father nodded, Levi floated into the sky, heading to meet his mate.

Clearing her throat, Circe kept her attention on the Shadow City coven. "They're straining."

And we didn't want to be here if Tom's wolves woke up.

Instead of heading to the driveway with everyone else, Mom hurried to Tom. She squatted beside him and hung her head as she brushed her fingertips against the fur on his head. She murmured, "I'm sorry I hurt you. That was never my intention. But as soon as I saw Bart, my entire world shifted. If I hadn't gotten to know him and had Jewel, I never would've known happiness. I'm sorry if my joy caused you agony."

Even after everything, Mom still cared for him. I didn't know much about their history; it was something she didn't talk about. The only reason I knew she had dated someone before Dad was because she had never visited PawPaw and Nana at their home. We'd always met them somewhere, or they would come and stay with us from time to time. When I was older, I'd finally asked why, and she had hastily informed me that an ex-boyfriend had made it clear that something bad would happen if she ever returned. Obviously, he hadn't been bluffing.

"Mom," I said gently, "they're waiting." I understood that look. She felt responsible for Tom. The sentiment was unfounded, but telling her that now when her feelings were so raw wouldn't be smart, especially as this was her last chance to tell him goodbye.

She straightened and took one last look at Tom. "Yes, of course." Turning to me, she almost tipped over. Her face was a shade paler, and her eyes were glassy with unshed tears.

Is everything okay? Killian linked. *They're already loading the buses.*

When I pivoted toward the driveway, I found him standing there, waiting. He hadn't left me behind.

Mom told Tom goodbye. Even though I hadn't spoken the words, they still felt strange. I said out loud to her, "The buses are being loaded."

That had her picking up her pace, but when we were about to pass Erin, Mom stopped in her tracks. She touched Erin's hand and said, "Please don't make him suffer."

Erin arched her eyebrow. "Do you know this man?"

The words Dad had repeated to me routinely over the

years replayed in my head. *Your mother is an emotional person, which is her strength and her weakness. She loves with all her heart.*

Oh, how wise Dad had been. He'd seen things that so many others didn't, and I strove to be half the amazing person he was.

"I did, but not anymore. His bitterness changed him fundamentally." Mom laughed harshly. "Believe me, if Cyrus and Sterlyn can forgive me for my behavior after Bart passed, I can wish Tom some peace. If it hadn't been for Annie and this group, I might have wound up just like him."

She'd told me a little bit about what had happened during my time away, when she'd essentially tried to break the silver wolf pack apart. She had so many regrets, and that could have been me, too, if I hadn't stayed with PawPaw and Nana.

"We'll handle them with as much respect as possible." Erin lowered her head and smirked. "I promise you that."

Having already averted her gaze to Tom, Mom missed the sinister expression on the priestess's face. Maybe I should tell her, but Tom's well-being was less important than us getting out of here before something worse happened. I clutched Mom's wrist and tugged. "You heard her. Let's go."

After a moment's hesitation, she relented and allowed me to drag her to where Killian was waiting for us. When I reached his side, he took my hand, and the three of us walked to the yellow school buses parked in a row behind the vehicles.

Half the people were already loaded, everyone eager to get away from this nightmare. PawPaw and Nana stood in the middle of the three buses with Sterlyn, Griffin, Annie,

Cyrus, Ronnie, Alex, Eleanor, Bune, and Zagan watching as the pack members boarded.

"Sterlyn and Cyrus suggested that Annie, Collin, Lowe, April, Mila, you, and I ride back in one of the Suburbans so we can head straight to Shadow Ridge and check on everyone there." Killian headed to the vehicle parked in front of the first bus.

Since Killian had been away for over a week, he needed to get back to the rest of his pack, and Annie was probably desperate to be with her and Cyrus's twins. But I felt bad leaving Nana and PawPaw to settle in. "Maybe I should go with my grandparents' pack."

"I will," Mom said. "I lived in Bart's brother's pack homes for a little while, and in a way, I felt closer to Bart there. You need to go home and rest with your mate."

Annie dodged through the last of the people boarding the first bus and strolled over. "And the silver wolf pack in Shadow Ridge is heading to the houses to prepare them, so there isn't much more you can do." She smiled as she slid between Mom and me and threw an arm over my shoulders.

"Besides, do you not realize everyone knows there's a new pack member?" said Mom. "And with your position, most have guessed exactly whose mate you are. Your priority should be going back and meeting your pack as the alpha's mate." She smiled with pride.

Stomach fluttering, I exhaled. "You're right." Though I hated the thought of all the curious stares to come, they were my pack now, and my priority should be meeting them. If the silver wolf pack would be there to greet the new packs while they settled in, that should be sufficient. PawPaw's pack all knew Emmy, my best friend in the entire world. She could comfort them as well as I could.

Killian's concern and pride surged through the mate

bond, adding to my emotional rollercoaster. I'd been so focused on rescuing my family and friends that meeting *all* of those in my new pack hadn't even registered.

If you want to stay with your family, we can, he linked.

Some of the tension in my stomach uncoiled just because he loved me enough to offer. But this was a moment where my decision would reflect the type of leader I was, and I wouldn't force Killian to choose between me and the other members of our pack. *They can handle it. Annie's right. I need to take my place by your side and meet the rest of the pack.*

Warmth exploded from him. *I really like the way that sounds.*

I do, too. I pushed my love toward him. A small part of me wished I could hide forever—a leadership role was the last thing I'd ever wanted—but although I wasn't the *alpha*, the alpha mate had responsibilities of her own.

We said our goodbyes, and I hugged PawPaw and Nana, telling them I'd visit them tomorrow. Chad took Mom's spot in our vehicle so he could get home and rest, while Bune, Zagan, and Eleanor drove the buses.

Finally, we all split up and headed to our destinations.

***

As soon as we were in range of Killian's pack, the connections in my chest flared. We passed the "Welcome to Shadow Ridge" sign, and the charming downtown came into view. The main street was picturesque and consisted of lines of brick shops that connected for miles. In the midst of the early morning rush of people heading to their jobs, numerous individuals with cameras pointed at anything and everything, probably seeking the shots that would further prove the town was full of supernaturals.

Humans.

"It's worse than when we left," Killian growled. His hands tightened on the wheel, causing his knuckles to blanch. "It's like they've multiplied."

I reached across the center console and placed a hand on his leg. "The news spread, and people had time to plan a trip down here. It'll probably get worse, especially since so many schools and workplaces are closing down for the holiday break."

The holidays.

In general, supernaturals didn't celebrate them. Because our kind lived so much longer, certain things didn't resonate with us as they did with humans.

Killian took the right that led from downtown toward the pack homes. His eyes flashed now and then, likely from his pack reaching out to him. They all knew he was coming home.

Sitting right behind me, Annie groaned. "I hope they stay away from our neighborhood."

"Me, too," Chad said from the middle-row spot behind Killian.

April sat in the back row between Collin and Lowe. The three of them had been mostly silent the entire way home, and I guessed it was because they'd been close to Scott.

We coasted by the thickening trees that led to the wolf pack neighborhood. Most of the trees were leafless, but the cypresses were still green and would provide some cover when the shifters ran in their animal forms. We took another turn, and glimpses of Craftsman-style houses broke through the bare trees.

A group of four humans standing where the supernatural battle had been caught on video had my lungs freezing. That...and the tall, shadowy form hovering over their heads.

"Fuck," Killian growled. "What are they doing out here?"

"The humans aren't the worst problem we have," Annie said urgently. "There's a demon with them, and it's got *red* eyes."

CHAPTER ELEVEN

A GASP SOUNDED from the backseat, likely from April. Then she said, "I...I can't see it."

That was yet another stark reminder that only Annie, Chad, and I could see the demon since we had angel magic running through our veins.

The demon dropped toward the unsuspecting group of humans as two of them faced the neighborhood with a camera raised, and the other two videotaped the area where the clip revealing the supernatural world had been shot.

I needed to get out of the Suburban, but I couldn't move. I sat transfixed by the demon. I'd never seen one with eyes that color, and they glowed brighter as they locked on us. So much negativity poured from its essence that the air seemed to have lost its oxygen, and my lungs worked hard to breathe.

Annie's and Chad's doors opened, breaking the spell that had immobilized me. There was only one demon, but that didn't mean something terrible couldn't happen. Chad and Annie ran past the front of the vehicle just as I swung my door open.

A large, warm hand caught my arm, and the buzz of the bond sprang to life.

Don't ask me not to go, I linked. Anything Killian wanted to say could be said via our connection, so for him to hold me in place told me he didn't want me to leave the car.

Our bond lost some of its warmth, indicating his displeasure with me. His reluctance added to the heaviness already swirling through me, but I couldn't run away from my destiny. Fate had chosen me to be one of Earth's protectors, and it was an honor I was determined to accept, especially after I'd failed so many people.

He didn't respond, and I pulled my arm from his grip. I didn't want to be an asshole, especially not to him. I wanted to respect him since he was my alpha and mate, but if I compromised too much, I would lose part of myself. He had to trust in my abilities at some point, the same as me. Besides, I couldn't sit back when I was mere feet away from a dangerous situation.

I hurried to catch up with Annie and Chad. All four humans stared at us as we approached, and the tallest of the bunch straightened his shoulders and placed the camera by his side. He said, "We have every right to be here."

The demon's shoulders shook as he laughed loudly.

The smallest human jerked her head up, her molasses-brown ponytail swaying. "Did you hear that?"

Rolling her light green eyes, the taller female muttered, "They're just messing with us."

"I—" The shorter male's bottom lip quivered, making him appear more childlike than the others. The camera shook in his grasp as he swiveled his head around, reminding me of a chicken. "I'm not so sure."

Swooping down, the demon pulled the smaller girl's ponytail. He had every desire to scare them.

Chad's back tensed as he approached them. "You need to get out of here—"

That seemed to be what the demon had been waiting for. Chad and Annie tapped into their moon magic, speeding toward the humans faster than a normal shifter could.

The smaller male's eyes widened, and the demon dropped, shoving the boy onto the asphalt.

"Booger!" the taller guy shouted. "What the *hell* are you doing? The two of you, videotape this now!"

Being taped would be awful, but if something happened to these humans, things would be worse. I tapped into my speed, racing to catch up to Annie and Chad, when another door shut from the Suburban.

I didn't have to look behind me to know it was Killian.

Annie and Chad were only a few feet away when the demon pulled out a long knife and slashed the tallest girl's cheek. She yelped as she reached for the wound, but he hadn't removed the knife, and she cut her hand.

"Bethany!" the taller guy screeched. "There's a floating knife there. Don't touch it!"

The shorter girl's face blanched.

"Move away!" Annie yelled as she and Chad barreled into the center of the group.

Three of the humans stumbled back, desperate to escape. The taller girl with the knife against her cheek stayed completely still, her tears mixing with the blood running down her face and dripping onto her white shirt.

Fur sprouted across Chad's arm as his wolf surged forward, but there wasn't much he could do. When he leaped for the demon, it soared high into the sky. It didn't want to fight, merely terrify.

I reached Annie and Chad as Annie reassured the girl,

"You're okay now. The demon is gone." She reached for Bethany, but the human flinched.

"Don't touch me," Bethany said, voice cracking, and covered her cheek with her hand. Blood oozed between her fingers. She jerked her head toward her friends. "I told you we shouldn't have come here."

I followed her gaze, and my stomach churned. The taller boy was recording again.

Chad's entire focus was on the demon flying away, but the fur on his arms had receded. Though I wished we could've killed the demon, the sludge that coated my skin from its negative presence eased.

"Get out of here," Killian growled at the humans as he reached my side. He glared at them. "Now!"

The smaller boy's mouth dropped open. "It's the guy from the news!"

Killian's jaw popped, and his breathing turned ragged. His surprise and guilt slammed into me, and I felt as if I were treading water. The situation could implode if we didn't de-escalate it quickly.

"They got video." I hated saying those words, but Killian might lose it if they didn't leave. These humans were stalking his home and pack, which would put any good alpha on edge. We couldn't let them leave without destroying the footage. If the public saw a young girl getting sliced by an invisible attacker, it would only instill more fear.

Annie pivoted toward the taller boy, who had the camera rolling. "You're right. They have video, and they aren't old enough to be reporters." She marched toward them, holding her hand out. "Turn it off and hand it over, *now*."

"What?" The taller boy clutched the camera to his chest. "No way."

"Roy, don't be stupid," Booger muttered. "They're supernaturals. Did you *see* how fast they ran?"

Feeding on the smaller boy's discomfort, Annie ran the few feet toward them quicker than humanly possible. She didn't blur like Alex, but it was fast enough to make it clear she was more than human.

"Did you seriously tape me getting attacked?" Bethany stammered as she backed away from Chad. Her chest heaved, and I guessed the terror of the situation was catching up to her.

"No," Roy exclaimed a little too loudly. "I mean, it was recording, but no one was aiming it at you until we realized you were okay."

Poor Roy. He actually thought that would make it better. Granted, most men my age would probably think the same thing.

Using Roy's distraction, Annie snatched the camera from him and pressed some buttons.

"She knows how to work a camera!" Roy gulped.

Annie tossed the device back at him and said, "I may be supernatural, but I was born in this century. I can use electronics just as well as you can."

"We all can," Killian emphasized, and marched past me toward them. He pointed at the three of them. "If I see any of you back here again, it'll be worse than getting your video deleted. I'll break the damn camera. Do you understand?"

Watching him go all alpha on them warmed my body. Even though we'd had sex not even twenty-four hours ago, with everything that had happened, it felt like months.

Roy's nostrils flared. He obviously had a problem with authority.

Bethany pulled her hand away from her face and flinched. She must not have realized how much blood she'd lost. Her hands trembled, and she nearly fell over as she rushed to her friends. "We understand." She grabbed the shorter girl's arm, tugging her away from us and toward downtown. "Let's go before they change their mind and don't let us leave."

My chest constricted. They still feared us. In some ways, protecting them might have made it worse, but we couldn't just let the demon play with them.

We watched them hurry away, and part of me wanted to go after them and talk to them and make them understand we weren't scary, but that wouldn't improve the situation. They would either fear us more or feel like we wouldn't follow through on Killian's promise if they returned. The best thing we could do was let them go and hope what they'd experienced had cured their curiosity.

The car's back door opened, and Lowe stood from the backseat. "I'll follow them and make sure they don't cause more trouble."

Killian nodded. "Just be careful, and stay under the radar unless they do something that requires you to reveal yourself."

"Understood." Lowe turned to follow the humans.

"Wait," Chad called out. "I'll go with you in case that demon comes back."

That was a good plan, considering Lowe couldn't see the demon. Annie wanted to get back to her kids, so that left Chad and me. "I can go. You've been—"

"No, J. I'm fine. Besides, you have your new pack to meet." Chad waggled his brows, pretending to be normal, but the circles under his eyes and his dingy hair told a different story. "If a demon shows up, you can't link with the silver wolf pack for backup."

My mixed emotions over no longer being part of the silver pack sucker-punched me again. There was no one in the world I would rather link to than Killian, but not being able to connect with my family pack made me feel cut off. I watched as Chad and Lowe stepped between a cedar and an oak and followed in the trees to conceal themselves from the humans' view.

Tingles ran down my back, and I glanced at Killian to find him observing me. His emotions were somewhat muted again, confirming I hadn't been crazy when I'd sensed the same thing.

"Come on, let's head home. We all need rest," he said as he forced a smile and took my hand.

Annie moved toward the neighborhood instead. "I'll walk the rest of the way." She took off at a jog, rushing to see her two little ones.

I allowed Killian to lead me back to the vehicle, not wanting to separate from him. I wasn't sure what was going on between us, but one thing was certain—he was hiding something from me.

We breezed into the neighborhood, and as we rolled around the final curve, the cozy houses in varying shades of white, blue, green, and yellow came fully into view.

Four people waited outside Killian's hunter green house. All four were older, probably around Mom's age. The tallest and most muscular man was bald with a kind face. Beside him stood a pretty woman with shoulder-length strawberry blonde hair. She was a little shorter than me. The second man reminded me of Collin. He wasn't as muscular as the other one, and there was a hardness to him that made me think he took most things seriously. The last woman was a few inches shorter than me with an athletic build.

Who are these people? I linked to only Killian as we pulled into his driveway. I hadn't wanted to pepper him with questions about what to expect when we got here, but I was nervous. At least it was a small group, but the looks on their faces said more than I'd have liked.

They were upset and tense.

I promise they'll love you almost as much as I do, he assured me. *The bald man is Billy. He's my beta and Lowe's father. The woman beside him is Pammy, his mate. The one who's slightly more muscular than me is Dylan, Collin's father. And the other lady is Gabbi, April's mom.*

They were here to get their children. I grabbed the door handle harder than necessary. *What about Scott's parents?*

They're getting things ready for Scott's memorial, Killian answered, sadness surging through him. *We'll have a campfire tonight to say our goodbyes, then welcome you into the pack.*

I'm glad we'll get to mourn with them. Though I hadn't been part of their pack long, Scott and I had shared that bond. The others probably felt more pain than I did, but I wanted to be there to share in his memory as well. We all had choices, and Scott had chosen to risk his life to help another pack. That wasn't a sacrifice I'd take lightly, especially since I was the one who'd asked for their help. Once again, I had failed to protect someone. The least I could do was honor his memory and say goodbye.

When we climbed out of the car, Pammy hurried over to me and pulled me into a hug. She linked, *I'm so glad Killian has found someone after all these years.*

Her unexpected warmth filled a void I hadn't known was inside me. Killian introduced me to the group, and all of them said warm hellos. I hadn't expected them to be so nice to me. After all, their family had risked their lives on my behalf.

The sun was ascending, lighting up the world.

"I hate to cut this short, but Jewel and I need rest. We'll wake in a couple of hours to help with the finishing touches for Scott's memorial," Killian said as he took my hand and tugged me to the door.

"Don't worry about helping. Just be there at six for the ceremony," Gabbi called as we stepped into the small foyer, which led to a large, open living room with blue-gray walls.

The door shut loudly behind me. Killian and I were truly alone for the first time with no one close by. He led me into the living room, with its long brown leather couch against the far left wall and a television hanging above a tilted chimney just across from it. A matching loveseat sat perpendicular to the couch, facing the five windows that overlooked the backyard and the closed-for-the-season pool.

From where we stood, I could see the sizable kitchen with its dark oak cabinets and circular glass table that seated four. A door positioned between the kitchen and living room led to the backyard. In the corner next to the couch sat a fishing pole and a tackle box.

I examined the portrait hanging over the couch. It showed a younger version of Killian, his sister, who was so close to his age that they could have passed as twins, and his parents standing behind them. My vision blurred as I realized I'd never get to meet these people who meant so much to my mate.

I turned back to Killian. Of all the places I might have expected him to guide me, I hadn't expected it to be here. Something had to be wrong. "I thought we were getting some rest." I placed a hand on his chest and stared into his eyes.

"We are. It's a little surreal having you in the house," he murmured. "It hasn't felt like home in such a long time, and with you here, it feels perfect. We just need to make it *our* space." His fingers brushed my cheek, and his love swirled through me, making my heart feel fuller. "This is your home, Jewel. If you want to paint the walls fuchsia, you don't even have to ask me."

Each day, I fell more for him. "Fuchsia?" I beamed. "That's an oddly specific color. I'm thinking that's a subliminal message."

"As long as it's what you like, I'm okay with it." He kissed my lips and pulled back. "But I want to fix us something to eat before we go to our room and crash." He brushed a finger along my cheek. "Sit down and relax while I make us something. We haven't eaten much, and you were severely hurt." He released his hold on me and moved toward the kitchen.

Between Killian calling it *our room* and wanting to take care of me, my heart grew two sizes. It'd been a long time since I'd felt so loved. "I can help." I took a few steps to follow him.

"For gods' sake, Jewel." His shoulders sagged, and he sounded hurt. "Can you not allow me to take care of you?"

CHAPTER TWELVE

MY EYES BURNED, but I blinked back the tears. I hadn't meant to upset him; I'd only wanted to help and be near him.

Acting in anger only led to regrets, and, boy, did I already have enough of those. Instead, I focused on my breathing and played Chopin's "Raindrop" prelude in my mind, searching for a sense of calm.

Killian grimaced. "Sometimes, I want to take care of you without you fighting me on it."

"I'm not trying to be difficult," I murmured, and rubbed my hands together. "I just want to be with you."

His face twitched with agony. "I'm being an asshole even though I'm not trying to. You damn near died tonight, and I want to take care of you."

"But you fought, too—" I didn't understand why that meant we couldn't cook dinner together.

"No, I *didn't*." His words were gruff, and he sounded as if he was in pain. "You wouldn't allow it."

I stared at him, my mind spinning. What was he talking about? I wasn't an alpha, so I couldn't command him. "You were fighting the enemy, just as I was. I don't understand what you're implying."

"You kept jumping in, protecting everyone before I could. You made it clear you don't think I'm as capable as you are because I'm not a silver wolf." He motioned at my chest, shoulder, and neck. "You wouldn't stop fighting even after you got injured and I asked you to stop multiple times. Do you know what it's like not being able to protect someone you *love*?"

I understood what he meant, but my actions had had *nothing* to do with him not being a silver wolf. Yes, he'd seen me get injured when he couldn't be beside me, but his reaction was misguided.

Frustration swirled in my blood, and I grew uncomfortably hot. I wanted to lash out, but that would accomplish nothing. "Kill, that's not fair. I only mentioned the silver wolf thing in regard to carrying one of the witches. You're more than capable in battle and in leading your pack, and you know I carry the guilt of not being here with all of you to fight while I was with my grandparents. I can't stay back when my friends, family, and pack are in danger. I wasn't trying to defy you."

His expression twisted, and he exhaled shakily. "I know that, but you have to remember my parents died because I chose to go to a party over helping them. I can't ever let someone I love die because I wasn't there for them again."

It hadn't hit me until now that we were dealing with very similar personal demons. "But if you would've jumped in and gotten hurt—" A sob got stuck in my throat. The thought of him being injured made me slightly insane.

"How do you think I felt seeing *you* that way?" He closed the distance between us again and placed a finger under my chin, tilting my head up so I stared into his eyes.

"Seeing you bleeding, and that wolf biting into your neck..." He closed his eyes and placed his forehead against mine. "I'll have nightmares about it." His fear wafted into me, chilling the chaos swirling inside.

"Did you really expect me not to jump in and aid you, my family, and our friends?" I hadn't been seeking out trouble, but I refused to be a bystander any longer. Maybe if Dad had brought the entire pack to help Sterlyn and Cyrus, he would still be alive. If I'd stayed with my pack instead of running off to lick my wounds, maybe all my family and friends would still be alive. It wasn't that I was that amazing of a fighter, and getting my ass kicked multiple times had been a humbling experience, but if we'd fought together like a pack should, maybe we would've been strong enough to survive the storms.

He sighed, his slight citrus breath hitting my face and tangling with his sandalwood signature scent, two of my favorite things in the entire world. My body warmed at his touch and proximity, the mate bond filtering through the confusion.

"I didn't," he whispered, and for a second, I had no clue what he meant until I remembered I'd asked him a question. "But that doesn't mean it didn't kill me to see you at risk and badly injured."

My hormones were taking control, and I was fairly certain I was losing brain cells.

"You can't expect me not to do the same thing as you in that situation." The urge to taste him nearly overwhelmed me. "You were born a leader and a fighter, and I was born a silver wolf. It's what we were made to do."

He licked his lips as his milk chocolate eyes darkened. "That doesn't make it easier."

"No relationship is easy, not even the ones blessed by

Fate." I took a step toward him, my breasts brushing against his chest.

"I love you so damn much. The thought of losing you—" he started.

"I'm right here. You haven't lost me." Though I was still upset with how he'd reacted moments ago, I wouldn't hold on to it. He'd been terrified, just like I had been the night he got shot after PawPaw's pack cabins had been set on fire. His heart had nearly stopped beating, and I remembered my desperation to save him. And that was before we'd completed our bond. "Remember, I almost lost you before our relationship even began."

He smirked, but it was full of sadness. "That's low."

"It's the truth." I arched my brow. "Maybe we need a pact that we will do what we feel is necessary with the least amount of risk possible." That was the best either one of us could offer the other.

Something unreadable crossed his face, which made me nervous, but relief poured from him, and the connection between us sprang back to life.

"I agree to that," he rasped as he brushed his thumb across my lips.

Unable to stop myself, I licked his finger. His salty taste alone made my body ready for him.

He groaned and fisted my hair gently with his other hand. "You're going to kill me. I need to make you something to eat."

There was only one type of hunger that weighed heavily on my mind. *We can eat after we shower. We need to get clean first.* I waggled my brows, making my intentions obvious.

His irises lightened back to the color I loved, and he kissed me. *You're right. We are filthy after all that fighting.*

Though I'd been in wolf form, blood dotted my shirt. The more I thought about it, the more I knew a shower was exactly what we needed.

"It's time to take you to *our* bedroom," he rasped as he picked me up like a princess and hurried down the hallway. I hadn't been in any of the bedrooms, but I knew the room behind the first door on the left had been Olive's, and Killian's old room was the second on the left. Straight in front of us was a full bath, but he turned right into the master bedroom.

This was the first time I'd seen his room, and the moment seemed right. His walls were the same gray-blue as the living room, and the tray ceiling was a light mustard. A huge ceiling fan hung in the center, and his king-size bed sat directly underneath it. His comforter was a navy that suited him perfectly—just like me. There was a large walk-in closet to the left and the master bath to the right.

He set me down lightly on the dark gray shag carpet and rushed to the oak dresser to the right of the bathroom door. He opened the top middle drawer and removed two shirts and two pairs of boxers.

More arousal coursed through me when I realized one set was for me. The thought of wearing his clothes made me feel more claimed.

When he sauntered to the bathroom door, I enjoyed watching the way his muscles contracted under his shirt. I could see every indentation of his athletic frame, and his chiseled face was to die for.

He stepped through the door and waited. When I didn't follow, he turned back to me and tilted his head. "Are you playing hard to get? Because I thought you promised me a shower." His over-the-top pout let me know he was teasing.

"Just enjoying the view, since it's harder to remember to

look when you're inside me." My eyes widened, and I clapped a hand over my mouth. I'd never said anything like that before.

Beaming, he snatched my hand and pulled me toward him. *You can ogle me afterward, but right now, I need you.*

He spun me so my back was pressed against the dark gray granite countertop. "I'm not above demanding," he cooed. Then he kissed me once more. My lips tingled, and my head grew dizzy as his mouth continued to work against mine.

Heart pounding, I watched as he shut the door and went to the gray-tiled walk-in shower. He turned the knobs, and dual showerheads sprayed high-pressure streams. As the water heated, he bent under the sink and grabbed two white towels. He tossed them on the rod next to the shower, then turned his attention to me.

Not bothering to go slowly, he grabbed the hem of my black shirt and peeled it from my body. As it passed over my head, the stench of blood reminded me that we truly needed a shower, and taking one together would make the experience pleasurable.

His lips found mine again as his arm wrapped around my body, and he unfastened my bra. His tongue entered my mouth, fueling my need.

I would never get enough of him.

My wolf surged forward, needing him as much as my human side did. Sucking on his tongue, I put my hands on his waistband. Getting him out of his pants was more of a priority than feeling his naked chest pressed against mine, though I wanted that, too. I eagerly unfastened his jeans and pushed them down, along with his boxers.

He chuckled, and warmth exploded through our bond. *Going after what you want, eh?*

I want all of you. Though I'd never been insecure, *confident* didn't truly describe me, either. But something had come over me, and I felt that way with him.

He stepped out of his jeans as his fingers worked on my pants. As I drank him in, he groaned and removed my jeans and panties, then gasped when I leaned back to remove his shirt.

The two of us stumbled into the shower, our mouths together. The hot water hit my back, unknotting some of the kinks from the fight and stress. He pressed me to the cold tile of the shower wall and reached beside me for a bar of soap from the cutout in the wall. His focus stayed locked on me as he rubbed the bar, creating suds all over his hands, which he then ran slowly over me. He washed my entire front, stopping at my breasts to fondle them. I moaned, enjoying his touch and encouraging him to keep moving lower. The water crashed over us, washing the soap from my body. When he reached between my legs, he remained and circled.

Tossing my head back with the sensations, I took the soap from him and cleaned his front as well. When I traced the curves of his abs, he sighed and kissed down my neck. The buzzing from his lips and the fingertips caressing my folds sent waves of pleasure coursing through me.

My fingers reached him, and I enjoyed his hardness. I stroked him as his mouth captured my nipple, and his tongue flicked against it. My body arched with need so crazy that the world hazed around me.

When I moved my hand faster, he responded with eager swirls. His teeth gently nipped me, and another wave of pleasure washed over me. My body quivered as ecstasy took hold.

Gods, Jewel. You are so damn sexy, he linked.

I tried to move away, sensitive to the pleasure he'd given me, but he locked me in place and continued to torment my body. His mouth and fingers were magic, and heat brewed again in my core. Stroking him faster, I wanted to take him over the edge with me. His hips rocked against me as mine swirled against his hand. Pleasure coiled inside me, urging me to move quicker.

He stepped from my grip, and I groaned in frustration. I wanted to touch him, feel him, and taste him. I wanted *all* of him.

He sat on the small bench built into the shower and tugged me toward him. His eyes glowed faintly, turning me on even more. Knowing that his wolf needed the connection as badly as mine did encouraged both sides of me.

I slipped my legs around him, straddling him, and he guided himself inside me.

I'd always thought being the one in control like this would be awkward, but I found myself eagerly rocking against him. Each time he filled me, he went deeper, offering the exact friction I needed. As I rode him, his mouth found my nipples again. He thrust against me, going deeper than ever before. My body adjusted to him, and I moved faster, closing my eyes and enjoying the feel of his hands on my hips guiding the pace.

My back arched as desire built. His fingers replaced his mouth and caressed my body as he kissed me. Our tongues collided, and an orgasm ripped through my body. Our bond opened, and his love and mine blended together, becoming one. There was no doubt about what he felt for me, and that was the reassurance I needed after the intense battle we had survived.

His pleasure mixed with mine as his body shook with

his own gratification, our combined ecstasy giving us our own personal high.

"That was amazing," he whispered, and pressed butterfly kisses on my nose.

Amazing didn't come close to describing what we'd done. I sighed as I gave him another long kiss before climbing off. I didn't want to move away from him, but the tile was cutting into my knees. "Let's get clean, eat, and cuddle."

He grinned, jumping to his feet.

And just like that, it seemed like everything was again right in our world.

FOR THE NEXT FEW HOURS, Killian and I got the alone time we so desperately needed. I snoozed in his arms, though I couldn't fall into a deep sleep. Every time I did, flashes of the battle sprang into my mind. This was the first time in days I'd been able to attempt to rest, and all the bad things I'd experienced since finding PawPaw's pack seemed determined to replay in my head.

Killian breathed softly beside me, and I tried to stay still, but no matter what I did, I wound up squirming. The last thing I wanted to do was leave his comforting arms, but he needed rest.

I inched away from his side, careful not to jar him, slid out of the warm sheets, and tiptoed into the hallway. I shut the door, wanting to buffer the noise of the television I planned to switch on. In the living room, I grabbed the remote and turned the volume to level one. I flipped to the news, wanting to know if anything had been broadcast about the government facility from which we'd freed the wolf shifters.

The first thing that flashed across the screen focused on an uptick in missing persons reports worldwide. The assumption was that human trafficking was on the rise, but the reporters all seemed puzzled by what it meant.

That was terrible, but if it took the heat off supernaturals, that was a silver lining. We didn't need the news to keep harping on about us and how we might destroy the world.

The bedroom door opened, and Killian shuffled into the living room. He glanced at me and the television, then asked, "Is everything okay?"

"Couldn't turn off my mind." I went to him and wrapped my arms around his neck. "It's almost six."

"That means it's time to get changed and head down to the training area for Scott's and Heather's ceremony," he said, and kissed my lips. "Olive might have something in there you can wear until we can buy you clothes tomorrow. I'd offer Mom's clothes, too, but I donated them when I moved into the master bedroom. Being around their things was too much of a constant reminder."

I'd hate to wear his late sister's clothes, but it was better than meeting everyone in his oversized shirt and boxers. "Won't me wearing your sister's clothes be the same thing?"

"No, I'll be fine. But maybe when things calm down, we can decide what we should do with those two extra rooms. Maybe we can think about his and her rooms?" His eyes twinkled.

I'd never thought about kids before, but it sounded perfect. Having children with him would be a dream come true, but at the moment, I had more of a priority—getting ready for the ceremony. "Yeah, we can. But let me go get ready." I hurried into his sister's room.

I'd never been in there before, and it was nothing like I'd expected. The white queen-size canopy bed with a plum comforter was centered against the farthest lavender wall, opposite a matching white dresser and flanked by night-stands. Just like Killian's room, it had dark gray shag carpeting.

A picture on one of the nightstands caught my atten-tion. It was of a younger Killian and his sister sitting on an embankment, fishing together. Just like the portrait in the living room, they could have passed for twins. Killian had his arm slung over her shoulders.

My heart ached as I imagined the memories this room must contain. I could still feel Olive's essence inside it.

Pushing away the strange emotions, I made my way to her closet. It contained mainly dresses that had been very much in style five years ago. I chose a simple black dress fit for the occasion and slipped it on. I didn't want to wear her underwear, so I kept on Killian's boxers. Her shoes were too small, so I opted for bare feet—not a big deal for shifters.

When I stepped out of her room, I found Killian standing at the edge of the hallway, wearing khakis and a black polo shirt. He smiled at me tenderly, though sadness showed in his expression. "You look gorgeous. That's the exact outfit Liv would've chosen to wear."

"I can change." I didn't want to cause him more pain.

"Don't. You look perfect." He held out his arm.

Not wanting to argue over it and make us late, I slipped my arm through his, and the two of us headed out the back door.

As soon as we walked outside, sludge coated my body.

We weren't alone.

CHAPTER THIRTEEN

MY VIEW WAS HINDERED by the side of Killian's home and the back porch's ceiling. I ran to the edge of the concrete porch.

Twilight had descended, and the air held a chill. Cedar and cypress branches swayed in the breeze, and the grass was still green despite the cold December temperature. Nothing seemed amiss, but the sludge still coated my skin. A demon was nearby.

What's wrong? Killian linked as he reached my side. His gaze followed mine, and his brow furrowed. As a regular shifter, he had no sense of the lurking evil.

A demon. I narrowed my eyes and tapped into my magic. Normally, I didn't have to do that to see better, but I had to be missing something because I didn't see anything nearby.

Killian tensed and tugged me toward the house as he linked, *Let's go back inside until Chad or Annie get here.*

He was making me feel as if I couldn't fight well on my own. I yanked my arm from his grasp, not wanting to move from this spot. If a demon was lurking nearby, I needed to locate it and make sure it wasn't wreaking havoc. *I can see them, too, you know.*

Oh, I'm aware, he growled. *You made that clear.*

I held back a snarl of my own. Whatever issues we had discussed hadn't been resolved, but I didn't have the attention to spare to address them. I ran down the few stairs, my hand sliding down the black iron railing on the right, wanting to get a view of the front of the house. Lo and behold, a demon was hovering over Killian's roof, its red eyes glowing brighter once it realized I had located it.

I couldn't tell if it was the same demon that had terrorized the humans earlier, but it didn't matter. A demon with those red eyes was never a good thing.

Its arm moved away from the blob of its body, giving it more of a distinct torso, and it raised its hand and spread its fingers, waving at me before laughing loudly and floating toward the sky.

Killian jumped the steps and rushed beside me. He mirrored my posture and desperately searched the sky as if the demon might appear, but the demon wouldn't do that. It was taunting us, knowing Killian couldn't see it and I couldn't reach it.

Damn nuisance. Mom hadn't exaggerated the havoc these things caused.

"It flew away." A shiver ran down my spine. "I think it was only here to torment us." I wanted to say more, but I swallowed the words. The fact that he had run out here despite not being able to see the threat worried me. Seeing him hurt or worse was my worst fear.

"Figures." Killian exhaled, but none of the tension left his body. "We need to get to the memorial. Then we can address the issue with Sterlyn and the others. I don't want this to take attention away from Scott and Heather."

My heart panged. Though Heather and I hadn't been super close, we'd forged a bond when we'd arrived back at PawPaw's and discovered the entire pack had vanished, including her parents and her brother, Sean.

He smiled sadly, and a touch of coolness from his pain surged through our connection. He took my hand and led me to the woods. Concern still surged through me from how he'd acted, but I locked it deep inside.

"I'm sorry for my rudeness. I know you weren't trying to throw the fact that you're a silver wolf in my face." He sighed and ran a hand through his short hair. "It's just hard when I can't see the very thing that's threatening you."

Here it was again, his need to protect me as if I were a helpless female. I gritted my teeth, frustration sitting heavy in my stomach, and tried to breathe evenly. Lashing out was not the answer and would only heighten our emotions. Since I didn't have anything nice to say, I remained silent and continued to walk at a steady pace beside him. I couldn't lie and tell him it was okay because the horrible smell would rat me out.

Instead, I listened to the rustle of flying squirrels and an owl stirring from its perch.

Our connection dampened slightly, and I realized he was holding back his feelings, too. The first time I noticed, I'd thought it might be a figment of my imagination, but this was the third time he'd done it. He must have learned that trick from being an alpha and needing to allow only the emotions he desired to filter through the pack links.

Dad had mentioned that sometimes, it was hard to hide your fear when you needed to the most. Maybe Killian was doing just that.

He didn't say anything, and neither did I, and we fell into an amicable silence. The cool breeze on my face with the crisp smell of fall, the dirt between my toes, and the love of my life beside me brought much peace, despite my frustration with him. As we strolled hand in hand, the lines of frustration smoothed from his face. Our troubles didn't seem as dire, even though we were heading to a memorial. For one peaceful moment, it was just him and me.

Walking parallel to the neighborhood, we eventually passed the entrance and continued toward the river. The twinkling stars indicated that darkness was imminent, and voices filtered through the leafless cypresses.

Do you think things will ever calm down enough that we can be a normal couple? I asked my mate.

His brows furrowed, and he looked at me. *What do you mean?*

Like going out to dinner and a movie? The things I'd rolled my eyes at when Dad and Mom had done them were the things I wanted to do with him. *Cook dinner together while drinking a glass of wine and talking about our favorite television show? Just relax without danger hovering over our heads?* We hadn't talked about it, but the government would continue to hunt supernaturals. Our fight was far from over.

Warmth flooded my chest, and I realized Killian had opened himself back up to me. He lifted my hand to his lips and kissed the back of it. *We will because I want those same things. When we welcome our children into this world, I don't want it to be full of uncertainty and terror.*

My stomach fluttered. I loved the sound of that. Obviously, we weren't ready—we had many issues to resolve, both with each other and with the supernatural world—but I very much wanted children with him. And I hoped it would be plural. Sometimes, silver wolves could only birth one child.

He tilted his head and paused. *What? You don't want kids?*

I do. I just hadn't thought about it yet. Ever since I'd laid eyes on him, our lives had been a whirlwind. We'd solidified our bond not even two full days ago, so beyond being close to him and having sex in our free time, not much had crossed my mind. *But now that you've mentioned it, that sounds like what I want as well.*

He grinned crookedly, and my pulse pounded in my ears. I reached out and brushed his shaggy scruff with my fingers. He hadn't shaved in a few days, and it added to his manliness.

His eyes glowed, and though I wished it was because of me, I suspected it was the pack reaching out to him.

His smile fell, and some of the warmth was replaced with the chill of despair. Our reprieve was over, and it was time to mourn the ones we'd lost. *Let's go.*

He wrapped an arm around my waist, pulling me to his side, and we continued toward the voices. The lightheartedness between us was gone as quickly as it had come.

We walked into a hundred-yard-wide open space where hundreds of wolf shifters were gathered. Green fescue grass contrasted with the red roofs and white walls of Shadow Terrace's buildings, the vampire town visible across the water through the bare oak and redbud trees. The murky Tennessee River ran past the edge of the land, and two small rafts, made of branches tied together side by side, bobbed gently in the water.

Sean, PawPaw, Nana, and Heather's parents stood in front of one raft, with PawPaw's pack of one hundred fifty spread out behind them. Killian's pack had gathered behind the second raft. The silver wolves were clustered between the two groups, bridging the gap.

As Killian and I drew closer, I noticed several items on the second raft that symbolized Scott, including a football and several pictures of Scott with a younger boy who looked just like him and with his parents and friends. It gave me a sense of who Scott had been: a football lover, a son, a brother, and a friend.

When I looked at Heather's, my heart constricted. Her raft was simply filled with various white flowers. The lack of personalization emphasized that the fire had stripped everything from PawPaw's pack. The humans and Tom had stolen so much from them.

Sierra hurried over and threw her arms around us. She linked, *Thank gods you're here. I don't know how much longer I can handle the pain of standing around, living through their memories.* The heartbreak she felt almost drowned me.

A few women from Killian's pack turned to me, and the urge to avert my gaze was damn near overwhelming. That would be the worst thing I could do. An alpha mate was meant to be a leader, especially for the same sex, which meant I needed to portray confidence. Though I was a strong wolf, I'd never had the desire to lead. I preferred to blend in with the pack and interject only when I had something worthy to contribute.

This was a whole different ball game.

A woman pulled away from the group and headed toward me. She was around Eliza's age, about sixty, and held such wisdom in her light hazel eyes. Her light amber bob bounced with each step, and her long black skirt flared behind her. When she reached us, she held out her hand to me.

This I hadn't been prepared for—it was a very human-like gesture—but I shook her hand. "My name is Jewel."

"We know," the woman said curtly. "Killian, Lowe, Collin, Luna, and Sierra have made us all aware. I'm Laura."

Did I say *nice to meet you* or *I wish we could have met under better circumstances?* Neither option felt right, especially since the two of us were already pack and this was a tense situation. My mind scrambled, and for like the millionth time, I wished Dad were here with me. He'd know exactly how to handle this situation.

"Laura has been the women's mentor since Mom died," Killian interjected, and tightened his hold on my waist. "She's a wonderful lady who I'm glad is overjoyed that I've found my mate."

She frowned before her face smoothed back into a smile. "She may be your mate, but I've been around this pack for a while now."

"Which is something I'm very thankful for." He kissed my forehead. "And we have an alpha mate once more."

Her mouth drooped, telling me what I needed to know. She hadn't expected Killian to back me, which was odd. Didn't she realize what type of man he was?

The older lady had a pure soul, but it was clear she took her role in the pack very seriously. She might feel threatened by me, but the point was that I didn't intend to replace anyone. I hoped to help wherever Killian and the ladies needed me to.

The best thing I could do was offer an olive branch. I straightened my shoulders and smiled. "I hope you're willing to teach me the way things are done here so the two of us can work well together." Though it was my destiny to lead the women as Killian's mate, that didn't mean I didn't need a close friend to aid me along the way.

The crease between her brows smoothed, and the tightness around her eyes faded. "I'd like that very much."

"Maybe you should join Killian and me for breakfast in the morning so we can spend time together." I wanted her to know I meant to follow through on my words.

She nodded, averting her gaze, and a weight lifted off my shoulders. Maybe she wouldn't challenge my position after all.

You did well. Killian squeezed my hand. *Laura is an amazing woman, but she doesn't like change. She was my mom's best friend before she died.*

Some of her concern could have been concern for the mate Fate had chosen for Killian.

Killian moved through the crowd, taking me with him. Chad locked eyes with me as I passed, and Emmy pushed by him and met my gaze. Her rosy complexion seemed darker than normal, and her dark brown hair framed her face. She was an inch shorter than me, coming in around five-foot-eight, and her satin-gray eyes held a promise. She mouthed, *I'm coming to see you soon.*

I nodded. I had no doubt she would. She and I had been inseparable, and when she'd returned here while I'd remained with PawPaw's pack, it had been the longest time we'd ever been apart. Spending time with my best friend and having her to talk to might make the burdens I carried more manageable.

I continued down the path with Killian, and we passed Sterlyn, Griffin, Annie, and Cyrus to take our place in front of Scott's raft.

Everyone quieted, and the ceremony began. Killian removed his arm from my waist and took my hand as he spoke to the crowd. "We're here today to celebrate the lives of Scott and Heather. I was one of the few who had the pleasure of knowing both of them, and that is something I will cherish for the rest of my life. Their sacrifices won't be in vain, and their memories will never be forgotten. They were brave, and getting to know them was a privilege."

He paused and took a deep breath, emotion swirling between us. "Scott and Heather were genuine and loved their families and packs. Losing them has made the world a darker place, but we can hold on to their light by never forgetting the love and joy they provided us."

Killian looked to PawPaw, who gave a brief speech, and then the ceremony was turned over to their families. We all took the evening to honor their memories by sharing stories, and their family members pushed their rafts into the current to carry their memories on.

THE EVENING HAD BEEN ROUGHER than I'd expected. Not only was I mourning the loss of Heather and Scott, but in a way, I was mourning Dad once more. That sort of grief was indescribable. I'd lost an alpha, which was traumatic on its own, but I'd also lost my rock. Thank gods I now had Killian.

Mom strolled over and threw her arm around my shoulders. She smiled sadly and said, "Hey, sweetheart. Want to go for a walk?"

There was honestly nothing I'd enjoy more. I needed a moment to collect my thoughts because the memorial was weighing on my soul. *Hey, babe. I'm going on a quick walk with Mom,* I linked with Killian.

My skin buzzed as his eyes focused on me. He replied, *Please be safe—you saw that demon just hours ago. Link with me if something goes wrong.*

A sliver of happiness eased the grief. He was trusting me to go on my own. *I promise,* I told him, then turned to Mom. "Let's go." I headed toward the cypress trees that led to home.

The two of us walked in silence until the trees thickened around us.

Mom sighed. "Your father would be so proud of you, even though I wanted to lock you in your room earlier today. Seeing you hurt like that petrified me. And I can only imagine how Killian felt."

"You think Dad would be proud of me?"

"Yes. You acted just like him. It's one of many reasons he and I fought on occasion." She chuckled. Her cognac-brown eyes searched the sky for a sign of him.

I rubbed a hand down my throat. "Killian wasn't happy with me, either."

"Oh, I bet." Mom dropped her arm down mine and took my hand. "Seeing your mate like that, knowing they could die, it's something even the strongest struggle with, especially with a past like his. He lost his entire family."

My chest tightened.

"He's a good man. I dare say almost as good as your father, and I feel blessed that he's your mate. He's one of the few I would approve of." She winked.

"Mom, what happened with Tom?" I hated to change the subject, but after everything, I needed to know.

She sighed and stared into the distance. "He wasn't cruel back then. He was ambitious, but he was a good man and treated me like gold." Mom pursed her lips. "After we mated, he was to take over your grandfather's pack once he stood down. But the night we were to claim each other, I saw Bart outside a grocery store, kneeling down to help a little girl who'd fallen. Something inside me snapped. There was no looking back, and I have no regrets. Being with Bart made all the bad things not matter."

I understood that. Even with the humans knowing about us, I wouldn't give up Killian for the world.

She dropped my hand and bumped her shoulder into mine. "But we don't have to worry about that anymore." Her eyes glowed faintly, and she frowned. "I've got to go help Martha with something. Breakfast tomorrow?"

"Sure, but Laura will be there, too." I smiled. "I'm going to head back to the house." I needed time alone.

THE NEXT WEEK passed in a blur. I was helping PawPaw's and Ruby's packs get acclimated and getting my bearings concerning my own with Emmy's help. Even though we weren't quite inseparable anymore, our friendship hadn't suffered, and she'd accompanied me while I made the rounds with Laura and the women of my new pack. Killian and I spent every waking moment together, and Sierra reclaimed the nightly activities of forcing Sterlyn, Griffin, Annie, Cyrus, Emmy, Luna, Killian, and me to watch romantic comedies with her. We all piled into either Killian's and my house or Sterlyn and Griffin's and took up every spot on the couch and floor to spend time together.

One morning, I woke to find Killian already out of bed. I threw my legs over the side of the mattress and hurried down the hallway to the kitchen. The smell of bacon, eggs, and biscuits made my mouth water and my stomach gurgle with anticipation. But when I walked into the kitchen, Killian was gone, and the eggs and bacon were already placed on plates.

Where was he? I sniffed the air, following his scent

toward the front door as panic swirled through our connection.

Something was wrong. Before I could open the door, I heard Killian say, "We have to be sure before we tell everyone."

"I am, but Dad doesn't believe me," Ruby replied urgently. "And if you don't do something about it, everyone will blame *you*."

My stomach dropped. What the hell was she up to now?

CHAPTER FOURTEEN

WITHOUT THINKING THROUGH THE CONSEQUENCES, I yanked the front door open and stalked into the front yard, where they stood just a few feet in front of me.

Their heads swiveled around, and Ruby averted her gaze to the grass as she tucked a piece of hair behind her ear. Killian didn't smile at me like he normally did each morning. His face was pale, and his cheeks were flushed pink with the shame swirling through our bond.

Before completing our bond, I might have thought that was because I'd caught him outside with Ruby while he'd thought I was still sleeping, but I knew better now. His love for me was undeniable, and I didn't feel threatened by her or anyone anymore.

She was up to something, and I needed to know what. Killian had enough regrets—she didn't need to be picking at his insecurities. The gods knew we had enough problems without her exacerbating them. I placed my hands on my hips and glared at her. "What the *hell* do you think you're doing?"

She closed her eyes. "This isn't what it looks like. He wanted to come out here so you could rest—"

"I'm not upset about that." I didn't want her to hold the illusion that I felt threatened by her. "I heard you tell him that people would blame him, which is manipulation to get what you want."

Lowe, Collin, Chad, and a few other guys from our pack were walking past our house toward the training area. A guy I hadn't met yet, who was in his mid-twenties, murmured, "Damn, Killian is a lucky man. Not only does he have that new girl hanging around him, but his mate is hot as sin."

Killian's attention swung toward the guy who'd spoken, making it clear he'd heard everything. He walked over to me and pulled me to his chest. *We need to go inside before I have to kill one of our own pack members.*

"Dude, Jewel's like my sister," Chad grumbled. "Either say that stuff through your pack link so I can't hear it, or better yet, don't say anything."

I mashed my lips together. Chad and I always hated it when we overheard people making comments about us. Humans had no clue what we could hear, so that had been a regular occurrence when we'd venture into the city and hung around people our age growing up.

Wearing a thin white cotton shirt of Killian's with only panties underneath wasn't helping matters. This was a good example of why impulsivity wasn't smart.

As if he sensed my embarrassment, Killian twisted us so his body shielded mine. He opened the door and led me back inside as he called over his shoulder, "Let me talk to Jewel. Then I'll find you. You can go train with Chad and the others, and we'll meet you there in a bit."

I was surprised he hadn't invited her inside to join us,

but he must not want her nearby when he informed the rest of us what she'd told him.

"That works," Ruby said with relief. "I need to work some frustration out, anyway."

He shut the door, and the two of us walked into the living room. The smell of the food made my stomach gurgle again.

Why don't you get dressed and come eat? he linked, and pulled me into his arms, kissing my lips. *I had planned on feeding you in bed and then ravishing you, but if what Ruby told me is true, we unfortunately don't have time for that.*

My stomach plummeted. I liked his original plan and wished Ruby had brought her information to him later. But if something was that wrong, who was I to argue with the change?

After returning the kiss, I pulled away and headed back into our bedroom. I had planned to meet up with Laura and some of the other women later this morning, but we had to handle the threat. I entered the walk-in closet and smiled, remembering Killian clearing out the right side for my clothes. I flipped through them and settled on a vibrant blue top that almost matched the color of my eyes and complimented my auburn hair. Then I snatched up a pair of jeans, a bra, and panties and quickly dressed.

Killian connected, *Sterlyn and Griffin are finishing their breakfast, and then they'll come over. Sterlyn's contacting Annie, Cyrus, Alex, Ronnie, and Rosemary.*

You'd better tell Sierra, or you'll never hear the end of it, I teased. Sierra hated to be left out, although sometimes, her presence caused more problems than anyone could have predicted.

She'll get over it, he replied. *If I were going to include someone else from the pack, it would be Billy since he's the next in command after us.*

I yanked my shirt over my jeans and headed back to the kitchen to find that Killian had the table set with steaming cups of coffee and plates filled with eggs, biscuits, and bacon for the two of us. Instead of sitting across from each other, he had placed our two chairs side by side.

Taking the seat nearer the back door, I kissed his lips before picking up a knife to spread the grape jelly and butter he had placed between us. I linked, *This looks delicious. Thank you.*

Only the best for my baby. He winked.

I popped a piece of bacon into my mouth and slathered the jelly and butter onto the biscuit. "I take it you're making me wait until the others get here before you tell me what Ruby said?"

He exhaled, and the area around his eyes tightened. "Let's just enjoy breakfast. It might be the last chance we have for a couple of days."

Patience wasn't my best quality, but for the reason he'd just stated, I figured I could use what little bit I had for us.

We ate in silence, enjoying each other's company and the food. Even though the eggs and bacon had been sitting out, they were still warm, so Ruby must not have been here long before I'd awoken. For all I knew, her knock could've been what had woken me.

As I took my last bite of food and sipped my slightly sweetened coffee, the front door opened. "See, I told you we should've come here for breakfast," Griffin grumbled, his and Sterlyn's footsteps heading down the hallway toward us. "He made his mom's biscuits. Those are from scratch!"

My eyes widened, and I looked at Killian and linked, *No wonder they're so delicious. Those are the best biscuits*

I've ever had, but I thought it was because you made them for me.

They were made with love and Mom's special buttermilk biscuit recipe, he answered as he took my hand in his. *I haven't made them in years. It was too painful before, but with you here beside me, the pain's more bearable, and I want to share things with you.*

I considered his words, and he was right. I still missed Dad terribly. The void would always remain in my heart, but with Killian by my side, things didn't feel as dire. It wasn't that I'd forgotten Dad or what he meant to me, but rather, I had someone on whom I could rely and with whom I could share everything...even my pain. *I will always be here for you to share your happiness, sadness, insecurities, strengths, and pain.*

He gave me that crooked smile I loved more than my next breath. *I know, and the same thing goes for you, because there's no way I'm even going to attempt to top what you just said to me.*

I beamed and teased, *Smart man. Maybe I can train you after all.*

"Uh...dude, did you bring us here to tell us something or so that Sterlyn and I could watch you and Jewel eye-fuck each other right in front of us?" Griffin asked, pulling me back to reality.

My face caught fire, and I turned my attention to them. Sterlyn wore her usual black shirt and jeans, with Griffin in his standard polo shirt and khaki pants. Sometimes, it was a little comical to see them together because Sterlyn was so down-to-earth while Griffin was preppy. It probably had to do with him growing up in Shadow City, where his late father had been the alpha wolf shifter.

"Leave them alone." Sterlyn smacked her mate on the

arm. "Kill is like our brother, and Jewel is family. They deserve to be happy, especially with all the crap we have to deal with."

The front door opened again, and Cyrus groaned as he and Annie made their way into the house. "What crap are we dealing with now?"

The sweet scent of vampires followed them, meaning Ronnie and Alex were in tow.

"Not sure yet," Griffin grumbled. "Killian is too busy staring at Jewel. He's about to go caveman and throw her over his shoulder and take her to their bedroom. I hope that's not why he called us over because I know what fated mates want to do all the time. He doesn't have to show me."

I giggled, unable to hold it back.

Sterlyn rolled her eyes. "See what I have to deal with?"

Annie and Cyrus stepped into view, and I almost lost it. Cyrus's dark gray shirt had chunky spit-up all the way down the front, and Annie's royal blue shirt didn't look much better.

Within seconds, Alex and Ronnie appeared behind them, and Alex scanned the room dramatically.

Brows furrowing, Killian asked, "What are you doing?"

"I heard a man's voice, but the words sounded like something Sierra would say." Alex lifted his brow. "Surely Griffin wouldn't be so melodramatic."

Mashing her lips together, Ronnie tried to hide her smile, but it didn't work very well.

"That was wittier than something *she* would say." Griffin puffed out his chest. "Tell them, baby." His gaze flicked to Sterlyn.

She shrugged. "Sierra is pretty witty."

His lips pursed, but the golden flecks in his hazel eyes brightened. "Here I thought you'd have my back."

"Lying wouldn't bode well for any of us in this house." She wrinkled her nose, but the corners of her mouth kept tipping upward.

I loved the relationship they had. It was nice to see that two alphas could still make jokes at each other's expense. Some alphas were too egotistical to handle it, but that was how well-matched they were.

At the sound of flapping wings, I glanced out the back door. Rosemary landed on the porch. Levi was right beside her in his demon form, and he flicked into view as he reached out to open the door. The two of them came inside, and Rosemary leaned against the wall by the door. Dirt covered her burnt orange shirt, and Levi had dirt crusted in the scruff on his face.

Killian took my hand and asked, "Why are you two so dirty?"

"We were helping with the construction of the shifter section of the city," Rosemary answered as she wiped her forehead with the back of her hand. "So many of them are homeless and having to double up in various sections. We're trying to help hurry the rebuilding process."

From what I'd been told, during the demon war, they'd opened the gate on the shifter side of Shadow City, so most of the damage from the battle was located there. I had yet to visit the city and had no desire to go. Bad things had happened to the silver wolves in there. To me, that city represented everything I never wanted to become.

"And we're trying to get a handle on things in Shadow Terrace, since a quarter of our population turned blood-thirsty." Alex hung his head. "I'd hoped we wouldn't face this issue again after Matthew's demise, yet here we are."

Ronnie laid her head on his shoulder. "It's not your fault. That was all the demons. We did the best we could."

She was right, but that didn't mean we didn't feel responsible for the fallout. I even wondered, if we'd all been together, would our current situation have been less severe?

"The blame game never accomplishes anything." Sterlyn strolled to the counter and leaned against it to see everyone in the kitchen. "All it does is waste energy that's needed elsewhere."

"Like now." Rosemary lifted her hand. "What's so important that Levi's and my presence were immediately requested? I flew so fast, I lost a handful of feathers."

Levi glanced at her adoringly. "What my love means is, what would you like to discuss?"

She narrowed her eyes and lifted her chin. "That's what I said."

"But not very politely." He kissed her cheek and winked. "Which we're working on?"

Rosemary lifted a finger, but Killian jumped in before the situation devolved. "This morning, Ruby informed me that she thinks more supernaturals have been kidnapped."

I wasn't surprised, but I'd hoped it would have taken longer.

"How would she know that?" Annie strode to the sink and snatched a few paper towels from the nearby dispenser. She dampened them and started wiping down her shirt.

"Good question." Sterlyn nodded. "First off, I've been watching the news religiously and have seen nothing about that, and second, even if the news did report a disappearance, I doubt they'd realize it was shifters."

Annie handed Cyrus some wet paper towels, and he dabbed at the spit-up. She said, "I don't know Ruby, but she seems to like attention. Could this be a tactic?"

I was glad I wasn't the person who'd asked. If I had,

Killian might have thought the question had stemmed from jealousy because of our past, when Ruby had tried to steal his attention from me before we'd mated.

Shrugging, Killian sighed. "I have no clue. She said she read it on a website."

"Nothing on the internet can be trusted." Rosemary crossed her arms and frowned. "They think angels go around carrying trumpets. I enjoy a good trumpet, but it's not something I lug around with me. How inconvenient would that be in time of war?"

For a second, I thought she was joking, but when her face didn't break from its scowl, I realized she was very serious.

"Some would argue that everything is true on the internet." Ronnie smirked. "So I'm sure you have a trumpet stowed away close by."

Rosemary's eyes bulged. "I do not! That would be as asinine as an angel cutting off their flight feathers."

I had no idea what she meant, but my mind focused on what Killian had said. I had an idea of what Ruby must have been talking about. I said, "One thing that my pack—er, my former pack did was to keep tabs on a local supernatural website." Not considering the silver wolf pack as my pack would take time. "We'd monitor them to make sure no one mentioned silver wolves." Dad had been overly cautious, but at the time, we'd wanted to remain hidden. "We were careful when we ran at night, and we never popped up on anyone's radar, but if something happened, we wanted to stay ahead of it."

"Wait. I remember Aurora talking about some website, too." Annie tapped her chin. "I wonder if it's the same one."

"It doesn't matter if Jewel can check it." Levi rubbed his

chin, and dirt fell to the wood floor. "Do you still have the information?"

"All I need is a laptop." Mine had melted in the fire.

Killian jumped up. "I have the one I used for college." He disappeared into our bedroom, and I heard the sound of a drawer opening.

"How come I didn't know about this?" Sterlyn pursed her lips.

That I had an answer for. "We kept it to ourselves. When Theo found Rudie and brought her into the silver wolf pack, she told us about the website. Her pack regularly communicated with packs across the United States, and in some cases, around the world, to discuss threats and anything out of the norm."

Killian came back with a black laptop and headed straight to me. He placed the laptop on the table. *The password is Olive2o.*

Heart constricting, I typed it in. The password was his sister's name and her age when she died. It was a stark reminder of how impacted he still was by his sister's and parents' deaths.

Swallowing the sob building in my chest, I tapped on the internet browser and typed in the web address. When the sign-in page for the supernatural intranet opened, I entered our pack's username and password. The various rooms for each country and region popped up on one side, and I selected the chat for the southeast region.

I found the thread Ruby had referenced. People were talking about kids who hadn't shown up to their high school for the past few days. They were concerned because each missing teen was tied to the same pack.

I skimmed down for the latest updates. Though the situation sounded suspicious, that didn't necessarily mean humans were involved.

But the last update had been posted just ten minutes ago, and it had vomit churning in my stomach. "This is so much worse than what Ruby read."

CHAPTER FIFTEEN

OUR TIME of normalcy was over.

The past week had been amazing. I'd met my new wolf pack and learned how things worked. Though adjusting to their ways had been stressful, Laura had been incredibly helpful, and I didn't want to let her down.

Now we'd all be under a whole different kind of stress.

"Any day now," Alex grumbled, and edged toward me.

He was right. I needed to get it out already. "Another pack has disappeared."

"*What?*" Killian leaned over to look at the screen. "Ruby said a few people."

My hand lifted to smack his arm. He was acting like he didn't believe me, but I had to remember that wasn't what he meant. He just didn't want it to be true. Sometimes, denial was easier, and no one knew that better than I did. "This morning, the chat group was speculating that it might be a few people. Like Ruby said, a few teenagers from the same pack didn't show up for a few days in a row for class. Then three of them also didn't show up for their job at a moving company. The owner is a wolf shifter from a different pack who likes to hire young supernatural kids. When they didn't show up for the third day straight after begging to work full-time over the holidays, he drove over to check things out. The entire pack is missing, not just the teenagers." I glanced up from the screen at Killian. "Sound familiar?"

"That's exactly what happened to your grandfather's pack." Killian placed his elbows on the table and put his head in his hands.

Exactly. "The only difference is that Heather and I were out when the pack was taken. Had we been home like usual, we would've disappeared with them."

Sterlyn placed a hand over her mouth and sighed. "They must have watched the pack to make sure the same mistake didn't happen. These are smart people we're dealing with."

"What bothers me most is that they were even able to find another wolf pack. Did Tom betray every pack he came across?" Cyrus crumpled the paper towel he'd used to make the spit-up situation worse and tossed it on the table.

It landed next to me, but I was too concerned with what was going on to give him a hard time. Besides, during the past few days, I'd grown attached to Arion and Eliza, who'd spat up enough on my clothing that I'd become immune.

"They likely have more than one pack helping them." Ronnie bit her bottom lip. "It could be other kinds of supernaturals, for all we know."

"Where did this pack disappear from?" Levi leaned against the back door.

"East of Knoxville, near the Smoky Mountains. About half an hour from Gatlinburg," I answered, scrolling for a more precise location.

He blinked as if my words weren't registering.

Griffin snorted. "You don't know where that is, do you?"

"Not at all." Levi shrugged and shoved his hands into his jeans pockets.

Ronnie tilted her head, examining him. "Then why did you ask?"

He bounced on his feet. "It's a logical question, and *if* I'd been raised on Earth and not in Hell, it would've been very meaningful."

"PawPaw's settlement was in Gatlinburg, and the government facility where they were held is southeast of Knoxville." I was never good at geography, so I hoped I was using the right compass directions. Regardless, *I* knew how to get there, and hopefully, that was all that mattered.

"So this pack's location is two to three hours away from here?" Levi bobbed his head.

"More like two and a half. It's only thirty minutes from Gatlinburg." I continued to scroll down and noted the location that had just been shared. The owner of the moving agency was panicked and wanted someone to come and check things out.

As far as I knew, our group was the only one who'd experienced anything like this.

"We have to leave *now*," Rosemary stated firmly. "If it's the same people who took Jewel's family pack, they'll burn the houses down to remove whatever evidence was left behind."

I'd been so focused on their disappearance that I hadn't thought that far ahead, but she was right.

"Griffin and I caught up with the rebuild in Shadow City and met with the council. We can spare one more day," Sterlyn said as she took Griffin's hand.

They'd been working hard to rebuild Shadow City, just

like Rosemary and Levi, during the morning and afternoons, and they'd been heading back over here every night to reduce the number of heads that needed a temporary place to sleep. Alex and Ronnie had opened up the royal mansion as a shelter because the need was so great due to the destruction.

"Are you sure?" Killian asked, and turned toward them from his seat at the table. "I hate to take you away when your people need you."

"It's fine. My mom and Kira are handling things well." Griffin waved a hand, dismissing his concern. "And if humans are taking more supernaturals, it could eventually affect everyone here. It's best if we head off the problem instead of waiting for it to arrive on our doorstep."

I linked with Killian, *Kira?*

That's our fox shifter friend in the city who also heads the police department, he answered.

Rosemary wrinkled her nose. "Look how well that worked out with the demon war. Most of the shifter side of the town has to be rebuilt, so I'm in agreement. Mother, Father, Bune, Zagan, and Eleanor can handle things while we go. Maybe not as efficiently, but the job will get done all the same."

"I wish I had half your confidence." Annie chuckled endearingly. "I just try to appear as if I have my shit together. Raising infant twins is nothing to sneeze at."

"And that's why you two should stay here," Sterlyn said. "You've spent enough time away from the little ones, so let us do some recon. We'll let you know if we need your help."

Alex pinched the bridge of his nose. "I hate to do this, but Ronnie and I really need to stay as well. Gwen and Joshua are doing an amazing job, but there is so much discord in Shadow Terrace and the city. I'd rather not go away again so soon if you're just going to scout the area. Gwen's and Joshua's entire focus is on the Terrace, and Ronnie and I are needed in the city."

From what I'd picked up on last week, Gwen was Alex's sister and the vampire princess, and Joshua was a vampire friend they trusted wholeheartedly.

"Unless you need us." Ronnie placed her hand on Alex's arm. "Then we'll come because Griffin is right. We need to stop the threat before it grows larger."

"If you're needed here, you should stay," Sterlyn assured Ronnie, and touched her chest. "Both are equally important."

"And we don't want more bloodthirsty vampires popping up," Griffin said as he punched Alex in the shoulder.

Narrowing his eyes, Alex hissed faintly. "Though we somehow became friends, I'd still prefer you not touch me unless it's a life-or-death situation."

In my short amount of time here, I'd noticed that Alex was standoffish except when it came to Ronnie. The rest of the guys would pat someone's shoulder to show affection, but he avoided casual touches. I wasn't sure if it was because he was a vampire, royalty, or just not that type of person.

"I bet Emmy and Chad would go with us." I hadn't gotten to spend as much time with Emmy as I was used to. The three of us had been one another's shadows after Theo got mated and stopped spending as much time with Chad.

Killian's eyebrows rose. "So I take it we're going?" Through our mate connection, I could feel the humor wafting through him, giving me the urge to laugh.

"I'm kinda the expert here." With that, I effectively ruined the mood and sobered him up. Only Heather and I had ever run into this situation before, and I was the only one alive to tell the story.

His shoulders sagged. "We should bring a few more people, though."

"Not so many people that if someone's watching the area, we give away our presence." Sterlyn rolled her shoulders. "If the owner of the moving company went by and didn't get taken or injured, we should be okay."

I hated to disagree with her since she had been my alpha, but I had to speak up. "Unless they're circling back to set fire to the houses."

"True." She ran a hand along the counter.

Rosemary stretched a wing, the edge of her dark feathers touching Levi. "They may have thought you were close by and used the fire to draw you out."

"Or the fire could've been a message that they can erase supernaturals from existence." Levi karate-chopped the air. "One thing I learned in Hell is that sometimes, it's not worth trying to figure out the message because we know they want to capture, torture, and kill us all."

His words seemed to remove all the oxygen from the room.

"You do have a point." Griffin snorted humorlessly.

Exhaling so hard that his citrus breath hit my face, Killian sat straighter in his chair. "I believe our best bet is to take a smaller group and park a few miles away so we can walk through the woods to the houses. If we sense danger or smell anything unusual, we can turn around and head back to the cars until reinforcements come."

That sounded like the safest course. "If the homes are

on fire, we'll know without having to get close, and we can leave without a fight," I said. "If we smell strong scents, we'll do what Killian suggested and call for reinforcements. Besides, they had the cabins burning within a day of capturing the pack. This is already day four, as far as the owner of the moving company knows." Perhaps they hadn't set the houses on fire because humans lived close by and they didn't want to draw attention. I was quite certain that the fire at my grandparents' cabins was set to lure Heather and me back. But as Levi had said, none of that mattered.

"Levi and I can do flyovers, and we'll know to be more cautious and make sure we examine everything, even the brush, for camouflaged humans." Rosemary sneered. "I won't make that mistake twice."

She was beating herself up, and I understood perfectly what she was going through.

Annie mashed her lips together. "Rosemary, it was smoky, too. There was a lot going on, and this is a whole new threat. None of us know what to expect."

"Don't minimize my mistake." Rosemary scoffed and fluffed her wings. "As a trained warrior, I'm supposed to be prepared for every possible scenario, and I failed."

The saying *ruffle one's feathers* took on a whole new meaning for me. But like in the supernatural books I enjoyed reading, much of the information in those stories was based on facts. The ideas had to come from somewhere, so of course, that would be true for expressions, too.

Pushing a piece of her copper hair out of her face, Ronnie stared at Rosemary. "What Annie is trying to say, only a lot more nicely, is stop beating yourself up and get over it. You learned. Now move on."

"I may be upset with myself, but I *never* physically

harm myself." Rosemary stood tall. "That would be point-less, and yes, I've learned that more training is required of me."

When he smiled, Levi's irises twinkled. "Clearly, you don't know how Rosey works. She's always hard on herself and rarely feels pride when she does something amazing. That's like asking her not to want to ravish me...impossible."

Rosemary paused as if considering his words, then nodded. "I can't disagree."

In many ways, I admired her and could see why Killian had been interested in her before me. She was direct, honest, and strove to do what was right for all. She wasn't embarrassed about her needs, and I wished I could embrace my sexuality like she did.

"All right, we need to get moving. Emmy and Chad are on their way to go with us." Sterlyn rubbed her hands together. "So we'll take those two, Killian, Jewel, Rosemary, Levi, Griffin, and me. It'll be a long day, but we should be able to make the entire trip up and back in a day if we move now. Pack a bag in case we need to shift or wind up being gone for a few days."

True. It wasn't like we would need to scope the area out for days. If the pack had been taken, the trail would be cold. There would be no way we could locate them since none of us were pack members, and we wouldn't even have a faint link to guide us. Hopefully, none of us would get taken like Chad had, which was the only reason we'd located PawPaw's pack so quickly.

Cyrus's expression twisted. "I hate not going with you, but I don't want to leave the twins behind *again*. Though Midnight is an amazing grandmother, I hate being sepa-rated from them."

I'd met Midnight, Annie's biological mother, several times. She had so much love for those two babies, and it warmed my heart.

"I feel the same way." Annie laid a hand on his shoulder and leaned against his chest, her head hitting right where the spit-up was mashed into his shirt.

"It's just a recon mission, remember?" Sterlyn smiled and hurried past Griffin, wrapping her arms around Cyrus and Annie. "Stay home and take care of my niece and nephew. And check in with the other packs."

"Hey, I want in on this." Ronnie blurred a few feet and got in on the group hug. I'd never seen them do anything like this before.

Rosemary shook her head. "Mortals are weird."

"Not going to disagree there, though I do like it when you press your body all over me." Levi waggled his brows.

A rare smile peeked through Rosemary's stern expression, and the faint scent of arousal wafted around.

Now I felt uncomfortable. "Okay, well, I'm going to go pack a few things so we can get out of here." I didn't want to see how this progressed since Rosemary seemed open to doing all the things, and I wasn't certain if that included a show.

"I'm with Jewel." Alex took Ronnie's hand and pulled her toward the door. "We'll keep our phones close by in case you need us."

Sterlyn stepped away, ending the group hug. "Sounds good. I'll head next door to get a few things as well."

Our group dispersed, with Griffin and Killian going to talk to Ruby, Rosemary and Levi waiting in our living room for us to leave, and Sterlyn grabbing some clothes and readying the Navigator so we could take one vehicle. It wasn't long before we loaded into the car with Emmy and Chad in the third row, Killian and me in the middle, and Sterlyn and Griffin in the front seats. Rosemary and Levi flew overhead, and I leaned toward the navigation system and plugged in the address the moving company owner had listed, asking for someone to come see if they could figure out what was going on.

We made the ride to the little town at the base of the Great Smoky Mountains in complete silence. Everyone was on edge. Normally, Emmy would have been trying to embarrass me with Killian, telling him about all the shenanigans we'd gotten into, but even she held her tongue. Soon, we were entering the quiet area of Wears Valley. Though PawPaw's pack had lived close by, I'd never heard of this pack, so they must not have communicated with them much. Most packs kept to themselves and worked together only when it benefited both sides.

The GPS led us toward the bottom of the mountains, exactly like the owner of the moving company had described. A few miles out, we reached a deserted school, and Griffin pulled off and parked in the lot. There were a few small restaurants and a gas station, but the town was so small, you could blink and miss it. In a way, it looked like a screenshot of the past.

The six of us climbed out of the Navigator and headed toward the towering mountain. A handful of people milled about, but no one paid us any attention as we crossed the road and hurried into the thick woods.

Stay close to me, please, Killian linked as he took my hand. We followed right behind Griffin and Sterlyn, with Chad and Emmy taking up the rear.

After all the drama from our last fight, he didn't have to ask twice. *Promise.*

Some of the tension released from his body, and the two of us moved in rhythm.

Just like Sevierville and Gatlinburg, which weren't far away, yellow birches, red cedars, and tall oaks made up most of the woods. The sound of animals scurrying had my body relaxing.

Griffin kept an eye on his phone, then stopped. He turned toward us. "The place is straight up, about half a mile away."

"If there is danger, it'll be close by," Sterlyn said, her face tense. "Luckily, the six of us can get messages out wide since we're all linked with someone who can communicate across the packs and we're all in range. Remember to be quiet and remain diligent."

"In other words, remember our training," Emmy said, echoing the words Dad had used so many times. She gave me a sad smile, but it was full of kindness. He'd meant almost as much to her as he had to me.

Chad's jaw twitched. "Yes, but remember, this is *not* training. If you get taken, it's not fun." He shivered.

I hated what the humans had done to him. "Hopefully, we won't run into anything."

"That's what I'm hoping for as well," Killian agreed, and tightened his hold on my hand.

"No verbal communication from here on out until we determine whether there's a risk," Sterlyn commanded.

We all nodded and moved at a slow and steady pace. I glanced overhead and saw Rosemary flying fairly close to the ground with Levi by her side. If a human saw her, they'd think she was a huge bird.

As we continued, I kept an eye on my surroundings as well as the sky. Something olive green caught my eye. I blinked, not believing what I saw, but no matter what I did, the image came back the same.

It was impossible. They were extinct. No one had seen one in centuries. And worse, it was flying right toward Rosemary.

I linked with Killian, *Dragon!*

CHAPTER SIXTEEN

THOUGH I'D JUST LINKED with Killian, I still couldn't believe it. The dragons that had migrated from the Fae Realm to Earth had died out centuries ago after other supernaturals had hunted them to extinction. The story was that there were still fae dragons, but fae rarely ventured to Earth. No one knew why, but it was safer that way. Fae were manipulative and elitist, and we had more than enough of those attitudes on Earth without additional supernatural help.

No matter how much I blinked, the dark olive dragon remained in sight...and then a second green dragon flew over the trees and fell in behind the first. The second dragon was slightly smaller and a few shades lighter.

Cold flickers of Killian's fear coursed through our mate bond, mixing with mine, confirming my fears. I wasn't hallucinating. Two dragons were flying toward us.

"Rosemary!" Sterlyn shouted, just as I saw Rosemary tense.

She and Levi had been searching below, not expecting a threat in the sky. There were bird shifters in the world, but they didn't typically get involved in battles because they were smaller and relatively easy to kill. Birds mainly acted as scouts and didn't attack.

Something snapped, and I turned to see a blur racing toward us. *Just a vampire*, I thought, and as I went to move my head to watch Rosemary again, my stomach lurched.

Vampire.

Alex and Ronnie weren't here, and neither was any other vampire from Shadow City or Shadow Terrace. Alex and Ronnie would have informed us if anyone was. So who the *hell* was this?

Fur sprouted on Chad's arms as his wolf surged forward. His smoky topaz irises glowed as he locked on to the vampire charging toward us.

The figure slowed, and soon a gorgeous woman stood about fifty yards away from us. She was of average height for a supernatural being, close to five-eight, and her dark hair was cut in a bob. She wore a silky black tank top and black jeans. Two other things made her stand out: despite being in the woods, she was wearing chunky black platform shoes, and her eyes, lined with heavy black eyeliner, were dark brown. This vampire still had her humanity, so there was that.

Killian stepped in front of me, blocking me slightly from the vampire's view. I took a deep breath and tamped down my anger. He was only trying to protect me, and if I acted the least bit agitated, the vampire might think we were hostile.

Reaching out to touch Chad's arm, Sterlyn inched forward and said, "We aren't here to cause problems."

The corner of the vampire's mouth tilted upward. "That's exactly what someone would say if they were here to cause problems."

She had us there.

"Well, I'm more worried about the dragons in the sky," Killian growled as he kept his attention on Rosemary. "And everyone here should be, too." His shoulders were so tense that his muscles twitched through his shirt. "They aren't supposed to be *alive*."

"And we're more worried about what looks like an angel," the vampire bit out. "They aren't supposed to exist!"

"Of course they exist," Griffin scoffed. "I grew up with them. But those two are a different story." He gestured wildly at the dragons, who were almost within fighting distance of Rosemary and Levi.

My entire mind focused on the one word she'd said —*we*. "Wait, the dragons are with you?"

"Yes, they are." The vampire lifted her chin. "I take it the angel is with you."

"You'd be right. If I were you, I'd make the dragons stand down before they get their asses kicked," Killian said through clenched teeth.

"Not even angels are immune to fire, I suspect." The vampire leaned back on her heels and crossed her arms. "And dragons can breathe that, you know."

How she didn't topple over was beyond me. I'd be tripping over my feet in those shoes, and that was with silver wolf agility.

Four sets of footprints sounded behind her. They weren't moving quickly enough to be vampires and were too soft and silent to be human, meaning they were some other sort of supernatural.

"Is this a trap?" Emmy asked as she looked past the vampire toward the sound. "Distract us while your four friends surround us and your dragons go for the angel?"

She was right. Since Tom and his pack were dead, the

footsteps could belong to members of a backup pack the humans had reached out to. If they had dragons on their side, they could probably abduct most packs without needing to knock them out.

Flashes of soft pink and vibrant red broke through the bushes and bare tree trunks as whatever was coming ran toward us. The colors were such a contrast to the winter woods that they stood out. After a few seconds, two women and two men came into view.

Killian inched forward, but I placed a hand on his shoulder. None of them, even the vampire, had a vile essence. *They feel like good people. If Sterlyn isn't attacking, let's give them a chance.* I grimaced. I'd just told him what to do, and he was *my* alpha, but I couldn't let him act rashly.

Fine, but if the dragons attack Rosemary and Levi or something seems off, we don't hesitate to attack, he replied.

Agreed. Though I wanted to get a read on them, that didn't mean I'd act foolishly.

The woman with rose gold hair caught my attention. Her hair was also styled in a bob, and her gorgeous ocean-blue eyes were almost as bright as mine. She was a similar height to the vampire, but her scent was musky vanilla, indicating she was a shifter. There was something different about her, though I couldn't explain it, and the strength of an alpha pulsed around her.

The woman next to her had long red hair that cascaded down her back. Her hazel eyes were narrowed, but mischief sparkled in them. She was about an inch shorter than the rose gold–haired girl, but where the pink-haired girl seemed strong and put together, this one sought to stand out from the crowd.

The man standing beside the pink-haired girl was her polar opposite. He was over six feet tall with shaggy, jet-black hair. His eyes were such a dark blue they looked navy, and some sort of tribal tattoo peeked out from underneath his short sleeves. Considering how closely they stood and the combination of their scents, it was clear those two were mates. They had to be in their mid-twenties, so a few years older than us.

"If we were going to attack you, we wouldn't waste time chatting." The red-haired woman tossed her hair over her shoulder. It was so long it hit the chest of the man beside her.

He didn't flinch, as if that were a normal occurrence. His own hair was buzzed shorter than Killian's, and his russet eyes had tightened in the corners. He was shorter than the shaggy-haired man but larger...almost as bulky as Griffin. Like the other couple, his and the redhead's scents were identical.

Also mates.

The vampire snickered. "Are you sure about that, Roxy?"

Clearly, the vampire was good friends with the wolf shifters, which was odd. Our friends were the only people I'd ever met whose friendships crossed over various supernatural races.

I tilted my head as I desperately tried to piece everything together. "I take it you all came here because of the intranet post?" If they were part of the missing pack and had been left behind, they'd either be desperate for help or attack us with questions. They were trying to get a sense of us, too.

The pink haired girl's focus zeroed in on me. "Yes. I take it that's why you're here, too."

"It is." Sterlyn nodded as her shoulders relaxed marginally.

There was no scent of sulfur. They weren't lying. But we had bigger issues to take care of. I glanced upright to check on Rosemary and found the two dragons hovering right in front of her. The dragons and Rosemary were staring each other down. Rosemary's wings were tenser than usual, ready for an attack, but so far, they weren't engaging in battle. I linked with Killian, *We need to fix the situation up there before it turns volatile.*

"Why don't you control your dragons?" Killian kept his attention on the pink haired woman.

She grinned, reminding me of Sterlyn. "They aren't my pets, just as I'm sure the angel isn't yours." An extra jolt of power surrounded her, something I'd never experienced before.

"I don't know." The vampire smirked. "Egan would look good on a leash."

The taller man exhaled. "Lillith, you can't say stuff like that. Jade would kick your ass if she heard you talking about her mate that way."

"Can it, Don." Lillith glanced over her shoulder at him. "She's not around, so we'll be fine."

Chad snickered. "I feel like I'm back at Shadow Ridge with Sierra, Luna, and Alex."

I chuckled. That was accurate.

The sound of flapping wings diverted my attention above us again. Rosemary's face was tense, her lips smashed into a line as she landed beside me. Levi was right beside her, but he remained in his shadow form. Rosemary kept her wings spread, ready to fight at any second. She examined the group of five in front of us and scowled.

"Your feathers are gorgeous," the red-haired girl said as she stepped toward the angel.

A large hand gripped her shoulder, and the man behind her murmured, "Roxy, don't."

They were just as enthralled by Rosemary as we were by the dragons, which had disappeared from the sky. A shiver ran down my spine. "Where are the dragons?"

"Don't worry," the pink haired girl said. "They're likely shifting into their human forms so they can talk with everyone. They can only link with their own thunder, the same way shifter packs do."

"Thunder?" Emmy bit her bottom lip.

"It's the dragon equivalent of a pack," Don answered gruffly. His body language mirrored Killian's—tense and cautious. He kept flicking his attention among us, waiting for the first sign of an attack.

"Dragons are fae creatures." Rosemary's hands clenched into fists. "So their presence here shouldn't be possible."

Levi stood close to her but remained silent. I was confident he wanted to remain invisible in case something bad happened, and they would have no clue that someone else was nearby.

At least we had the insight that none of these people were angel descendants.

Someone to our right cleared his throat, and our heads jerked in that direction just as the tallest and most muscular man I'd ever seen stepped from between two red cedar trees with his arm around a woman a few inches taller than me. The pupils of the man's golden eyes changed to slits before becoming human-like again. His long, honey-blond hair was gelled upward, and with his free hand, he rubbed his sandy scruff. "The dragons who live on Earth were once from the Fae Realm, but over the centuries that we've been here, our magic has evolved to be part of this world."

These had to be the dragons, Egan and Jade.

The woman fitted against his body as if Fate had designed her for him, her lush dark hair vibrant against his pale green shirt. She narrowed her honey gold eyes as she examined us one by one. She and the man next to Roxy seemed the most uncomfortable with us. She arched a brow and addressed Rosemary. "And I was told angels weren't real."

"We're the oldest beings of this dimension." Rosemary straightened her shoulders. "Any supernaturals from this world would know that we exist, just as I know that dragons are fae, so I assume you're the one who was human before the fated-mate bond was complete."

Jade took a step away from Egan, but then Egan's golden eyes glowed faintly. They had to be using their connection to speak telepathically. Jade stopped in her tracks.

"We saw that a pack has gone missing, and we wanted to find out if something bad went down," Sterlyn explained, and smiled, providing the illusion of calm. "We just want to see if someone needs our help."

The pink haired girl let out a huge breath. "That's why we're here, too. We don't live too far away." She walked slowly toward Sterlyn.

Don followed closely behind her, his jaw twitching. There was no question he didn't like her approaching us, but I suspected the girl had a mind of her own.

She extended her hand to Sterlyn. "My name is Sadie, and the man behind me is my fated mate, Donovan."

Donovan nodded his head and rolled his shoulders, readying for a fight if it came to that. He pointed behind him. "The vampire is Lillith, the redhead is Roxy, and the man beside her is Axel. And the dragons are Egan and Jade."

Sterlyn introduced our group in the order we stood—Griffin, herself, Emmy, Chad, Killian, me, Rosemary, then Levi.

The friends glanced at one another uncomfortably as Rosemary fluffed her wings. She hadn't wanted us to bring attention to Levi, but I understood where Sterlyn was coming from. If we didn't want to be perceived as threatening or untrustworthy, we had to let them know a demon was in our midst.

"Is that a joke?" Jade gritted. "Or is that your way of telling us someone is about to attack?"

This woman had severe trust issues, and I wondered what she had endured in her lifetime.

Levi flickered into human form, and Roxy started, jumping a few feet off the ground. She gasped. "Maybe Lillith was right, and I've completely lost my mind. But did anyone else see a guy just *appear* in front of us? Sadie, a little bit of fae warning would be nice."

"He's *not* fae." Egan frowned and pulled his mate slightly behind him.

Familiar indignation strummed through me. What was it with these supernatural guys? Did they really think that us wee womenfolk couldn't fight?

Grinning wickedly, Levi waggled his brows. "I'm a demon."

"Whoa." Axel lifted a hand, his olive complexion paling, and homed in on Sadie and Roxy. "You said there weren't any angels and demons, yet here I am, *looking* at one of each."

The emotions were growing more heightened again. If it

was this bad with Sterlyn introducing Levi at the first oppor-
tunity, I couldn't imagine how they would've reacted if they
had found out about him later. It would've eliminated any
hope of an alliance, which Sterlyn wisely had known.

"People forgot angels exist because they were
sequestered in Shadow City for the past thousand years,"
Griffin spoke slowly. "There's nothing to be afraid of."

"And demons have always been around, but when we're
in our shadow form, you can't see us. Until the demon war
at Shadow City, we didn't want the world to know about
our presence." Levi shrugged as if that explained it all.

*I understand we're trying to make these people feel
comfortable, but if the local pack was taken, there's a chance
whoever is responsible will come back,* I linked with Killian.
I didn't want to rush things since we'd just learned dragon
existed, but we needed to move this conversation elsewhere.

"That's why he looks so familiar!" Lillith snapped her
fingers and pointed at Killian. "He's the man who told the
entire world about us!"

Guilt and shame slammed through our connection. I
was so tired of people making Killian feel bad when he'd
tried to do the best thing for our entire world. "Wouldn't
you rather it be *him* than some supernatural who wanted to
instill fear so they could gain power?" I pushed past Killian,
wanting this accusation to end. "He told the world the truth
—that we're just like humans and have lived beside them for
centuries. At least it was a comforting message."

Warmth oozed through the bond, overpowering the
emotions he'd been feeling moments before. He linked, *I
love you.*

I love you, too. Those words were so simple, but the
meaning behind them held the most power.

"Jewel's right." Sadie placed a hand on her chest. "We

weren't part of that war and only knew about the city beforehand because of a bear shifter who escaped."

Griffin's head jerked back. "I remember Dad talking about a bear who escaped and that a vampire clan found him. The former vampire king, Matthew, held that over my dad's head until he died."

Our worlds had been connected even before this moment. That was strange, but not surprising in all the craziness of our lives.

Chad and Emmy glanced at Sterlyn, eyes glowing. They were linking with Sterlyn about something.

She shook her head slightly and said, "If this pack has vanished, we need to look around. The longer we delay, the riskier this entire situation could become."

"What are you talking about?" Jade asked as she stepped beside her mate again and glared at Sterlyn. "Do you know something about this?"

"Let's just say this pack isn't the first one this has happened to." Griffin raised his chin, his alpha power pulsing around him. "And the longer the humans have them, the more time they'll have to do...*things*." He glanced at Chad.

To Chad's credit, he didn't move, except for the vein pulsing between his eyes.

"We just came from there." Roxy rubbed her arms and shivered. "They're gone. A few televisions were on, and a back door was left open. It's like they up and vanished."

"Did the settlement smell of humans?" Out of everything that night, the scent of humans was what stuck most in my mind. It had been so odd and unexpected. Now it was bone-chilling.

"So faint we thought it was coincidental," Egan answered. "But there were a few spots near some deep tire tracks where it was heavier. The tracks could have belonged to a semitruck."

My heart thudded against my ribs. "The humans must have taken them." I'd bet they'd snuck in and caught them, and a huge truck had pulled up so they could fit all the bodies inside and maybe even regulate the knockout gas in there.

"Wait." Lillith lifted a hand. "You think humans took an *entire wolf pack?*"

A white falcon flew erratically toward us, breezing past an oak tree and a yellow birch. It landed on a branch a few feet away and screeched, "*Kuck, kuck, kuck.*"

Rosemary rose from the ground, ready to strike the bird. "That has to be a shifter!"

"It is," Sadie exclaimed. "He was watching for threats, and he's telling us something is wrong."

CHAPTER SEVENTEEN

THEY HAD a bird shifter acting as their scout. This group was even more diverse than I'd thought.

"We'll shift," Jade said, and took her mate's huge hand.

Rosemary spread her wings. "Or you can let Levi and me handle it since we don't have to change forms like you two do." She took to the sky as Levi shadowed into his demon form.

Jade's chest heaved, and her nostrils flared. "Your friend has a horrible attitude."

"She doesn't mean to come off that way." Killian rubbed his temples. "Angels are very blunt and factual. Believe me, if she wanted to insult you, there would be no question about it."

Jade placed a hand on her small waist. "I wasn't questioning if she was."

The falcon cawed and flapped its wings erratically. If I hadn't known better, I'd have thought it was having a heart attack.

"We can talk about all this later." Sterlyn turned in the direction we'd come from. "This threat shouldn't be ignored. The falcon is uneasy, and with what we've experienced, something is coming."

"But if it's human..." Lillith started.

Chad cut her off, "They are worthy adversaries. They kidnapped me, and I went through intense training. These humans have weapons, dart guns, and training of their own."

He left out the part about being a silver wolf, which was for the best. Though our heritage wasn't a secret anymore, that didn't mean we should provide that information up front. Besides, there was something different about Sadie, and she wasn't sharing that information with us, either.

Trust took time.

"We could've shifted and been in the sky by now," Jade growled, and stomped her foot like a horse.

Levi floated toward us, but it wasn't as if the others could see.

"Levi's on his way down," I said to be reassuring, but I regretted it as soon as the words were out.

Egan stared skyward and squinted. "How do you know?"

There was no getting around the reason; they'd all know if I lied. "I can see him in his shadow form."

He homed in on me and tilted his head. This man was intelligent, but there was no fear or judgment in his eyes. Rather, it was curiosity.

Jewel, Killian warned.

This time, he had every right to talk to me that way. *I'm sorry. It slipped out.*

Levi landed next to me and changed back into his human form. He normally didn't do that with us, but with the newcomers, he must not have wanted to startle them.

"There's a group of wolves heading this way." Levi

frowned and tugged at the hem of his black shirt. "There don't appear to be any humans, but I'm not sure if that's a good thing."

"Of course there would be more than that pack working with the humans." Griffin's nose wrinkled, and the breeze blew, ruffling the sides of his hair. The longer gelled section on top stayed firmly in place.

Emmy sneered. "What the *hell* is wrong with this world where people willingly turn against their own kind?"

A sharp, humorless laugh escaped Sadie. "You'd be surprised. Some people are willing to turn against their self-proclaimed daughter and take her and everyone she loves down just to make a point."

Bitterness laced her words, and I had a feeling she was speaking from personal experience.

"How many are there?" Sterlyn asked, skipping straight to strategizing.

Levi ran a hand through his hair. "At least fifty."

Fifty. This supernatural group had decided to come hard, just the same as Tom's.

"That means they suspect someone is here," Killian rasped as he stood closer to me. "But how would they know?"

"Our groups are both here because of the intranet, *and* they're supernatural." We could've walked right into a trap. "The owner of the moving company could be the person in charge, or they're monitoring the boards and saw his post." And who knew if either scenario was the truth? It didn't change the issue.

We were being hunted.

"There are eight on our side and eight on theirs, unless they have more people close by." Chad gestured to Sadie and her friends. "Now would be the time to fill us in."

"This is all of us." Sadie glanced at her friends. "But we'll fight alongside you."

Roxy nodded and squared her shoulders. "You said you've fought this group before? Tell us what to do."

"Within reason." Lillith patted her chest. "Just remember, I can't shift into a wolf."

"We know what vampires can do." Emmy chuckled. "Some of our closest friends are the king and queen of vampires."

Lillith's body stilled. "How is that possible?"

"All things for another time," Egan interjected, and removed his shirt.

If I hadn't been mated to Killian, I would have very likely been drooling. The man was stronger than I'd realized, and the magic swirling from him was something I'd never experienced.

Dragon.

Wings sprouted from his back, and his pupils turned to slits as his dragon peeked through.

Where Rosemary's wings were fluffy feathers, his were muscular scales. Though Rosemary's wings could deflect bullets and slice through someone's neck like butter, they appeared nonthreatening. Egan's wings looked dangerous, and the urge to step back nearly took over.

"What are you doing, man?" Axel asked. "We said the angel and demon would do this."

"That was before we realized we were fighting supernaturals." Egan flapped his wings and elevated several feet from the ground. "I'm not worried about keeping the existence of dragons secret since they aren't humans."

"I'm shifting, too." Jade ran back between the oak and yellow birch, opting for privacy and probably the preservation of her clothes.

"What do we do?" I asked.

Griffin removed a pistol from his waistband. "I'll stay in human form on our side so we can communicate with the others." He checked his ammo and unfastened the safety lock. "I'm better with a gun, anyway."

"I'll stay in human form, too," Sadie said from her side. "Egan is only half shifting, so that will make things easier."

"In case anyone doesn't already know, Lillith will stay in human form," Roxy added while sticking her tongue out at the vampire.

Lillith rolled her eyes. "You're the only one who thinks it's funny."

"And that's all that matters." Roxy smirked. "My goal is always to make myself laugh. I don't care if it misses the mark for other people, though it seldom ever does."

That girl was so freaking similar to Sierra that it was scary.

"Where are they coming from?" Sterlyn, used to having to redirect conversations, settled into the role naturally. "I'm assuming they're spread out and running toward us."

"They've circled the entire neighborhood." Levi changed back into shadow form. "I'll help fight since they can't see me. The closest ones are near, so if you're going to shift, you'd better get moving." He soared through the trees.

Donovan scowled. "It's freaky as hell when he disappears right before our eyes."

"Please, it's not like you haven't been around something similar." Roxy arched an eyebrow.

I had no clue what they were talking about, and frankly, I didn't care.

"Everyone, go shift while Sadie and I keep an eye out," Griffin commanded as he clutched his gun tighter.

Let's go this way. Killian nodded to the two red cedars a

few feet away. They would provide enough coverage for us to shift in private.

We headed in that direction while the others spread out to do the same. A small hand snatched my upper arm and forced me to stop and turn.

Emmy.

"I heard what happened when you were breaking Chad and the others out—how, despite your severe injuries, you continued to fight." Her gray irises darkened as she spoke through clenched teeth. "And I know why you did it because I feel the same way. But Jewel...you have *nothing* to make up for."

My head snapped toward Killian, and I linked, *You talked to her*. There was no way it had been Chad because the two of them would have ganged up on me.

She asked me the other day, based on something Chad and Mila said. What was I supposed to say? Killian held my gaze but lowered his head.

And it spoke volumes.

I'd spent a little time with PawPaw's and Ruby's packs, helping to get them settled, but not as much as I would've liked. I'd been more focused on getting settled with my own pack and figuring out my place in it, so Killian had been checking in more with them than me. And this was what I got for it.

Jade, in dragon form, shot into the sky, breaking the tension among the three of us. She flew high, rushing toward her mate, refusing to be left behind.

It was exactly what I'd needed to dampen some of my exasperation and become rational. "I love you, but now isn't the time for this discussion. We have enemies charging toward us." I pulled my arm from her hold and headed toward the cedars. She hadn't been there. If she knew the full story, she might not have wasted those seconds talking to me.

As soon as I stepped behind the tree, I heard bones breaking and repositioning. At least everyone else was taking the threat seriously.

As I yanked off my shirt, Killian rushed beside me and ripped off his shirt. *I'm not sorry that I talked to her, but I should've told you.* He removed his jeans and boxers.

His nakedness distracted me. Even in battle, it was hard not to take in his muscular body, his full lips, and the way his skin rippled from the raw power underneath.

When I realized I was devouring him with my eyes, my blood heated more, and I had to force myself to look away. He was being a jerk, after all.

The corners of his mouth tipped into a cocky smirk. The butthead realized I'd been checking him out.

I called my wolf forward, and she came with a vengeance. These wolves would learn we were silver—if they even knew what that meant. I almost wondered if the history of our species had vanished while we'd hidden for centuries and Shadow City had closed its gates. From what Sterlyn had said, even Griffin had thought the silver wolves were long gone before he'd met her and learned who she was.

My skin tingled as silver fur sprouted on my body. *Yeah, you should have.* I wanted to say more, but not with frustration swirling inside me.

Paws pounded faintly close by. The enemy was getting closer. As my bones broke and I found myself on all fours, the enemy's breathing became audible. The moon was around a quarter full, so I was only slightly larger than a normal wolf. Hopefully, that wouldn't give our new acquaintances pause or make them ask more questions.

Despite being upset, I didn't want to leave Killian, so I waited until he trotted to me in his wolf form.

Sterlyn and the others are out there with Sadie's pack, Killian linked as he edged ahead, leading us back to the group.

As we trotted out, Emmy ran from behind a smaller oak tree, with Chad hurrying behind her in human form. His eyes were tight, and Griffin said, "I thought you were shifting."

"I have to stay like this," Chad said, and his forehead lined with worry before he could smooth his expression into a mask of indifference.

None of us had time to argue with him. Granted, I couldn't in this form.

With the red of her coat, Roxy's wolf resembled a fox. It was as vibrant as her hair in human form. Though most wolf shifters' fur was similar in color to their human hair, there were certain exceptions, like the silver wolves. I'd assumed she and Sadie dyed their hair. Clearly, I was wrong about at least one of them.

Lillith held a knife and stood stoically next to Sadie. What troubled me most was that Sadie had no weapon in her hands, nor was she in wolf form. I hoped she had strong combat skills. Surely her mate would be tenser and more protective if he thought she was at risk. He was hovering close to her, but no more than Killian was to me.

Chest constricting, I nearly growled. Maybe he wasn't confident in her abilities after all.

The incoming wolves would be here any minute. The falcon flew through the trees in front of us, but this time, he didn't make a noise. Instead, he flapped his wings urgently and landed on a branch. I wasn't sure what good he could do, but he intended to watch. Maybe if we got overrun, he could alert Egan and Jade that we needed them.

Killian edged in front of me to block me from the incoming wolves' view. From what I could tell, two were heading right for us, but they were likely linked to more wolves nearby, so it wouldn't be long before they all descended.

A beige wolf and a dark gray wolf appeared. They had their noses to the ground, sniffing out our scents.

The sound of more wolves rushing forward told me they were coming.

My wolf wanted to move in front of Killian, but I forced her to stay back. Though I didn't like how he was trying to keep me from the front line, I'd bide my time and move when it mattered. Unlike Mom, I chose my battles, and now wasn't the time to exert that energy.

When the beige wolf noticed us, she threw her head back and howled.

My heart pounded. I'd hoped one would be in human form so we could talk. We couldn't strike because it could be another pack here doing the same thing as us—trying to help.

"We're here searching for the pack. We aren't here to cause harm," Griffin said reassuringly, and raised his hands in surrender.

Both wolves bared their teeth and snarled as they pawed at the ground.

That wasn't a good sign, but their intent was clear when they lunged.

Griffin pointed the gun right at the beige wolf's head and pulled the trigger. The bullet made its mark right between her eyes.

The dark gray wolf ran through the trees in a sporadic

path so Griffin couldn't aim at it easily. Griffin shot, but the wolf pivoted behind a slender yellow birch for cover. A shadow form appeared behind him. When the dark gray wolf surged forward again, Levi jerked his legs so he tumbled to the ground only a few feet in front of us. Sterlyn didn't hesitate. She lunged in and ripped out his throat.

Loud mourning howls filled the air as the pack felt their links dissolve, and the rest of the wolves barreled toward us.

"Spread out and form a circle," Griffin commanded. "That way, we can protect everyone's back."

"Maybe we should spread out and attack them," Sadie said from behind.

After a moment, Griffin spoke again. "That would be detrimental. We're outnumbered and need to stay together and fight. Most of them are coming here, anyway. This way, they can't gang up on a few of us and take us out slowly."

And that was exactly what they would do. They would target the smaller groups, one by one, until we were all dead, captured, or gods knew what else.

"That makes sense," Sadie replied. Though I couldn't see her, she sounded sincere, and my lungs worked more freely. She was an alpha who was open to reason and wasn't ornery just because she had something to prove.

We all backed up to each other, and Killian's displeasure surged through our bond, likely because he couldn't stand in front of me in this formation.

Emmy flanked my other side. They were both going to keep an eye on me and were treating me like a child.

I'm fighting, I linked with Killian. *I don't know what the two of you are planning, but I won't stand back while everyone else fights. We've already had this conversation.*

His large wolfy head turned to me, and he replied, *We aren't up to anything. She's just worried about you, too. Ster-*

lyn's made it clear we each have to focus on our fights, so don't be too alarmed.

In other words, they wouldn't be able to hover over me.

Good.

"We see them!" Lillith called from the opposite side of our circle.

"Same here," Griffin answered from his spot beside Sterlyn, who was next to Killian.

Sadie confirmed the same thing just as ten wolves appeared in front of me. Something about them was familiar, but I couldn't wrap my brain around it.

Then a wolf ran through the center, its cold ice-gray eyes staring right at me. The light blond fur and the cruelty its soul emitted were something that could never be duplicated.

It shouldn't have been possible. But when he gave me a wolfy smile and threw back his head and howled with such hate, my insides turned cold.

Killian, we have a huge problem. The more I watched the wolf, the more I knew without a doubt who it was. *That's Tom.*

CHAPTER EIGHTEEN

THIS WAS A NIGHTMARE. *Erin said she would take care of him.*

Erin chooses her words wisely. Killian growled as he crouched beside me. *Even with supernaturals hunting down our kind, she can't be trusted.*

His white-hot rage mixed with my shock, making the world spin. I had to get control over my emotions, or I'd become a heaving, panicking mess—similar to being comatose, and I wouldn't be able to protect myself, let alone the people I loved. That would prove to Emmy and Killian that they had been right to tell me I couldn't fight.

"Shit," Griffin rasped, and he swung his gun at Tom.

Out of the corner of my eye, I saw Lillith tense. Sadie was the only person in human form I couldn't see because she was behind me. Lillith said, "What's the problem?"

"This pack attacked us when we rescued the first pack that was taken. They're supposed to be dead." Griffin fired his gun.

Tom moved sideways faster than should have been possible, and the bullet missed him by inches.

"Well, you did a piss-poor job of killing them," Lillith gritted out as she held her knife in front of her. "I hope your follow-through is better this time around."

Her words cut, but obviously, someone should've stayed behind to confirm that Erin and her coven had handled the wolves.

The wolves charged all at once, with no hesitation.

Tom's attention was locked on me, making it clear he knew who I was. He had to be tracking my scent because my fur was the same color as Sterlyn's and Emmy's—the same as Sterlyn's natural hair color. Our irises remained the same shade as when we were in human form, but that tended to be harder to track. You had to make a conscious effort to identify a person that way.

Tom and four of his wolves ran right at me, and I knew they wanted to kill me.

I took a few steps forward, eager to start the battle, but I couldn't let instinct take over completely, or our circle formation would be in vain.

Damn it, Jewel, Killian linked, his frustration bleeding through already. He inched forward to stand beside me. He tensed as if he thought I was going to argue with him, but that was the thing.

I wouldn't.

He was standing beside me, not in front of me to hide me from danger. That was when I realized what the entire problem was between us in these moments. When he stood in front of me, I felt like he thought I wasn't capable. It wasn't that I wanted to fight anyone all by myself; it was that I wanted him to treat me as an equal and not some fragile flower.

As the five reached me, four targeted Killian, and another four lunged for Emmy. With fifty of them, each person would have three or four wolves to fight at one time. My heart thudded as I prayed that Sadie and her friends knew how to fight. Otherwise, this could be a disaster.

The falcon took off, I hoped to find Egan and Jade. With Levi fighting close by, Rosemary should be here at any second.

Tom's cruel eyes locked on my neck. Then the two wolves on either side of him bolted at me.

They meant to take me down fast and hard.

I stumbled back a few steps so the two wolves closest to Tom would fall short, but the wolves on the far left and right had attacked my back half, which meant they would reach my front.

Standing on my hind legs, I watched from the corner of my vision as each group of four wolves launched their attacks on Emmy and Killian. My stomach dropped. I desperately wanted to help them, but I had to end my fight quickly.

The two wolves lunging toward me opened their mouths and aimed for my sides. I swung my front paws and swiped at their faces, pushing them down. The gray wolf on my left scraped its teeth down my side, but luckily, it did nothing more than that.

With my right paw, I slammed a walnut wolf to the ground so hard his eyes rolled back. A little relief washed over me, but I couldn't completely disregard him. He could be faking.

The adrenaline pumping through me numbed my body to pain, which helped me focus on the yellow and dark auburn wolves closest to Tom. They were primed to strike again.

The whooshing and flapping of wings grew louder as Rosemary and the dragons arrived, the angel sounding almost like a melody and the dragons like a metronome, keeping the beat of the altitude they desired.

Thank gods. We needed all the help we could get. Sadie and the others didn't seem power-hungry, and I worried they'd never had to fight against an enemy like this.

As the yellow and dark auburn wolves attacked again, I hunkered close to the ground. I had to time my move perfectly.

At the last second, a flash of pink shot past me and slammed into the chest of the dark auburn wolf, forcing it backward.

I had no clue what the hell that was, but it had been targeted at the enemy and not me, so I'd go with it. I pivoted, changing my strategy now that there was only one wolf on top of me.

The yellow wolf's head jerked in her pack mate's direction, giving me a slight advantage. I lunged onto the yellow wolf, and her attention swung back to me, but it was too late. My teeth slashed into her shoulder, and I dug deep to make the wound bad enough that she wouldn't be able to move without experiencing severe agony.

I'd had that type of wound before and was aware of exactly how it felt. Even though these wolves meant us harm, there wasn't a negative essence wafting from her, unlike Tom. She was just a wolf obeying her alpha like any pack member had to. I'd kill her if it came down to it, but if I could incapacitate her and take out the real threat, that would hopefully fix the problem.

The yellow wolf whimpered and yanked away, making the wound jagged and deeper.

Jewel, watch out! Killian linked as his terror increased my heart rate.

Warm liquid dripped down my snout, and the metallic

stench of blood entered my nose. Though my wolf didn't enjoy the taste and smell, it didn't bother me in wolf form. If I'd been on two legs, I'd have been vomiting up everything in my stomach.

As I pivoted toward the gray wolf, something heavy hardened in my stomach. The wolf was almost on me, her mouth mere inches from my back left leg. She'd been strategic, going for the back section so she'd stay out of my peripheral vision.

Stumbling to the right, I tried to move so the impact wouldn't be as direct as she planned.

Jade soared down from over my head and caught the gray wolf a second before she could make impact. She wrapped her arms around the wolf and sank her claws into its belly as she took flight again.

Maybe this group wasn't as unprepared as I'd feared.

A flash of light blond fur caught my attention, and my gaze landed on Tom, who was moving away from me.

Coward. He wanted to watch me die, or maybe kill me, but since Jade was near, he was running away. I should follow him, but that would break the circle, and there were enough enemies left to fight that it could be detrimental to our side.

The scent of brimstone swirled around us, and I glanced over my shoulder to check on everyone and find out where the smell was coming from. It was strong and dried my throat, but I didn't see anything burning.

What I did see transfixed me.

For the first time in my life, the world didn't make sense. Sadie was shooting pink beams from her palms, not only fighting off her attackers but also helping everyone else. Now I understood where that flash of pink had come from earlier.

Donovan, Roxy, and Axel were holding their own in wolf form, with Sadie stepping in as needed. Egan had completely shifted into his dragon form and was fighting ten of the wolves several yards from the circle. He had to be drawing them away from us. Smoke trickled from his nostrils, floating skyward and confirming that those paranormal books had been based on truth, even if the authors didn't realize it.

Dragons breathed fire, but that wasn't what disturbed me the most. I had no clue what Sadie was. I'd never heard of any wolf shifters who could conjure magic like that. Maybe she wasn't a wolf after all. But then...what was she?

Something that needed an explanation later.

A snarl sounded, and I turned forward in time to watch the gray wolf splat. Her body bounced and cracked in a way that shouldn't have been possible.

This time, my stomach lurched, even in animal form.

The dark auburn wolf struck at my neck. I dropped to the ground, and the enemy wolf's mouth caught air as he tumbled over my body. His claws dug into my back, causing sharp pain, but it was better than the alternative—death.

I bucked like a bull in a rodeo, needing to get him off me before he caused worse injuries. He grunted as I leaped hard from my back legs to my front, but he held on.

The walnut-brown wolf at my feet stirred awake.

I was on borrowed time.

The dark auburn wolf had dug his claws deep into my back and was barely budging. Each time I tried to buck him off, his claws dug deeper, and his negative essence seeped all over me. Not only was he hurting me, but he was also making me feel tainted. This wolf craved something sinister. I had to get him off me.

Dad had told us that when a plan wasn't going as expected, change the strategy.

Though it wasn't ideal, I had one option, though it would leave me exposed. Not wanting to overthink the decision, I rolled onto my back, exposing my belly.

Due to the quarter-moon boost from my angel blood, I was heavier and a little larger than the other wolf. He groaned from the impact, which sounded odd in animal form. His claws receded as he tried to squirm out from under me—which was exactly what I wanted.

Jumping back onto four paws, I whined slightly as agony shot through my shoulder muscles. He'd clawed me in a very tender spot, but it wasn't anything I couldn't handle. I had to push through the pain.

He lurched forward, and my wolf reacted before I could process what I was doing. I ripped out his throat, and warm blood gushed over my face and chest. The usual nausea that accompanied a kill churned uncomfortably in my stomach.

A stabbing pain emanated through Killian's and my connection, and I pivoted to face him. A hickory wolf had sunk its teeth into Killian's left side, while a khaki-colored wolf bit into his right shoulder. They had coordinated their attack, and Killian was in so much pain, he couldn't swat them off with his other legs.

This was unacceptable.

With a deep bellow, I cleared my vision and ran to my mate, tapping into my angel speed. I slashed the side of the hickory wolf's neck with my teeth, hitting the artery. I wouldn't rip his throat out. He deserved to die a slow and painful death for doing that to my mate.

The wolf hadn't sensed me until I'd been on top of him. He released his jaws to get away, but the damage was done.

I rammed my head into his side, forcing him out of my way. I had to get to the other one.

A shadowy figure appeared on the opposite side of the other wolf, and I watched as the outline of a demon sword rammed through its heart. The wolf yelped, but the sound cut off as death took hold. He hadn't seen the demon coming, and he should've known better. They'd fought us before, and now they were determined to fight even with dragons and a girl who could shoot beams out her palms fighting against them. What could possibly be that important for Tom to risk his pack members this way?

You're going to be okay, I linked with Killian. *They aren't fatal wounds.*

I know, baby, Killian assured me, but his attention was still focused in front of him. *I'm just glad it was me instead of you.*

Guilt nagged at me. I hadn't been quick enough to fight off my enemies to help him. The one person I loved and treasured most in the world had been injured right beside me. If only I'd trained harder and focused more.

"They're retreating!" Lillith yelled, and I scanned the area again.

No one had attacked me while I'd been helping Killian, but I hadn't thought much about it.

Enemy wolf after enemy wolf raced away from us. Something must have happened to cause them to retreat so rapidly. I found at least thirty dead enemies with no casualties on our end. I wasn't sure how we'd managed that, and we did have some injuries on our side. My back throbbed from where the one wolf had gotten me, and Killian was worse off.

A bush was on fire near Egan, and the ground in front of Sadie and her friends had chunks torn up from where

Sadie had focused her beams. The most disturbing thing was the blood that coated the ground all around us and puddled under the wolves.

A gurgling sound came from the hickory wolf. Now that the fight was over, I was ashamed that I'd been so cruel as to force someone to die that way. I moved to finish him off, but he took one last shaky breath.

Guilt churned in my stomach, and my limbs grew heavy.

We have to find Tom, I linked. This wouldn't stop until we killed him. Maybe not even then, but at least we'd be safer.

I'd moved forward to chase after them when something crashed to the ground behind me, stopping me in my tracks. Heart racing, I whirled around.

It was Sadie, and she was unconscious and pale.

CHAPTER NINETEEN

UNCERTAIN, I was torn about what to do. I didn't want Tom and his pack to get away, but I didn't feel right leaving Sadie like this after she'd helped so significantly to save us.

Griffin watched the wolves run off, then glanced back at Sadie, who was slowly sitting up. Sweat beaded her forehead, and Donovan tensed beside her.

"Are you okay?" Griffin asked, and I could have hugged him for it. I wasn't able to speak, and unlike Ruby, I preferred not to walk around naked in front of others now that Killian and I had forged our mate bond.

"I'm fine." She used her forearm to wipe her forehead. "I just drained myself."

"If you're sure, then I'm going after them." Rosemary expanded her wings from her spot in front of Griffin, Donovan, and Sadie. "We don't need to let them get away, or we can follow them and see where they're heading."

"Go," Sadie assured her, and glanced at Egan, who ascended into the air as well. "Jade and Egan want to go with you."

Though we'd fought together, both sides still had some

questions. It was hard to trust when the other side had their secrets. A pack having the exact same fur color wasn't normal, nor was a pink-beam-shooting woman who also smelled like a wolf shifter.

"We don't need observers," Rosemary sneered. "Levi and I can handle this on our own."

Jade growled low and threateningly as smoke trickled from her nose.

The last thing we needed was to fight among ourselves while the enemy got away.

Levi landed underneath Rosemary and transitioned back into his human form. He lifted his hands in front of him and said, "What my love means is we'd hate to take away some of your people when you aren't feeling well."

Thankfully, I was in wolf form, or everyone would know I wasn't buying that. The only reason it didn't smell like a lie was because Levi meant it. *Why doesn't she want their help?*

She's not super trusting, and the way Jade reacts to her doesn't help. Killian huffed, and pain floated through our bond. The wolf must have gotten a good hold on him. He continued as if he hadn't felt anything, *She and I didn't get along until after Sterlyn arrived. She's blunt, and for a long time, I was like Jade and took her as insulting. I just hadn't been around angels before.*

Nor had Jade, obviously. Killian's assessment was probably fair.

"I'm sure you're more than capable, but Egan and Jade are used to doing that sort of thing for us, as I'm sure the two of you are for your group." Sadie pressed a hand to her stomach as if trying to get her bearings.

"Fine," Rosemary rasped as she ascended higher. "But if a human sees a dragon, remember that I was against it." She soared in the direction in which Tom had run, not bothering to wait for Levi.

Jade exhaled, causing smoke to flow around us as she took off, following Rosemary.

Scratching his scruff, Levi winced. "Well, this will be fun." He changed back into his shadow form and said, "Egan, we better go before they fight each other." He darted skyward, chasing after his mate, with Egan right behind him.

"We'll get Sadie back to the cars," Lillith said loudly enough for Egan and Levi to hear.

I wanted to go after Tom, too, but it made more sense for our friends who could fly to follow him. For all we knew, he could be leading us to their backup.

Despite my self-control, my attention kept flicking to the body of the wolf I'd killed in the worst way possible for hurting Killian. Saliva pooled in my mouth, but spitting was impossible in wolf form. Skin crawling, I tried to look away from what I'd done, but no amount of willpower could force me to avert my gaze.

Blood had puddled under his head, and his eyes were open, reflecting the moment of fear when death had taken over. I suspected this would haunt me.

Something nuzzled my neck, and when the buzz of our connection started, it confirmed it was Killian. That was enough to finally allow me to look away, but when I focused on him, his concern filtered more strongly through our bond.

Are you okay? He stepped away so he could watch me reply.

Though we weren't in human form, he could still read me, not only by my animal actions but also because of the alpha and mate bonds.

There was no point in lying. *I...I killed him.* I hung my head. He'd know it was more than that. *And not in a very nice way.*

Some humor flitted through. *There's a nice way?*

He was trying to make me laugh, but this was not the time or place. *Can we get out of here?* I wanted to leave the body, and quickly. The longer I stayed here, the deeper the memory would be seared in my brain.

Let's shift back so we can talk to the others, he linked.

I noticed that Emmy was the only remaining wolf. Chad stood beside her. All the other wolves had vanished, likely to shift back into human form.

Is Emmy staying in wolf form in case a threat appears again? I linked. Having someone in animal form would provide more protection if a few enemy wolves circled back toward us. Even though that likely wouldn't happen, the silver wolf motto was to always be prepared.

Not missing a beat, Killian hurried to the red cedars we'd used for cover before. He replied, *It's just a precaution.*

Here, I could only link with Killian, which was less than ideal when decisions were being made.

Focusing, I pulled my wolf back into my center. I tried not to yank on her too hard and have the shift be quick and draining, but the urge to change so I could get the smell and taste of the enemy's blood off me was tugging at everything inside.

Agony dug its claws into my body as Killian began his shift. His injuries weren't fatal, but they were deep enough to make his shift very uncomfortable. I wished I could heal him, but since I wasn't a full-blooded angel, the only angelic magic I had was extra strength and speed.

Unable to stop and check on him, I shifted far too slowly. My spine readjusted until I stood on two legs, and my skin tingled as my fur disappeared. When I finished, Killian's pain was already gone, indicating he was back in human form.

As I reached for my clothes, the stench of blood wasn't nearly as strong. I dressed quickly, desperate to get away from here. We knew that the humans who had taken PawPaw's pack had also taken the local pack. Hanging around would only allow them to call in reinforcements, and none of us needed that right now.

You didn't do anything wrong out there, Killian linked with me, and his gigantic hands cupped my shoulders. *You protected me. They attacked us.*

I turned toward him, noting he was dressed as well. His citrus breath hit my face as his sandalwood scent surrounded me, making me feel safe and comforted. I hadn't been aware that I needed his closeness, but we didn't have time to spare. We still weren't sure about the actual enemy we were fighting or their goals. *I could've killed him quickly and not let my anger take over.* The same anger I tried to control. Normally, I'd try one of my calming techniques, but the thought hadn't crossed my mind when I'd seen he was in danger.

Maybe I was more like Mom than I feared.

Every one of us has made a decision in battle that we've lived to regret. Killian tucked a piece of hair behind my ear. *We've allowed people to live who wound up wreaking havoc and killing people. Did that wolf have negative energy?*

Reflecting on the chaotic situation, I realized the wolf's energy had been as bad as Tom's, but all I'd seen was him hurting my mate. I nodded, unable to speak even through our bond.

Then all you did was allow him to exit the world in the

same way he's done to others. Killian kissed my forehead and linked, *It could have been Fate intervening.*

I sighed and relaxed. Even though guilt continued to churn inside me, it wasn't eating me alive as it had been moments ago. Either way, I should've been the better person—a person more like Dad—and acted with grace. Just because that wolf might have hurt and killed others didn't mean I needed to become him.

I had to preserve that part of myself.

Every time I proved something to myself, I went and did something like this. Then everything got worse again. The thoughts I tried to control and move past attacked me like a rabid raccoon. If I'd fought alongside the silver wolves when they'd needed me, maybe I would have had more patience and not acted rashly. Maybe if I'd fought alongside them, the pack would have been at its strongest, and we wouldn't be in this mess. I'd failed again, and it all came down to *me.*

Hey, where'd you go? Killian asked. He placed a finger under my chin and tilted my head up. *I felt as if I got through to you, but then it all vanished.*

Regret, anxiety, and guilt were all bitches, and they'd become my master. *We need to move. None of us are safe here.*

His brows furrowed, and he sighed. "You're right, but this conversation isn't over."

If I had anything to do with the situation, it was. Instead of responding, I pivoted and rushed back to the others.

Sterlyn, Donovan, Roxy, and Axel were back in human form. Sadie was on her feet, and she leaned on Donovan, allowing him to support her.

My chest burned. One day, I hoped I'd be confident enough not to feel weak when in pain or in need of help.

When the need to prove myself wasn't overwhelming and I could just *be*.

Busy battling some internal war, I didn't look over at the one wolf shifter who would always be with me.

"Where did you park?" Sterlyn looked around.

"At the edge of town," Donovan answered as he wrapped an arm around Sadie's waist. "Lillith is going to get the vehicle and pick us up on the road that leads to the pack neighborhood. It's half a mile that way." He pointed in the direction Tom had run.

Griffin loaded his gun. "We can walk with you since Sadie isn't feeling well."

"You all need to get out of here, too." Sadie stood taller as if to prove she could. She pulled out her cell phone and tapped the screen. "Do you mind if we exchange numbers so we can stay in touch? If either of us learns anything or something strange pops up, I'm thinking our groups working together might be a good solution."

After everything we'd gone through, I had to agree with her. Though I wanted to learn where this pack had been taken, I'd rather we not find the location like we had last time, when they'd gotten Chad.

"Excellent plan." Sterlyn rattled off her number, and soon, the two of them had each other's contact information saved.

"We better get moving. Lillith will start honking if we make her wait too long," Axel grumbled as he took Roxy's hand.

Donovan snorted. "She will not. This isn't her first ro—" He stopped and tugged at his collar. "Ride. It isn't her first ride."

That was definitely not what he had been about to say, and that comment and how they handled themselves made it clear that these people weren't new to dangerous situations.

It was also clear that even though we'd exchanged numbers, we weren't ready to reveal our secrets.

"And they say I have the big mouth," Roxy said as she tilted her head toward Sadie and raised both eyebrows. "Maybe I'm not the one whose lips can't stop moving."

She and Sierra would either love or despise each other. There would be no in-between.

"If you need us, just shout or howl." Killian took my hand and tugged me behind him. I didn't complain.

I wanted to leave this scene behind.

"Later, bishes." Roxy snickered as the four of them moved toward their destination.

Emmy edged in their direction, but Sterlyn shook her head. Her irises glowed, indicating they were communicating via the alpha bond. Since she reminded me of Dad in so many ways, I was fairly certain Sterlyn was telling Emmy that we would respect their wishes and keep an ear out for threats.

The six of us hurried back to our vehicle. A few deer ambled by, which comforted me. If they had sensed a threat, they wouldn't have been hanging around. With each step we took away from the battle scene, my body relaxed a little more. My chest expanded more easily, and my legs didn't feel as heavy.

The scents of Tom's pack hung heavily in the air, along with a bit of the maliciousness that wafted from their souls. Though not all of them emanated that level of negativity, at least half did—a problematic sign.

As the sun shone on us and the crisp December mountain breeze whipped past us, I still couldn't find any peace. I was pretty sure this situation had made my struggles worse.

Suddenly, the scents vanished. They were just gone.

Chad sniffed, confirming he'd experienced the same thing. "There's no trace of them."

"How is that possible?" Griffin asked.

"I don't know." Sterlyn tapped her fingers on her jeans, and her silver irises shone brighter. "The only explanation I can come up with is one we won't like."

Killian clenched his teeth. "Erin."

I'd been around that coven only once, and I already disliked them as much as my friends did. What kind of priestess allied with people outside her own city? One who didn't have a moral compass.

"That's what I'm thinking, too." Griffin holstered his gun. "Putting that away before I shoot something just to do it." His nostrils flared as he quickened our pace. "It's time to get home."

THE RIDE back to Shadow Ridge was as silent as the ride over had been. Everyone was stewing over what we'd learned. The coven hadn't handled Tom as promised, and he'd somehow vanished into thin air.

Sterlyn had spoken to Rosemary, who had a similar story. They hadn't been able to find the wolf shifters to follow them, and neither could Jade and Egan.

Rosemary and Levi were flying back to Shadow City to do some investigating while we drove home.

When we passed the "Welcome to Shadow Ridge" sign, Sterlyn picked up her phone and typed out a message. The response dinged almost immediately.

I looked out the window and watched humans with video cameras walking the streets of downtown Shadow

Ridge, the sun setting behind them. I hadn't gotten a chance to explore much of the town and didn't want to until things calmed down. People continued to flock here.

As we turned toward our home neighborhood, Sterlyn continued to message on her phone. "I've always been impressed by Rosemary, but this might be the most spectacular thing she's ever done," Sterlyn murmured.

She'd said that out loud for my benefit. I was the only one who couldn't link with her. "What's up?"

As we entered our subdivision, Sterlyn chuckled and pointed at a black sedan parked in front of her and Griffin's home. Rosemary and Levi were standing at the driver's door, glaring at the person inside with their arms crossed.

"Who's that?" Emmy asked as she leaned between Killian's seat and mine and squinted.

"Erin," Sterlyn replied. "We're going to get some answers."

CHAPTER TWENTY

I WASN'T sure what to make of Erin's presence. For her to show up at the shifter neighborhood without a large portion of her coven surrounding her meant she expected this conversation to go in her favor...unless they were hiding in the woods.

Griffin turned into the driveway of his and Sterlyn's white Craftsman-style house. Though their house had a similar floor plan to ours, there were two differences. Their three bedrooms were split with two on one side of the house and the master on the other, and they had the wraparound porch with a round, black-wire table and matching chairs positioned where they could watch the road.

Stomach heavy, I tried to take a calming breath so I wouldn't fling open the door, march over to the witch, and punch her. She'd put my mate in danger, as well as some of my most precious family and friends.

I understand your anger, Killian linked, his frustration adding to my already frayed nerves. *But Erin is a Shadow City council member and helped us defeat the demons, and unfortunately, she has a lot of influence. Though I hate poli-*

tics, we need to let Sterlyn, Griffin, and Rosemary handle her.

Don't worry. I already let my emotions get the best of me once today. The memory of the wolf gurgling on his own blood flashed into my mind, sickening me.

As Griffin killed the engine, Sterlyn turned around in her seat. She took a second to look each of us in the eye. "Remember that controlling oneself prevents the other person from feeling as powerful."

Again, she sounded like Dad, and my eyes burned with tears. It wouldn't take much for me to fall apart, and I bit the inside of my cheek to hold myself together.

"Chad and Emmy, go check in with Mila and the others," Sterlyn commanded. "They may need your help, and I don't want Erin to feel ganged up on." She got out and rushed toward Levi and Rosemary.

It was time to confront the witch.

As I followed her lead and climbed out of the car, I played *Prelude to the Afternoon of a Faun* in my mind. The one time I hadn't used the coping mechanisms I'd employed my entire life, I'd done the very thing I feared—made a poor decision I'd have to live with. I refused to make that mistake a second time.

The thrumming of an approaching vehicle roared louder, and when I looked toward the street, headlights hit my eyes. I blinked, adjusting to the change of vision. Though wolf shifters could see easily in the dark and light, a bright flash during twilight required adjusting, the same as if I were a human. The vehicle pulled in behind Erin, and when my vision acclimated, I saw it was Alex's Mercedes SUV, with him driving and Ronnie beside him. A blonde girl I'd never met sat behind Alex, with Eliza next to her.

I wasn't surprised that Alex and Ronnie had shown up.

They were just as integral to this group as Killian and I were, and both of them were council members.

Griffin and Sterlyn stood next to Levi and Rosemary, but Erin hadn't emerged. I didn't see anyone in the car with her, but witches could conceal themselves if needed.

Emmy crawled out of the Navigator and hurried to my side. She murmured, "I hate not being able to pack link with you anymore. I saw that wolf launch his attack on Killian and couldn't get to him or warn you. And now you won't be able to fill me in on what's going on."

Despite the dire situation, a grin spread across my face. "I'm sure you'll hear all about it later." Though I preferred not to get caught up in drama, Emmy always enjoyed being in the know. As an alpha's mate, not only did I need to know about threats and drama to support Killian and help him navigate the pack's issues, but Killian wanted me involved in the conversations. Though PawPaw was a great man and an amazing husband, he operated in the antiquated ways of the wolf pack and rarely asked for Nana's opinion. Killian and Dad were the opposite—both of them cared what their mate and pack members had to say.

"I'm counting on it," she said as she hugged me. "You may be an alpha mate, but damn it, you were my best friend first. I get that you don't have as much time for me as you used to, but I'm kinda really missing you."

Though we'd been hanging out in the evenings, it had been with everyone. She was slowly becoming part of our group, but we hadn't had much alone time since I'd returned. "You're right. I'm sorry. I miss you, too, and I'll come fill you in later." She was my best friend and had spent months with me to help me grieve, not wanting me to be separated from everyone in our pack. She'd made time for me, and I needed to make sure I made her feel special, too. Now we didn't even have our link and couldn't chit-chat throughout the day. I had to make more of an effort because her friendship was one of the most important things in my world.

"There's my bestie." She released me and winked. "I knew she'd come back around."

Chad marched around the Navigator, reaching us as Ronnie, Alex, and the blonde got out of the car.

"Be safe," Chad said as he patted my shoulder and took Emmy's arm.

As the two of them walked off, I inhaled and walked back around the Navigator. Killian finally stepped out, his hand stretched toward me.

You waited for me, I linked, though I wasn't truly surprised. *Why didn't you come over?*

He intertwined our fingers. *Because with the hugging and telling you she missed you, it was clear Emmy wanted a moment alone with you.*

My face burned. Of course he'd heard us. *She's used to having my undivided attention and being able to talk to me whenever she wants.*

Then you'd better spend some time with her. I've very selfishly dominated all your free time. He kissed my cheek and led me to the group as Levi banged on Erin's window.

Ronnie, Alex, Eliza, and the blonde girl were waiting behind Rosemary and Levi with Sterlyn and Griffin.

And I loved every minute of it. Being with him made me the happiest, but I'd seen what happened when mates lost themselves in each other. After Dad's death, Mom had fallen apart, and it had been from more than losing her fated mate. She'd lost her entire world. Though she loved me, Dad had anchored her and leveled her out. Killian was, without a doubt, the most important person to me, but I couldn't lose my entire self to him. We needed to love each other unconditionally but also keep a piece of ourselves. *But yeah, I need to take time for Emmy, Chad, Mom, and my grandparents—which will include dragging you with me from time to time.* I just needed to make sure it wasn't the entire group every time like it had been.

I like the sound of that. The warmth of his love filled our connection.

"Is this mortal humor that I don't get?" Rosemary asked, glancing over her shoulder as we stopped next to Sterlyn.

When I'd first met Rosemary, I hadn't known how to take her. She was very blunt, and I'd been jealous of her friendship with Killian, but I'd realized she had an amazing heart and was just awkward. I understood awkward.

Ronnie chuckled. "No, that's not mortal humor."

The blonde girl between Ronnie and Eliza rolled her chestnut eyes and pursed her ruby-stained lips. "It's called control." She flipped her messy, shoulder-length ivory hair over her shoulder and placed her hands on her hips over the top of her black, satin, Sofia-style dress. Her four-inch ruby nails matched her lipstick and high heels perfectly.

She was gorgeous, and her sharp cheekbones and posture reminded me of Alex.

"You must be Gwen," I said without thinking.

A slight smile graced her face, making her more beautiful. "Yes, and *you* must be Jewel."

"I forgot you hadn't met." Ronnie cringed. "I'm sorry. That was rude."

Alex placed an arm around his wife's shoulders. "Do not be hard on yourself. We have a very pressing issue."

The door clicked, and we all turned to the sedan as Erin opened her door. She climbed out of the vehicle, squared her shoulders, and met our gazes head-on. The maliciousness of her soul slammed into me, coating my skin with that familiar sludge.

"It's about damn time," Griffin rasped from Sterlyn's other side. He stood between his mate and Alex.

Erin flipped her wrist and ran her free hand over her French twist. She wore a skin-tight, scarlet, sweetheart-cut dress that had her breasts on proud display. She and Gwen looked ready for a gala instead of an impromptu meeting to discuss betrayal, death, and threats.

The car door shut from whatever spell she'd cast. She said, "I was waiting until you all were here. I don't want to have to repeat anything."

"And that meant you couldn't get out of your vehicle?" Sterlyn lifted her brow and tilted her head.

"Please," Erin scoffed, and leaned against her door, making it clear she had no intention of moving. "As soon as I stepped out, you'd have started making accusations and asking questions. All of you are rather young—well, except for Rosemary." She smirked as her attention flicked to the angel.

"You forget that Alex and Gwen are older than you, too." Rosemary's feathers ruffled, and one floated to the ground.

Levi stepped beside Rosemary and placed an arm around her waist. "Love, age is like a fine wine, and I can promise that *you* taste exquisite."

My face burned, and he hadn't even directed the comment at me.

Sterlyn coughed as well. "Let's keep this conversation on track. We discovered something disturbing today."

Glancing at her black nails, Erin didn't seem bothered one bit. "Rosemary and Levi already informed me that you all found Tom."

Eliza hissed, the most witch-like sound I'd ever heard from her. She pointed a finger at Erin and said, "I knew we couldn't trust you."

"I said I'd *handle it,* and that's what I did." Erin shrugged. "I don't see what the big deal is."

Not even the song I'd been playing in my head could calm this anger. "Let's see," I snapped. "He had my grandfather's pack, Mom, and Chad taken to a human government facility where scientists experimented on them. Is that not a *big* deal to you?"

"I swear to the goddess, your group continues to grow with new additions just as unimpressive as the rest of you," Erin complained.

"Watch it, Erin," Alex gritted as crimson bled into his irises. "You are talking to council members and other people we value. There's only one person here that none of us like, so I'd say your opinion isn't required."

Laughter bubbled in my chest, and I had to swallow hard to prevent its release.

Erin lifted her chin. "I did not come here to get insulted."

"We didn't ask you here to insult us," Rosemary countered, and stepped toward her. "So watch your mouth, witch, or I'll do it for you."

"And you wondered why I remained in my car." Erin glared and lifted her hand. "*You'd* better watch it, angel. Azbogah is no longer here to protect you, and the only reason I haven't zapped you is that he was a dear friend. However, my patience is running thin, even if you are my elder."

Rosemary jerked forward, but Levi tightened his hold on her, keeping her in place.

"If you do *anything* to any of us, I will put you in your

place, as I itch to do every time I see your face," Eliza said slowly, and there was a power in her voice I'd never heard before. "There was a reason my ancestors' coven was meant to live in Shadow City, and I'd be more than happy to show you why."

A sinister smile slithered across Erin's face. "I'd like to see you try."

Killian, you need to do something. I didn't want to step in, but emotions were high, and everyone was losing sight of the real reason she was here. *If a fight breaks out, there's no telling what the consequences will be. She's already lied to us once. Who knows what she's capable of?*

His hand tightened on mine, but despite the turmoil surging within our bond, he relaxed his shoulders. He linked, *You're right. We're feeding off each other. Thank the gods you're here. I think even Sterlyn is struggling to remain calm.*

My wolf brushed my mind, her pride mixing with mine. His praise meant so much to both of us. Maybe I could be more like Dad on occasion. My absence from Shadow City might have been a bonus at a time like this. I wasn't as emotionally tied to Erin as the others, who'd seen betrayal after betrayal, were.

"Erin, we just need to understand why Tom is still alive," Killian said, and released my hand as he moved in front of Eliza, protecting Erin.

I could slap him. When I'd said he should take control, I hadn't meant for him to put himself in harm's way. I had to do something.

As I was about to rush toward him, Erin huffed, "Fine. Since you asked nicely."

Some of the tension boiling through everyone eased,

and Eliza dropped her hands. With no clear threat, I forced myself to remain stationary.

"There is a reason I didn't kill him that none of you can see because you're blinded by right and wrong." Erin steepled her fingers. "That's the problem with this *entire* group. You can't see all the options. In your minds, there's only one clear path, and because of that, you miss out on opportunities."

"We're looking for answers, not a lecture." Ronnie clenched her hands at her sides. "Unless this is your way of avoiding answering the question. But surely you know that won't work."

Gesturing toward Ronnie, Erin pushed off the sedan. "That's my point. You deem me bad and expect me not to answer when all I'm trying to do is discuss your..." She trailed off and searched the sky for an answer.

"Our shortcomings?" Alex hissed.

"Sure." Erin shrugged. "That works."

"For your love of all things vile, will you please shut up?" Levi groaned. "You're purposely antagonizing us. After living most of my life in Hell, I recognize the signs."

I'd read enough books to know Erin was grandstanding, though it would gain no favor among our group. It was an ego boost for her.

"Allow me to reveal one of my finer skills," Rosemary rasped, and she flipped her feathers over.

Erin was going to milk this for as long as she could, and we had to be smarter. What could she gain by keeping Tom alive?

A lightbulb flashed in my mind, and my blood ran cold. "She never intended to kill Tom or his pack. She wanted to keep them alive," I murmured. This woman was an evil genius, but she shouldn't have hidden her plans. "When she was asked to kill them, she made it clear she would take care of it. We assumed she meant she'd kill them." We'd all been so eager to take care of the ones impacted by the facility.

Rosemary inhaled sharply. "But what was the point of keeping them alive? So they could continue to attack us?"

I opened my mouth to answer, but Gwen beat me to it. "She is using him to uncover who took the pack."

Silence descended as everyone processed what we'd just learned while Erin examined me.

She tapped a finger on her lip as an evil smirk formed. "You've surprised me, wolf girl. Maybe you aren't like the rest of your friends after all."

Pulse racing, I immediately understood her implication. I could see gray...like *she* could. I clasped my hands to hide their trembling. What if what boiled inside me wasn't just anger but something more insidious? Maybe there was something jaded about me, and that was why I struggled to be like Dad.

My vision dotted, and it wouldn't be long before I passed out.

CHAPTER TWENTY-ONE

KILLIAN'S strong arm held my waist tightly, anchoring me to the present. He linked, *She's messing with you. Don't let her get to you.*

His reassurance lessened some of my hysteria, but my stomach churned with nausea. I couldn't be weak, especially as the alpha's mate. Though I didn't have to be *the leader*, I still needed to be strong and prove I was worthy of Killian's love and my spot in the pack.

"Or maybe she can see the bigger picture more easily than the rest of us can," Killian growled. "Don't come here and try to create chaos to get yourself out of trouble."

Having him stand beside me, both physically and emotionally, had my wolf howling inside. He was fiercely protective of us and wouldn't tolerate anyone hurting us in any way.

The sound of footsteps informed me we had newcomers, and I glanced over to see Annie and Cyrus rushing toward us. Sterlyn must have told them what was happening.

"Trouble." Erin barked out a laugh. "Please, you all

think you hold more influence and power than you do. Yes, the angels respect Rosemary and even the *demon*, and Gwen, Ronnie, and Alex have formed a tighter bond with the vampires. The shifters have rallied around Griffin, Sterlyn, and Cyrus because of everything you sacrificed for the city and surrounding areas. But your support is already fading. Between the crazed, bloodthirsty vampires you have locked up in cells, the disappearing packs, and the escalating demon attacks across the world, things are looking bad for your group. Add in the alpha of Shadow Ridge—the shifter council members' *best friend*—informing the world of our existence, and the tides are turning. It's my coven that has remained within the city to help rebuild and hide it once more."

There it was. She was using the disappearing packs to gain control over Shadow City. The urge to punch her nearly stole my breath, and I'd met her only twice. I wasn't sure how the others were holding back.

"Everyone knows the *demons* outed us." Sterlyn stood rigid, but her face was smooth and relaxed. "We even told the city what happened after things settled down. They saw the humans in the city with video recorders."

Annie and Cyrus stopped at the edge of the yard a few feet short of the Navigator. I wasn't sure why, but having them near made things less intense.

Erin nodded. "That's my point. The angels created the demon problem, then the vampire and shifter council members aligned themselves with the angels, so it became your problem, too. In fact, the residents have asked the witches to focus on repairing the gate the demons damaged to get inside so the city can shut again."

"We all know your coven had a helping hand, but regardless, that won't solve *anything*." Griffin tapped his fingers on his legs, giving away his frustration. He wasn't nearly as composed as his mate. "The humans know we're there now, and supernaturals beyond the city are disappearing. We can't turn a blind eye."

"Why not?" Erin glared in challenge. "We've done it for over a thousand years."

"She does have a point," Gwen said as she gestured to Erin.

"Gwen..." Alex warned.

Ronnie stepped forward. "Just because it was done that way doesn't mean it was right. Are you seriously thinking about locking down the city again and letting chaos ensue?"

"Isn't our priority our *residents*?" Erin arched her brow. "That should be where our loyalties lie."

With a long exhalation, Annie licked her lips. "My understanding is that only the strongest supernaturals live in Shadow City."

Erin grinned as her attention flicked to Eliza, and she cooed, "Your understanding is correct, proving that my coven is the strongest."

Nostrils flaring, Eliza tilted her head back. Ronnie placed a hand on the older lady's shoulder, and Eliza sneered but remained quiet.

"Azbogah was desperate to shut the city off to protect the world from *you* all." Annie smiled sweetly. "But now you don't know how to acclimate to the outer world and have to train nonstop to even battle demons. So it makes sense that the residents are desperate to lock themselves up again. I mean, you couldn't even hold the protective spell to keep the city hidden, so I get it, and the rest of the world will, too. If you're asking for our blessing—"

"That's *not*—" Erin said viciously, and stopped, her face turning pink. She placed a hand on her stomach and cleared her throat. With a slower and steadier voice, she said, "That's not why we want to shut the gate."

Cyrus smirked and moved closer to his mate. He chuckled. "Then why do you?"

Erin opened her mouth and closed it again. Her forehead creased. "Because we...want to be left alone."

That was the weakest excuse she could have come up with without telling an outright lie. But I wouldn't be the one to call her out on it.

"Do you really think that will happen now?" Eliza raised her arms out beside her. "Back when the city was created, no one knew about it unless they were invited inside. No one came knocking on its gates, and the few living outside, whose family and friends did move in...well, they eventually died off, and the city was mostly forgotten until the doors partially opened a few years ago. Now the *entire world* knows about the city. Do you believe that if you shut the gates, you'll be safe? You may be a strong coven, but if multiple covens attack, they can overpower your magic and get inside."

Eliza was right. There was no more hiding. Humans had learned about our existence, and Shadow City and the surrounding areas had become a target. We could hope that things would calm down, but the last time I'd turned on the television, Killian's face had filled the screen as much as it had before.

"It's a good thing I saved Tom, then." Erin crossed her arms, pushing up her breasts. "We can track him and see who he talks to, or even what he eats for supper."

Sterlyn rubbed the back of her neck. "What have you learned in the past week?"

Erin's expression smoothed, similar to Sterlyn's. They were both employing their poker faces, which made my skin crawl. Sterlyn didn't want Erin to know she was rattled, but what was Erin trying to hide?

"Nothing worth sharing." Erin rubbed the corner of her eye. "But if anything newsworthy comes up, you'll be the first I tell."

Each word sounded calculated. There was no doubt in my mind she was hiding something from us, but unfortunately, she had power on her side. We had no way to obtain the information other than from her. There had to be a way around it, but I was lost as to what that could be.

"You should've told us," Killian rasped, his eyes hardening. "Tom poses a threat to *my* mate and her family, which is unacceptable."

Erin glared at him. "This is why I didn't confer with Sterlyn and the other council members. They would feel the same as you. However, I don't have to tell *you anything*. You aren't a council member, and you don't live in the city."

She was *vile*, and as her anger rose, sludge thickened on my skin. I needed a shower, pronto, but first, I had to stand beside my mate. "No, his pack is the one your ancestors chose to protect you outside the city," I said. "He deserves to know what's going on in the city and any decision a council member makes, the same as you. Don't talk down to him when he's a far better person than you." She didn't get to dismiss him as if he was nothing. He and his ancestors had done the job the silver wolves had been meant to do: protect the city and every supernatural in this world.

Warmth exploded through our bond. He linked, *Having you stand up for me turns me on in all kinds of ways.*

Hold on to that feeling until we're alone. I couldn't have him distract me.

"Are all silver wolves this mouthy, or is it just the ones close to this group?" Erin scowled. "Actually, no. The vampire queen, Rosemary, and the demon wolf always have plenty to say as well."

"We're as mouthy as you are," Ronnie said sweetly, batting her eyelashes. "You know what they say—birds of a feather flock together."

"That makes no sense." Rosemary pinched the bridge of her nose. "Birds can't flock with *one feather*."

Unlike my friends, I had no interest in politics. "You don't trust or like us, and the feeling is mutual. That's why you didn't tell us. You knew we wouldn't go along with the plan. So tell me, why should we trust you now?" I hated speaking up so much, but something wasn't right. We were missing a piece of the puzzle.

Erin examined me, and a shiver ran down my spine. I forced my body not to react as I held her gaze. She said, "You don't have much of a choice. Do you?"

"I wouldn't call that trust, then." Rosemary spread her wings.

"Not my problem." Erin turned back to the sedan and climbed in. "I'll let you know if I learn anything worth sharing. Until then, don't threaten me or call me away from my city. Unlike you, I won't abandon the residents." She drove off, leaving the rest of us staring after her in the yard.

"I'd trust a prince of Hell over her," Levi said, his attention locked on the car until it turned out of sight. "Which is saying something, because those assholes were hideous."

"Her soul is darker every time we're around her." Rosemary pursed her lips. "I knew better than to leave that day at the farmhouse."

Sterlyn strolled to the center of the group. "It's no one's fault. We had over two hundred shifters to get to safety, and Rosemary and Levi were dealing with burying Scott's body in the respectful manner he deserved. We did the best we could, and if we could go back, I doubt we'd change our strategy."

"Take it from my experience," said Alex. "I fully supported my brother as king, and when I learned he'd been doing unspeakable things, I had similar thoughts. What if I'd questioned him more? If I'd done my due diligence, would Matthew have lost his humanity? And the thing is, all that does is waste energy and cause you to spiral. You learn from those mistakes and move on so you don't make them again. At least none of our loved ones perished from leaving Erin and the others to handle the pack."

Not yet, but if Tom hurt anyone, in a way, that would be on us. I understood his point, and I remained quiet.

"Now that's the man I love." Ronnie beamed at him and kissed his cheek.

"Griffin and I should head back to Shadow City and check in with our people." Sterlyn yawned. "If the shifters are questioning things, we need to spend more time there. After fighting today, I don't think we plan on doing anything special tonight."

With getting acclimated to my new pack, trying to be there for Mom and my grandparents when I could, learning that Tom and his pack were still around, and having that huge confrontation with Erin, I was pooped. I didn't even have the energy to watch a movie.

"Since I'm technically the third council member, I should go with you, too." Cyrus groaned and leaned his head back. "Kira has been filling in a lot as the acting shifter member, which isn't helping matters."

"You all stay at the mansion with us." Ronnie winked. "We have plenty of room, and that's where Sterlyn and Griffin are. We can ride back together."

"After you drop me off," Eliza cut in. "I will *not* go into that city. Not with the Nightshadow Sisters there." She crossed her arms, her frown set.

Killian tugged me to him. "We should be good for the night. My priority is taking my tired mate home and getting her rest."

We all said our goodbyes, and the two of us walked into our house. It was silent, which was heavenly after being around so many people today. Though I loved my friends, I needed time alone to recharge. I didn't mind being around Killian—his presence was calming—but that was it.

He stopped in the living room and released my hand. "Want to take a shower and get comfortable? I gotta do something, but it won't take too long."

I'd hoped that we would shower together, but it made sense he had things to take care of; we had been gone all day. I swallowed down my selfish wish and nodded before heading to our room.

Within ten minutes, I'd showered and changed into my pajamas, the bed calling my name. When I opened the bathroom door, the smell of grilled cheese and tomato soup infiltrated my nose, and my stomach gurgled.

Killian walked in with a wooden tray, carrying a single sandwich and a large bowl of soup as he took the last bite of the grilled cheese in his free hand. He set the tray on his side of the bed, leaving my side open so I could crawl in. He grinned. "Dinner is served."

My heart expanded with so much love that my chest ached. I hadn't even thought about food. He'd let me shower so I could crawl into bed and get comfortable and eat. Tears burned my eyes, and I thanked Fate she'd given him to me.

I wasn't worthy.

Thank you, I linked, not trusting my voice not to break

from the emotions surging through me. I got into bed, and he placed the tray on my lap.

You never have to thank me for providing for you. He kissed my lips and sauntered to the closet to grab some clothes, then made his way to the bathroom.

The shower turned on as I ate my meal, and I couldn't believe how good a grilled cheese sandwich and soup could taste.

When I finished, he came out of the bathroom wearing plaid pajama bottoms and no shirt. A bead of water ran down his face and dripped onto his chest.

All my tiredness vanished as my body warmed.

I placed the tray on the nightstand as he made his way to his side of the bed, and I crawled toward him as he stood there, facing me. I placed a hand on his warm skin, enjoying his classic sandalwood scent, and ran my fingers over his pecs.

Goosebumps spread across his skin. *You're tired. You need some rest.*

First, I need something else. I placed my free hand around his neck and guided his lips to mine. When they touched, the buzzing intensified the need inside me.

He growled and lowered me onto my back slowly, our mouths never parting. I ran my hands down his back and stilled when my fingers found the rough patch where he'd been injured while in wolf form. I linked, *You're hurt.*

I'm fine. It's already scabbed over, and I don't feel any pain. His tongue brushed my lips, begging for entrance.

Unable to deny him, I opened my mouth, and his faint citrus taste filled my mouth.

His hands slipped under my pale yellow nightshirt and caressed a nipple. My hands immediately went to the waistband of his pants and pushed them off his hips. He chuckled as he kicked them onto the floor while he continued his perusal of my body.

I lifted my hips, removing my shorts, desperate to feel him inside me. After he took care of me, I wanted to do the same for him.

We aren't in a rush, he linked, but I begged to differ. After everything he'd done for me, I needed to connect with him. I wanted to make him feel the same amount of love for me as I did for him.

I pushed him over so he sat against the headboard and straddled him.

Wait, he linked as he pulled my shirt over my head. *I need to take care of you first.*

You've already done that. It's my turn, I demanded.

After helping him remove my shirt, I tossed it to the floor and slid him inside me. He filled me, and his lips sucked on a nipple.

He chuckled, making my head dizzy, and linked, *You are ready*.

Oh, I know. I rocked against him, needing the friction only he could provide. He was the only one who could satiate me, pleasure me, make me feel as if I were the only person in the world.

Increasing the pace, I spread my legs further so he could reach deeper. We normally went slowly, but this was more frantic. I needed him like a drug.

I was desperate. Addicted.

My hands threaded into his short hair, and I pulled at the ends. He moaned, making me dizzier.

He removed his lips from my breast and reclaimed my mouth, his tongue colliding with mine. Both hands covered my breasts, sending warm quivers through me as we lost ourselves in each other.

I rolled my hips, and he whimpered against my mouth. It was the sexiest noise I'd ever heard in my life, and I made the same movement faster.

Gods, I love you so much, he linked as his hands gripped my hips, guiding me and increasing the pressure. He opened up our connection, and his love for me slammed into our bond.

He loved me as much as I loved him. The kind of love that was almost painfully blissful.

I love you, too, I replied, though that didn't feel like a strong enough word for what I felt for him.

As we pushed our devotion through each other, my entire world focused on him and this moment. The friction grew stronger, and he bucked wildly underneath me. We both needed the other person in this special connection we'd share with only each other for the rest of our lives.

His pleasure collided with mine, and soon, we shook with ecstasy. The wave was like a storm from which I never wanted to be saved. This was the rare moment when I couldn't tell where he began and I ended, and there was no other way I'd ever want to be. We were two halves of a soul, and this was how we connected to be complete. This was the gift we were able to give each other.

As I collapsed against his chest, exhausted and happy, he pulled me into his arms, and we drifted off to sleep together, as it should always be.

A FEW DAYS LATER, Emmy and I sat at the kitchen table, enjoying time alone together.

I'd spent two days with my grandparents, checking on the pack and seeing what I could do to assist them. They all seemed to be acclimating, though Heather's family, especially Sean and his close friends, were growing restless, wanting to find the people who had done this to them. Sitting by while a threat hunted us didn't sit well with any of us.

My grandfather's pack and Ruby's pack were getting along very well. Birch and Sean had become close friends, and by the way Ruby clung to Sean, I was fairly certain they were mates, which would be terrific. If that were the case, she wouldn't cause problems for any other couples.

"So, what does sex feel like?" Emmy asked as she leaned over Killian's and my kitchen table. Her eyes were almost as bright and shining as the silver bling coffee cup she'd brought over.

I beamed. Killian had gone to meet with Billy and other pack leaders to talk business, but it was partly a ruse to give Emmy and me some alone time. "I don't know how to describe it, but it's like the closest thing to Heaven I've ever known."

"Well, that's cheesy." She took a sip of her coffee. "But I shall let it pass since you're newly mated and all. Maybe in a few weeks, I'll ask again and get a better answer."

I stuck out my tongue and laughed. "I doubt it, and I honestly don't want to go into details. That's private between him and me." I'd never want to talk about him in a disrespectful way. What we shared was special and only for us.

"Whatever." She set her cup on the table and rolled her neck. "All I know is I'm glad you have him. When we were fighting, I saw how he kept checking on you. He was determined not to let anything happen to you, no matter the cost. One day, I hope I can find someone with half that devotion."

Though she was trying to be supportive, her words bothered me. That was the one problem he and I had in our relationship, and it was a big one: I wanted him to trust me to handle things on my own. It wasn't that I didn't want him to check on me from time to time, but apparently, a *lot* of his focus had been on me, and that was probably how he'd wound up getting hurt.

She tilted her head as she examined me. "What? You act like it's a bad thing."

"It *is*. He doesn't think I can handle my battles on my own. It's one thing to check on me occasionally, but he's, like, waiting to step in because he expects me to lose." I leaned back and ran a finger along the rim of my coffee cup.

Emmy bobbed her head. "Have you talked to him about that?"

"Yeah, but it never goes well." I shrugged. "It's like he thinks I'm saying he can't defend me." That was the cycle we were caught in.

A knock sounded on the front door right before it opened.

"Jewel? Killian?" Sterlyn called as she entered the house. She'd spoken out loud for my benefit because she couldn't link with me anymore.

"In the kitchen."

Sterlyn and Griffin stepped into view, and Sterlyn's face was lined with worry as her eyes glowed. She had to be linking with Killian.

I stood. Something was wrong. "What's up?" I was surprised Killian hadn't already linked with me to give me a heads-up.

"We'd just pulled into our driveway next door when I got a text from Sadie." Sterlyn's face turned pale. "Another pack's gone missing, and they need our help."

CHAPTER TWENTY-TWO

YET ANOTHER PACK HAD VANISHED. It surprised me how quickly it had happened after the previous pack's disappearance. Either the humans had a larger building or there were multiple locations.

I hoped for the first option. The more locations they had, the harder it would be to rescue everyone.

Kill, I linked. I wanted him to get back here. He'd be more likely to know what to do.

He replied immediately, *Sterlyn just linked with me when she saw I wasn't there. I'm heading back now.*

Some of the heaviness fell from my shoulders, and I stood. "Let me get Kill's laptop and see if there's anything in the chat about it.

"Good idea." Griffin headed to the far right corner, where the Keurig stayed. "I'll make coffee for Sterlyn and me, if that's okay."

I rocked back and cocked a brow. "Would you ask Killian if he were here instead of me?"

He puffed out his cheeks. "I want to say yes, but you'd know I was lying."

"Then you don't need to ask me, either." I narrowed my eyes at him, then hurried to the bedroom to get the laptop Killian kept stowed under his nightstand. I'd asked why he didn't keep it in a central room, and he'd informed me that he didn't want too much technology around. It made him uncomfortable and often found more trouble, and we didn't need any help with that.

I was beginning to see his point, but the disappearances were something we all needed to be aware of.

Griffin chuckled. "Though she's quieter than the rest of you, she sometimes surprises me with what she says."

Emmy said, "One thing you'll learn about Jewel—if you haven't already—is though she may not be the first one to speak, when she does, she usually has something important to say."

"Many people equate silence with weakness, but that's not the case with her," Sterlyn added, and then a chair slid across the floor. "When she talks, you listen."

My cheeks burned as I entered the bedroom, thankful they couldn't see how their words affected me. Though I appreciated being valued, I preferred more discreet recognition. I wouldn't be ungrateful and complain when they were being kind and supportive.

I pulled open the bottom drawer and removed the laptop, then stepped into the hallway and faced the kitchen. Sterlyn had seated herself with her back to the sliding glass door. The scent of freshly brewed coffee greeted my nose, and I returned to my seat at the table. Griffin made a second cup of coffee while I booted the laptop.

I wanted to ask Sterlyn several questions, but I remained quiet. There was no point in asking before Killian got here. As I opened the web browser, the front door clicked, and our bond tugged as Killian entered.

Multiple footsteps sounded with his.

As I logged on to the supernatural intranet, Killian, Billy, Lowe, Chad, and Darrell came into view.

He'd brought the cavalry.

Without missing a beat, Killian took the vacant chair across from Sterlyn and moved it so he sat beside me. Our legs brushed, and heat coursed through my body.

"I hope you don't mind, but I figured it wouldn't hurt for all of us to hear." Killian nodded toward the men he'd brought with him.

"No, we keep underestimating the other side, so it's best if all heads are in on this together." Sterlyn bit her lip as her phone dinged. She glanced at the screen and leaned back in her chair. "Ronnie, Alex, Annie, and Cyrus are leaving the city as we speak, and Rosemary and Levi are heading this way."

I'd been focused on action, but now I took a moment to look at Sterlyn and noted the dark circles under her eyes. We were all stretched thin. They'd spent the past few days in Shadow City to temper the fear Erin and her coven had been stirring up. Their presence had calmed the panic to a degree, and they'd remained to help rebuild the city, so some things had gone back to normal. Even though the destruction had affected mainly the shifter side of the city and a little bit of downtown, it had inconvenienced everyone. So many shifters had been displaced and needed to find shelter elsewhere. Apparently, the wolf shifter condominium had been ruined by a fire the late angel Azbogah had planned, and the flood of shifters into the vampire section was causing more disgruntlement. The small population of bird shifters who lived within the city had taken up a few homes in the angel condominium, but they were the only ones who could live there because there weren't any stairs or elevators. And the witches weren't allowing anyone to stay with them, stating that their coven was already low on space with the space that they had. So the brunt of the problem had fallen onto the vampires.

Even though Shadow Ridge and Shadow Terrace weren't having housing problems, we were dealing with the influx of humans, especially with Christmas around the corner. Many humans took a vacation this time of year, and with the universities out, too, the town was brimming with humans and their cameras. We had several wolves running the perimeter at all times to keep humans from getting too close to anything supernatural.

Killian placed a hand on my neck, and our connection buzzed between us. If it hadn't been for him, I was certain I wouldn't have found much calm.

As I inhaled his scent, my nerves settled, and I found the courage to scan the various pack chat threads for any updates related to the disappearances. "I don't see anything concerning, other than people talking about the pack we scoped out the other day."

"What are they saying?" Emmy leaned over the table, nearly spilling her coffee.

Sterlyn reached out and caught the cup right before it would have tipped over. Thank gods for supernatural reflexes.

I scanned the paragraph. "The wolves who know the missing pack swear something is wrong. It's a small pack, but the wolves are strong and content with everything they have. People suspect something is amiss, and they're tying the timeline to the supernatural news that broke out."

"Do they define 'small'?" Darrell asked as he stepped into the kitchen and made his way behind Emmy. His eyes were bloodshot, giving his blood orange irises a sinister edge.

Good question. Depending on the wolf and the size of their pack, small could be a wide range. The silver wolf pack had been twenty-five, the definition of paltry, but if a pack had five hundred members, anything less than two hundred could be considered small. Then I stumbled upon the answer. "One hundred five."

Grabbing her phone, Sterlyn typed out a message. "Maybe if this second pack is smaller, too, they took them to the same building. I'm asking what she knows about the new pack."

That would be the best-case scenario, but lately, things hadn't been going in our favor.

Killian leaned against my shoulder and took a deep breath as he skimmed the website with me. Nothing else caught our attention except for the growing paranoia that gripped the domain. I wanted to reassure people, but that could result in them lowering their guard, which could be detrimental. Staying on high alert was best.

Sterlyn's phone dinged as Griffin carried two cups of coffee to her. He set one cup in front of his mate just as the sound of flapping wings grew louder.

Rosemary and Levi were almost here.

"That's her again." Sterlyn swiped her phone and chewed on her bottom lip.

Wings appeared beyond the sliding glass door behind Sterlyn as Rosemary landed on the concrete porch. Her burgundy hair flew behind her, and her burnt orange shirt reminded me of a sunrise. She pulled her wings into her back as Levi transitioned from shadow to human form beside her.

"I don't know how long it'll take for me to get used to

seeing angels and demons out here." Lowe tugged at his ear. "I knew angels lived in Shadow City, but we rarely saw any until we integrated the silver wolves into this neighborhood."

"It is a sight to see," Killian agreed, and the temperature dropped. Though I knew he didn't have romantic feelings for Rosemary anymore, his words reminded me that he had at one point. Then he continued, "It's the same as seeing a silver wolf, especially in the moonlight."

He ran a finger across my cheek, and a shiver ran through me. He had a way of making me feel special, and I was ashamed I'd gotten upset at his words.

Angels were majestic. Both Rosemary and Eleanor came across that way, and I'd bet that any other angel, man or woman, would seem the same.

The glass door slid open, and Rosemary and Levi joined us, but Rosemary didn't bother to shut it again, ready to take flight at any time.

Chad leaned against the wall on one side of the kitchen. "What's wrong, Rosemary?"

"You tell me." She leveled her gaze at him. "Sterlyn asked us to come here right away. Normally, when there's no notice, something awful's happening. So forgive me if I don't want to come inside and sit if this is an urgent matter."

Tugging her more into the room, Levi shut the glass door. "We've been working nonstop inside the city to get the dome working again so Heaven's light can filter through and recharge the angels more quickly. We're a little tense even without the concerned tone of Sterlyn's message."

Now *that* was something we all could understand. We were trying to work through things here, but we were on tenterhooks waiting for Tom's next move. Killian, Chad, Lowe, and Billy were discussing heading to the latest missing pack's neighborhood to find a belonging so Eliza or Circe could locate them.

"I didn't mean to alarm anyone." Sterlyn clutched her mug with both hands. "It's just...dealing with the Shadow City repairs and politics, I haven't slept much. Then Sadie's message came. I hate that it took another pack going missing for things to start moving forward again."

"You don't think *you've* slept much?" Chad laughed humorlessly. "Why do you think I've been harassing Killian and Darrell about going back to find something from the pack neighborhood? I know what they're going through, and let me tell you, it's horrible."

My breakfast revolted in my stomach. Everything Chad had said was true, and we shouldn't have waited to go back to get more answers.

An engine purred louder the closer it came. It had to be Ronnie, Alex, Annie, and Cyrus...or so I hoped. We didn't need any more surprises.

Lowe paced inside the threshold between the kitchen and the living room. "If we go anywhere, we need more people. Between what happened at the farmhouse and the other pack location, small groups won't cut it."

The front door opened, and the four people we'd been waiting on barreled inside. The corners of Annie's eyes were tight, and Cyrus was so stiff, I was certain he wasn't bending his knees. Ronnie and Alex seemed paler than usual, which was saying something.

Sterlyn launched into the backstory, filling everyone in. "And Sadie just informed me that the new missing pack is smaller, too. About one hundred fifty members, and only about an hour and a half away from the other location in the mountains near Knoxville. Apparently, this pack lives relatively close to her stepbrother's pack."

"Did her stepbrother alert her?" Billy asked, rocking from his toes to his heels across from Chad.

"Yes," Sterlyn answered. "They went by to drop off some food, and when they drove up, everyone was gone. The scents were faint everywhere."

The same story once again. The humans had to realize we would eventually catch on, but maybe that was the point. They wanted to instill fear in us like they feared us.

"Then we have no choice." Ronnie stood at the edge of the living room, but her voice was clear. "We have to figure out what's going on."

I hated to be this person, but if I didn't ask and something happened, I'd have yet another thing to feel guilty about. "When we met Sadie and her friends, I trusted them. They seemed concerned and honest, and they helped us when Tom attacked. But what if..." I trailed off, remembering that their essence had felt pure, but that didn't mean they were on our side. They could be working for a cause they believed was good. Intent meant everything when it came to measuring one's soul.

Cyrus interjected, helping me get the words out. "They might be setting us up." He cleared his throat and took his mate's hand. "That would be an effective strategy."

I hadn't considered that, but it's a good point, Killian linked with me, his pride wafting through our bond, making me sit up taller.

I was glad I'd spoken up. Everyone seemed to consider that a valid concern.

"But we felt their essence." Emmy tilted her head and glanced at her dad for reassurance. "We would've known."

"Not necessarily, dear," Darrell said as he placed his hands on her shoulders. "Sometimes, it's not that simple."

Sterlyn tapped a finger against her lips. "Just like the

girl we held hostage. Savannah. She was trying to capture us, but she was also afraid of us and thought it needed to be done. Her soul wasn't evil, and she thought she was doing what was best for the humans. It could be similar for Sadie and her friends. We simply don't know."

"Either way, the possibility isn't something we can ignore." Annie shook her head and stepped forward. "But if people are in trouble, we have to help them. We can't just say it could be a trap and turn a blind eye."

"That's not what any of us are suggesting." Alex tugged at the collar of his pale blue button-down shirt. "Of course we will check things out, but we have to be cautious, especially after the last two attacks."

Ronnie looped her arm through her husband's and beamed adoringly at him. "I so *love* the man you've become."

"And this wouldn't be possible if it weren't for you," he replied, and he kissed her.

Annie smiled at them, then turned her attention back to the rest of us. "Let's not forget they're probably focusing on wolves right now because of Tom. Soon, other supernatural races will be taken, too."

That was something I hadn't considered.

"What's the plan?" Billy asked. "Take half our best fighters? Because we need to leave some here to handle the humans and the demons if they decide to act up."

"With the damage Sadie's pink light beams can do, if she were to fight against us, we would need a lot of manpower. Especially if Tom attacks alongside them." Griffin frowned. "I'll bring some of my pack members, too."

"We can't risk that." Sterlyn shook her head. "Not with Erin working the city. We also don't want her to know we're up to something. Even though she says she's following Tom,

I don't trust her. I think Cyrus and Annie should stay in the city to cover for Griffin and me. They can stay with the twins and the silver wolves in case something happens."

"But—" Cyrus started.

"She's right," Annie jumped in. "We need to pull our weight in the city, and we have the babies to think of. If backup's needed, we'll leave and help our friends and family." She cupped his cheeks. "I hate it, but Erin is using your new position on the council to gain leverage since you weren't raised there. We need you present and active so she can't say you aren't knowledgeable about the city. I'll call Eliza and see if anyone from the coven might be willing to help."

"I'll take twenty of my best fighters, including Lowe," Killian said as he placed a hand on my knee. "Billy, I need you to stay back and lead since Jewel will be going with me."

"Understood, though I hate not being there to fight alongside you." Billy pushed off the wall. "I'll go get nineteen of the others and tell them to start packing."

"Since Luna, Sierra, April, and Collin have fought against Tom before, make sure they're part of the twenty," Killian commanded.

Sterlyn rubbed her hands together. "Cyrus, what if I take Emmy, Darrell, Chad, Theo, Rudie, and Mila?"

My stomach dropped, and though I hated to speak out against her, I couldn't remain silent. "Mom. Tom's after her."

Her iridescent lavender eyes softened. "I know, but she knows him. She might guess a move none of us would be prepared for."

I wanted to argue, but she had a point.

Killian linked, *We'll keep an eye on her.*

That would have to be enough. Their decision was made.

"I'll ask the other two wolf packs to send some of their people with us." Chad offered, heading to the door. "Mila's over there now and can begin the discussions."

Alex and Ronnie stared at each other, having a telepathic conversation. After a moment, Alex faced us. "We'll bring thirty of our fighters with guns to help. It's the least we can do, and I hate that I can't spare more with the demon chaos on the Shadow Terrace side and the bloodthirst that's taken hold."

"Rosemary and I will talk to Zagan and Eleanor. The angels are helping with the demon situation and the rebuilding efforts, so I'm not sure how many we can pull away without alerting Erin," Levi offered as he opened the sliding glass door.

"Eleanor." Rosemary scoffed. "Why her?"

"You know why." Levi grinned. "Zagan won't go without her, and she's a good fighter."

"Don't remind me." She hurriedly stepped out onto the porch.

We had a plan, and everyone was ready to move. I just hoped it would be enough.

Sterlyn stood and placed both hands on the table. "Everyone who's going needs to be ready in the next hour. Pack for a few days. We don't know what's ahead of us."

We dispersed, eager to see what was going on while fearing that things might be worse than we knew.

As I headed into Killian's and my bedroom, he walked in behind me. He turned me around and touched my face. His touch buzzed with ecstasy, and I forgot about the dire situation we were in, even if only for a minute.

I kissed his lips, breathing in all things Killian. Who

knew when we would have a chance to do this again? It could be days, and I wanted to take a moment to enjoy being with just him.

He kissed me gently and with so much love. Warmth filled my chest until he murmured, "Gods, Jewel, I adore you. Nothing can ever happen to you. Is there any way I can convince you to stay here?"

Familiar hurt soared through me, churning into anger. But Emmy's words replayed in my mind. It was time for us to have a heart-to-heart and hash this out.

CHAPTER TWENTY-THREE

I INHALED DEEPLY and ignored the urge to play a classical song in my mind. That would only distract me from choosing my words wisely. If he and I were going to have a productive talk, I would have to move past my hurt and tell him how I felt.

Taking a step back, I locked eyes with him and said, "Killian, how many times are we going to have this conversation?"

He took my hand in his. "It was more wishful thinking. The words just slipped out."

At least he'd acknowledged that me staying behind wasn't even a remote possibility, but that didn't do much to calm the storm brewing inside me. I wanted to yank my hand out of his, but that would only escalate the situation. Instead, I focused on my next words. "I get it. I do." I placed my free hand above my heart. "Don't you think I want *you* to stay here and remain safe? But the difference is, I would never hint at it even half-jokingly."

"Gods." He hung his head, but his grip on my hand remained strong. "I gave Griffin hell for acting like this with

Sterlyn, yet here I am, doing the same thing to you. I'm an asshole, but it's only because I don't want you at risk. The world would be a darker place without you in it."

My blood thawed, and the rage vanished, but not my exasperation. "As long as we're together, we're less at risk of losing each other." I tilted his face up so his eyes met mine. "And who's to say I would be any safer here? This location is the epicenter of supernaturals, and there could be an attack at any time. Nowhere is safe anymore."

He exhaled, his breath fanning my face. He lowered his forehead to mine and rasped, "I should've never agreed to go on television. I didn't have a mate and didn't want anyone else to take that risk. Within days of that decision, you waltzed into my life, and I wish I could take it back."

Regret was a bitch. That was something he and I understood. "You did the right thing. If you hadn't, the demons would've taken control of the message through terror. You did the very thing they didn't expect, and though it's less than ideal, it was the best choice. You are such an amazing man, alpha, and friend, and I'm honored to stand beside you." I pushed my emotions toward him, wanting him to feel my sincerity.

Just as much as he regretted being the face of the supernatural world, I hated that I'd given him so much grief after my grandparents, their pack, and my mom were taken. It wasn't fair, and he'd been an easy target.

"There's no one else I want by my side," he murmured as his fingers tangled in my hair. "Ever. You're the most important person in my entire world, which is why I was acting like an ass and praying you'd stay behind. But you're right. Who's to say you would be safer here?"

My chest expanded with hope. Maybe this time, we'd

resolved this issue. "And I need to feel like you believe I'm capable and worthy of fighting beside you."

His face fell. "Yeah, I know. You're a strong silver wolf. You've made that clear."

I hadn't meant that, but during a fight, I became defensive, though that didn't make it right. "I'm sorry if, by bringing up the type of wolf I am and my training, I made you feel as if I thought I was a better fighter than you. That wasn't my intention. I was trying to get across that I am worthy to be out there fighting *with you*."

He chuckled and shook his head. "In other words, we're feeding off our insecurities."

The way he'd put it was a lot less wordy. "How do we get beyond that?"

"For starters, I could stop asking you to stay behind and not fight so you'll be safe." He grimaced. "And I have to understand that you were made to protect and you'll inevitably get hurt. But to do that, I need something from you."

My lungs froze. With anyone else, I would expect a trick, but not with him. But my skin crawled as I waited for what he'd say next. For him to have worded it that way, I was certain he'd ask for something I wasn't willing to do. "Which is?"

"Confide in me when you're in over your head?" He tucked a piece of hair behind my ear as he whispered, "I know what you're going through. You're determined to make up for all the people you let down...all the deaths you're taking the blame for. I get it. I have the same issues, but you could've died when we fought Tom the first time, and let's not forget how you risked your life at your grandparents' cabin by going after Chad. I get that he's like your brother, but I *need* to know you'll ask for my help if you need it. I need to trust you will. That's the only way I can have you by my side without panicking."

His words were like a slap to the face. As expected, I hadn't wanted to hear them, but also as expected, he wasn't trying to trick me. He spoke the truth, and it was hard to hear. My irrational attempt to retrieve Chad in the middle of burning cabins while guns were aimed at me had led to *Killian* almost dying. If it hadn't been for Rosemary...I couldn't even finish that thought.

I wanted to lash out, but that wouldn't be right. I had to own up to my mistakes.

"Babe," Killian breathed. *I didn't mean to upset you. Sorry if I'm still being—*

You aren't. I'd wanted the open conversation to resolve our issues, and sweeping problems under the rug was not the way to work through them. *You're right, though it's hard to hear. It's just...when you want me to stay back, that makes me more determined to prove I can handle it.*

His hand ran down my face, and his palm settled against my neck. He linked, *You're right. We're just fighting over the same things.*

I nodded, not needing to add anything.

I guess that means we both have to work on it and learn to trust each other. He smiled sadly, concern wafting from his end of our bond. "I promise to work harder on my overprotectiveness. I never thought you couldn't handle a battle. I just don't want you to *have* to. I want to protect you, but you feel the same way as I do."

I'd known we had similar struggles, but this conversation had made me realize they weren't just similar—they were the same. He blamed himself for not being there when his parents and sister died, and I blamed myself for abandoning my pack when they'd needed me the most. We'd let down the most important people in our lives, and we were determined never to let it happen again. That was why he'd become the face of supernaturals and I'd almost died to protect the people I cared about.

Killian sighed and chuckled darkly. "Knowing that my actions and words made you feel invaluable changes everything for me. That was never my intent, and I got more belligerent when I felt like you were being reckless. Now I know I drove you to be that way, and I—"

"Stop." I wouldn't let him take all the blame. "My actions were *my choice*. There are always external influences in the world, but if it rains and I hit a car, the fault is mine, not Mother Nature's. Yes, your words influenced me, but I am my own person, even if you're my fated mate. Do *not* take away the things I need to be accountable for—that won't fix the problem between us. You need to stop trying to protect me and anyone who's fine standing on their own, and I need to realize I don't have to put myself in harm's way just to prove something. It's that simple."

A rare, crooked grin spread across his face, and I forgot to breathe. His chiseled features had an extra edge that made him even more manly. He was, hands down, the most handsome guy I'd ever laid eyes on, and most importantly, he was all mine.

My body warmed, and the urge to force him onto the bed and have my way with him had my jaw clenching. We didn't have time for that; we had to grab our clothes and take care of pack business outside. "We better get moving before I stop caring that we're supposed to be leaving."

He kissed me and linked, *I want to tell you to forget leaving, but it wouldn't look good for the alpha and alpha mate to disappear when battle decisions are being made.*

I hated that we were both responsible, but with the

possible disappearance of another pack, things were escalating. If we didn't intervene, our future together might be cut short. Forfeiting a quickie for a lifetime together wasn't as hard when I put things into perspective.

Begrudgingly, I kissed him, savoring his taste one last time, and pulled away. "I'll pack our things while you run out and make plans with Billy."

"Fine, but we *will* be finishing this moment together." He winked and strolled out the door.

I watched his ass until he turned down the hallway and disappeared from view. It was one of the qualities I loved best about him.

Forcing myself to march to the closet, I got to work. With another pack missing, we needed to locate some of their items to track and rescue them.

A FEW HOURS LATER, we wound up with a hundred and twelve people heading toward this latest pack neighborhood, including twenty from Birch and Ruby's pack, thirty from PawPaw's, twenty-two from Killian's and my pack, thirty vampires, including Ronnie and Alex, six witches, and the people we'd already counted on from our meeting. Rosemary, Eleanor, Zagan, and Levi were flying ahead of us to ensure we weren't heading into a trap, while the rest of us were divided into sixteen vehicles.

Killian drove one of several Suburbans the vampires had loaned us, with me riding shotgun. Lowe sat behind Killian, with Sierra behind me, and April, Luna, and Collin sat in the back row.

We were close to the address Sadie had given Sterlyn, and

we hadn't passed a restaurant or gas station for miles. We'd been climbing up a mountain on a two-lane road so narrow that passing another sizable vehicle was a tight squeeze.

Thank gods I wasn't driving.

"Is the plan really to pull up in sixteen vehicles?" Sierra leaned forward, sticking her head over the center console and Killian's and my joined hands. "Like, 'Here we are, suckers. We brought the cavalry because we don't trust your asses.'"

Killian rolled his eyes. "*Or* we could say we brought reinforcements because we're worried Tom's pack could show up with larger numbers."

"Let's go with Killian's suggestion since it's not untrue." Lowe groaned. "I swear, Sierra. Sometimes you want to cause drama just for the sake of entertainment."

"And you're welcome for that," Sierra said as she glanced over her shoulder at him. "Think about how boring this ride would've been without *me*."

Luna snorted. "My ears wouldn't be hurting right now with how tone-deaf your singing is. And who still sings 'The Song That Doesn't End'? Are you six or something?"

Sierra sat back. "First off, it's a classic and perfect for any long road trip. Do you want to scan the stations tirelessly, looking for a good song? No? I got you covered. Do you want a childhood song that everyone remembers all the words to so everyone can sing along? It'll take care of that, too."

"You brought back childhood trauma," Collin said from his spot behind her.

April laughed. "The trauma she even created back then! Remember, that was her *favorite* song. She sang it *everywhere*."

Unable to stop myself, I turned around to see what was going on.

"What did I say?" Sierra glared as she pounded her chest. "It's a classic. Who wants to hear a song about Johnny cutting down an apple tree or the wheels going 'round and 'round? A freaking lamb sang my song."

Lowe rubbed his temples. "A lamb named Lamb Chop. I mean, come on, that's *sick*. That's like having a pig and naming it Bacon."

"Those are cool as hell names for a lamb and a pig." Sierra flopped back in her seat and crossed her arms. "There is something *wrong* with every one of you."

In less than a mile, we'd be pulling into a neighborhood where an entire pack had potentially vanished, and our passengers had decided to fight over children's songs. If I hadn't been here, I would've thought someone was making this up. *Does she ever simmer down?*

Oh, gods, no. Killian's shoulders shook with quiet laughter. *There are two things that are constant with Sierra. She enjoys going for the shock factor by saying outlandish things, and when she's worried or stressed, she amuses herself. But the few times she's serious, take heed because she has something important to say. That's when you want to listen. Until she starts joking around again. Then you can tune her out.*

Now that he'd explained it, I could read her like a book. In the short time I'd known her, Sierra had proven to be a force to be reckoned with and a loyal friend.

"Everyone, focus. I'm interrupting your important discussion," Killian said as his hands tightened on the wheel, his knuckles turning white. He then linked with all the pack members within range. *Griffin and Sterlyn are linking with me and talking with Ronnie and Alex via phone. Half the cars are going to pull over a mile out.*

Is that necessary? Lowe asked. *What if they aren't bad guys?*

Even if they're good, if Tom shows up, we want to catch him unaware. Killian slowed the vehicle and followed Levi into a small lot that was part of a state park. It offered access to a river that ran about half a mile away, though no one else was here now—unsurprising with how cool the temperature was. The parking lot was big enough to leave all our vehicles. *He likes to spread out and attack from all directions. We need to counter that with our own strategy.*

My stomach grew heavy. I hadn't expected Tom to be here, but that had been wishful thinking. He'd been at the other location, so he would likely be keeping watch here as well. If this was a setup with Sadie, the same strategy would work.

Collin linked. *Do you know how we're going to split up?*

Sierra and Luna will stay with us. The rest of you need to get out and head to Sterlyn and Griffin's vehicle to trade places with them and Chad.

Lowe would be in charge of those in our pack who stayed behind, while Darrell would lead the silver wolves.

Lowe jumped out, with April and Collin right behind him. When Sierra's door opened, Griffin glared at her and commanded, "Move."

Crossing her arms, she shook her head. "I was here first."

"Dear gods," Chad growled as he moved around Griffin and climbed into the vehicle. He leaned over, picked Sierra up, and placed her over his shoulder before moving to the back seat.

I expected her to yell and threaten, but instead, she laughed manically and sang, "This is the most I've been touched by a man in a while."

Chad tossed Sierra on the right side of Luna. He shivered and rasped, "You're pretty but like a sister to me. Never say that again."

And that's exactly why she had. I spun forward to hide my smile as Griffin and Sterlyn took their seats behind us.

"What's the plan?" Luna asked, getting us back on task.

"The seven of us, Rosemary, Levi, Mila, Ruby, Birch, five of their pack members, Hal, and ten of Hal's pack members are going with us," Sterlyn answered as Killian pulled back onto the main road. "So there will be three cars."

It was weird to hear people call PawPaw by his given name—Hal—instead of Alpha.

"So twenty-eight of us." Chad nodded. "That's about the same numbers we had each time Tom attacked, so that shouldn't seem strange."

We wanted to pretend we were doing things the same way. Tom was angry enough to expect it. "Do we really have to bring Mom, though?" I asked.

"He'll be more irrational that way." Griffin fidgeted in his seat. "So it will be better for us. Also, remind me to drive next time. Sitting back here is damn uncomfortable."

"Now you know how we feel, man." Killian glanced into the rearview mirror and smiled sweetly at his best friend.

When Killian pulled onto the road that led to the pack neighborhood, the vehicle became silent. I played Debussy's "Prélude à l'après-midi d'un faune" in my mind to calm down.

I hoped Sadie was trustworthy.

A few minutes later, one-story brick homes came into view between the red cedars and oak trees. Each home had about an acre lot, and the yards were well maintained with pansies and primroses.

I searched for threats in the woods—signs that Tom or Sadie had people waiting to attack us.

"Holy shit," Killian rasped. "Maybe we *have* been set up."

My head jerked forward again. At least fifty people stood behind Donovan, Sadie, Egan, and Jade. Half of them were huge like Egan, and my head screamed *dragon*. They stared us down, the larger men's and women's pupils turning into slits.

Five people rushed out of a house on the left side, while five more came from the house on the right.

Two of them aimed guns at us.

I could see it in their eyes. They were going to shoot. Sadie was a foe.

CHAPTER TWENTY-FOUR

MY HEART POUNDED, and my skin tingled where the fur sprouted over my body. I wouldn't be able to shift and attack them before shots were fired, but I couldn't just sit here and do nothing. We weren't close enough that Sadie and the others could attack easily, but bullets and her beams could travel faster than a car.

Killian slammed on the brakes but couldn't back up due to how closely the car behind us was following.

Cold tendrils curled in my center as my fear combined with Killian's through our bond. We'd brought backup, but we hadn't expected an attack like this on arrival.

We should've known better.

A figure dropped from the sky with large black wings expanding from her back—Rosemary. The two people fired their guns just as Sadie yelled, "Stop!"

Rosemary circled around, her form blurring like a tornado as she hovered in front of our windshield. I watched in disbelief as the bullets bounced off her wings and landed five feet away on the cement driveway.

A lump formed in my throat. I didn't want her to get

hurt protecting us, and I didn't have time to scream for her to move.

When no other shots were fired, she straightened and landed midway between the Suburban and Sadie, crouched with her wings spread behind her. Her mahogany hair appeared more purple in the sunshine. A shadowy figure hovered beside her, and even though I couldn't see his eyes, I knew it was Levi. He wouldn't be anywhere but beside his mate at a time like this.

Sadie's piercing eyes landed on her, and she shouted, "These are the people I asked to come here. They aren't our enemy!"

Some of the panic uncoiled in my stomach, but not by much...just enough for my fur to disappear. The two men still had their guns aimed at us. The muscular one standing in front of the house on the right twisted his face in confusion. He was close to six feet tall and in his mid- to late twenties. His long dark hair was pulled into a low ponytail, and his hunter green eyes narrowed. "Are you sure we can trust them?"

"This is a conversation you should have had *before* she asked us to come." Rosemary's feathers fluffed, making her wings look larger. "And maybe you shouldn't shoot at the very people you asked for help."

Jade snorted. "We did discuss this, and Sadie asked them to come. Drop your gun, Torak, and tell your pack to stand down."

Torak lowered his weapon, and his green eyes glowed. He was an alpha, but Sadie was, too, so they couldn't be part of the same pack, meaning he was likely the step-brother.

Once the men had aimed their weapons at the ground, Rosemary stood and moved aside so Killian could proceed.

"Do we still want to stay after they shot at us?" Luna asked. "If that's not a red flag to get the hell away, I don't know what else could be."

"The pack doesn't know us, and our windows are tinted." Killian pressed the gas, lurching the vehicle forward. "We would've been nervous as well."

"But we wouldn't have shot *first*," Chad grumbled. "I agree with Luna."

Even though they had a point, we couldn't just leave over the strangers' bad judgment.

Someone moved in their seat, and Sterlyn said, "These packs aren't trained like we are. They won't have the same level of control that we expect from one another. It's not that they're weaker or less intelligent; they just haven't had the same opportunities, and we can't fault them for it, especially when they're scared."

Her words moved me, and they hadn't even been directed at me.

Griffin added, "Even Shadow City guards are trained to assess threats. If a pack is content with what they have, they don't have a need for the same sort of training we've had. We always prepared for the day someone would try to take over the city."

Even during the week we'd spent at home, most members had trained every day. Some people hadn't trained in the past, such as Sierra's family and several others who worked day jobs, but after the demon attacks, changes had been made pack-wide. Now everyone was getting some sort of training, even those with day jobs. We all needed to be able to protect ourselves.

Stay— Killian linked with me, then paused. He exhaled and clenched his jaw. *Remember, we're staying close to each other.*

A slight smile tugged on my lips. He was trying to make things better between us, and I loved him for it. *I remember.*

When we pulled up to Sadie, Killian parked the vehicle and cut the engine. Everyone climbed out of the vehicles. Having Rosemary and Levi nearby and watching the others in Sadie's group gave me comfort. Rosemary wouldn't hesitate to react.

As we gathered, I noticed one of the men standing near Sterlyn. Strength wafted from him, emphasized by his muscular form, but that wasn't what had caught my attention. He was missing one of his forest green eyes. Something horrible must have occurred for a man like him to get injured that way.

The back passenger door of the Suburban slammed, and I turned around. Sierra marched toward the man on the right with the gun. Her gray irises brightened as she made a beeline to him and asked, "Your name is Torak, right?"

Grinning, the guy scratched the back of his neck. "The one and only. And who are you, Sunshine?"

"Outraged." Wielding her pointer finger like a weapon, Sierra growled, "What the *fuck* is wrong with you? Do you always shoot your allies like they're worthless scum, or did you reserve that crap for me?"

The guy's jaw dropped, and he blinked several times.

"Whoa," Chad murmured. "I know she's mouthy, but I've never seen her that confrontational."

Luna snorted. "You didn't see her the first time she saw me after Rosemary and I escaped Shadow City."

I had no clue what she was talking about, but now wasn't the time to ask for clarification. We needed to calm Sierra.

As if reading my mind, Killian linked, *Sierra, stand down.*

Sierra's body stayed rigid as if she hadn't heard him, and she continued, "Are you reckless or just stupid?"

Torak holstered his gun at his waist. "I thought you were whoever took this pack. Sadie told us you all appeared in the woods at the last pack location where you met. I didn't expect you to pull up in cars."

"So just stupid. Got it." She crossed her arms, giving him a death stare.

PawPaw stood behind me, with Sean next to him. Their other four pack members stood behind him, while Birch, Ruby, and their pack filed in behind Chad and Luna.

"It's my fault," Sadie said. "I couldn't make out Killian's and Jewel's faces until our guys already had their weapons drawn. I should have considered you would drive up. After all, you knew we'd be here."

"And with quite an army." Killian nodded to the group behind them.

There was no mistaking Roxy's striking red hair. She was next to the man with the missing eye. I grimaced. I needed to learn the man's name.

"Last time, those wolf shifters attacked us," Egan said, his strange accent alluring. I'd never heard anything like it before, but then there was no telling where he'd been raised, especially since everyone had thought dragons were extinct. "So we wanted to make sure we had adequate backup in case they brought more people with them."

That was one reason we'd left the largest part of our group elsewhere.

When Sierra didn't make any swoony comments over Egan, who was just her type, I glanced at her. She was still glaring at Torak, who had his chin lifted in defiance.

"And who are you?" Ruby purred, and stepped between Luna and Chad to get closer to him.

"Taken," Jade seethed, her pupils turning to slits as she stared the wolf shifter down.

This entire situation was a disaster. I linked to Killian, *Maybe bringing everyone was a bad idea.*

A vein in his neck bulged. *Sure seems like it.* He then linked Sierra in with our connection: *If you don't calm down, I will force my will on you. The situation is already tense without you going—*

She spun around, her glare landing on him.

Oh, no. He'd better stop there. I jumped in, *Without you allowing your emotions to rule you. Torak was an ass, but he wasn't trying to be. He's trying to protect his pack and friends. You know how that is. Haven't you ever made a mistake?*

Her shoulders sagged. *I've never shot at anyone who didn't deserve it.* Her words, though, had lost their punch.

Because you've never fired a gun, Killian added, and I wanted to smack him.

I was trying to calm her, but he was riling her up all over again. I linked, *Focus on Sadie and her allies. I'll handle Sierra.*

His head tilted back as his attention landed on me. The right corner of his lip curled upward. *Yes, ma'am. And is it bad that I like it when you get a little bossy?*

You only like it because I'm performing my duties as the alpha's mate, I teased, despite the less-than-ideal situation.

Damn straight. I love it. The heat of his approval pulsed through our connection as he turned his attention to the current threat.

Forcing my attention back to Sierra, I caught Torak biting his lip. He said, "I'm sorry. Had I known you were in the vehicle—"

"You'd what?" Sierra turned toward him, placing a hand

on her hip. "Fire more rounds?"

She wasn't listening to reason. These two men needed to leave her alone and let me deal with her. *Sierra, please. Remember we're here because supernaturals are missing. We need to focus on that.*

"I—" Torak started.

Sierra raised a hand. "Just forget it. We need to pay attention to what's going on." She spun on her heel and stormed back to our group.

Now that I could focus, I scanned the people with Sadie in more detail. The men and women behind Egan were the tallest and had a hint of brimstone scent to them. Well, all of them except for one short girl with long chocolate brown hair that fell over her shoulders. She smelled like a strange combination of vampire sweetness and dragon brimstone. She stood close to the second tallest man there, who came in just shy of seven feet.

"What have you found?" Sterlyn asked, redirecting the conversation from Sierra's meltdown.

Donovan frowned. "Nothing. We got here about fifteen minutes ago, and we searched the perimeter first. We were about to break up and search the houses when you pulled up."

I sniffed the air. All I could smell were our groups. The local pack must have disappeared more than a few days ago.

"Did you smell anything unusual?" Rosemary's wings were still extended, but they'd gone back to their normal size. "Nothing stuck out when we flew over."

"So your little invisible friend is beside you, eh?" Roxy asked as she leaned around Sadie and narrowed her eyes, searching the air around Rosemary. "It freaks me out that I can't see him. That's not *normal*."

"Nor is shooting pink beams from your hands, yet here

we are," Sierra shot back.

Killian grimaced. *Sierra, please, for the love of all our pack, be quiet. We told you about that, but that doesn't mean it's okay for you to blurt it out in front of them.*

"That's fair." Roxy placed her hands on her hips. "But how many wolves have the exact same shade of fur, huh?"

"About as many as the dragons that are supposedly extinct." Sierra wrinkled her nose.

These two were in some sort of pissing match, and I wasn't sure how it would end.

"Both sides have secrets," Sterlyn said, and glared at Sierra. "But that's not why we're here. We're here to figure out whether another pack has been taken."

PawPaw placed a hand on my shoulder and squeezed. "When they attacked our pack, it was coordinated. There was a bang on our door, and when I opened it to check things out, something rolled into the house. That's the last thing I remember. It had to be a gas canister or something that knocked us out."

The woman behind Sadie gasped. "*You* were taken?"

"Remember, Winter, that's why Sadie and Donovan wanted them to come." The man with one eye took the woman's hand.

"I know *that*, but I didn't know that the pack was here with them, Titan." She huffed. "Why didn't you tell us that, Sadie?"

"Mom, I didn't know. He wasn't with them last time." Sadie shook her head, causing her bob to sway. "But their presence here now is helpful."

Axel placed a hand around Roxy, turning her away from Sierra, and said, "Well, that must be what happened here, too. How else could an entire pack have vanished *again*?"

"I hate to be Miss Negativity. After all, this is all good to know, but remember how we were attacked last time?" Lillith stepped forward. "I'd rather not have to fight like that again in unfamiliar territory. I don't know how to find them, but let's do what we're going to do and *go*."

If they were going to attack us, they wouldn't be eager to leave. I'd felt like we could trust Sadie before, and seeing how they were acting now made more of my unease vanish.

"We have a simple solution for that so we don't have to linger and risk Tom's pack outnumbering us again, especially as your group has proved how unskilled your members are." Rosemary straightened and marched toward Torak.

Jade scowled and clenched her hands. "What the *fuck* is your problem? Keep talking, and I'll show you how *unskilled* I am by kicking your ass."

Heart racing, I racked my brain for the best way to de-escalate the problem.

"Even if you were skilled, it is unlikely that you could defeat me." Rosemary waved her hand dismissively. "I'm a Fate-blessed warrior."

"What Rosemary is trying to say is that many of us have been trained for battle since we could walk, and we still struggled against Tom and his pack," Sterlyn said as she moved to stand between Jade and Rosemary. "Angels are blunt, and though she comes off as rude, that's not her intent."

"How was that rude?" Rosemary's brows furrowed. "You said the same thing I did."

Egan wrapped an arm around his mate and pulled her to his side, his golden eyes glowing.

"We're all trained, but it's been a few years since we've had to fight, so we're on edge," the almost-as-tall-as-Egan dragon shifter said. "But do not worry. We are already working on remediating the problem. It's important that our king and queen are protected."

"King and queen?" Birch rocked back on his heels. "I thought all the strongest supernaturals lived in Shadow City. What king and queen don't live there?"

"The dragon king and queen is what Draco means," the small girl next to the large man replied. She looped her arm through his. "Sometimes, my mate forgets that dragon facts aren't common knowledge."

The men by the house on the left hurried to join the group behind Sadie, keeping an eye on the area. The tension brewing between our two groups was palpable. If we wanted to work together well, we would have to learn to trust each other, but that likely wouldn't happen until after our witches had performed the spell and verified where this pack had been taken.

Torak motioned to the house. "How will going in there accomplish anything?"

"She's getting an item that belongs to the owners so some of our nearby friends can perform a location spell." Griffin clasped his hands together. "They should provide us with answers."

Donovan leaned forward. "So we aren't the only ones who brought more people."

"Seeing as we were shot at when we got here, are you surprised?" Sierra arched her brow.

"What my pack member means," Killian said, giving Sierra a stern look of warning, "is the last two times we've come across Tom, he's had large numbers. We wanted to be cautious, the same as you."

Sadie lifted both hands in surrender. "I'm just glad you trusted us enough to come. In fairness, none of us know each other well."

The front door banged open as Rosemary exited the house and held up a brush. "I'm assuming this should be enough. It has the dead hairs of multiple owners."

Despite being in shadow form, Levi snickered. "You have a way with words, love."

Torak and the wolf shifters standing close to him jumped and frantically looked around for the demon.

Roxy flipped her hair over her shoulder. "I told you that one of them could be invisible."

"Being told and experiencing it are two different things," the smaller man next to Torak growled.

Rolling her eyes, Sierra answered, "You build up a tolerance eventually."

The sound of an approaching engine had my body stiffening. *Are some of our allies coming here already?*

No, why? Killian asked.

He didn't hear the noise yet, but he would soon. The moon was less than a quarter full, which meant my senses weren't that much stronger than his.

Before I could answer, he tensed. *Someone is coming.*

"Are you expecting anyone else?" Titan cupped his ear. "You said you had others close by."

"They aren't on the way yet," Sterlyn answered, and turned to face the road.

Rosemary soared into the sky. "I'll take a look." When she was perhaps half a mile skyward, she went still. "Wolves are circling the entire neighborhood, and five Suburbans are heading toward us, blocking the road so no one can leave."

Dread pooled in my stomach. There was no getting out of this.

We were about to battle with Tom once more.

CHAPTER TWENTY-FIVE

I HAD HOPED that Tom wouldn't show up, but that was silly. Between his attack at the government building and him finding us at the other pack's location, he had to be staying close by, watching for us to arrive.

Killian linked with me and our other pack members, *We're already surrounded. Since I haven't heard from you all, I'm assuming everyone is okay.*

We are. No one passed by here, so it's a good thing you brought backup, Lowe replied. *Is it the same guy as the last two times? It's like they have an alert system or something.*

Blood chilling, I wanted to smack myself. I hadn't considered that. *You're right. He could be monitoring the intranet or posting the notifications about disappearing packs himself.* I'd grown up inherently trusting the information there and hadn't considered that Tom could be the source. All he'd need would be multiple aliases. His entire pack likely had access to the portal for years, so he'd look like an established and reliable member.

Killian grabbed my hand, and tingles from our bond burst to life. He linked, *Even if we had known he was planting the information, we would've come here to scope out the area. It's not like we would've ignored the worsening situation.*

He was reading my emotions, and I hadn't bothered to hide them from him. But his point, while valid, didn't change the fact that I was responsible for not considering the complication. Dad had praised me for my ability to see things others didn't, and here I was, in my first leadership role, failing to do just that.

The engines were humming louder, and the fight was almost upon us. The problem was that we couldn't easily communicate across the different groups if we all shifted.

"Anyone have a plan?" the chocolate-haired girl with the weird scent asked. "Because now is the time to discuss it."

"Katherine's right," the second-tallest dragon shifter said, and took the woman's hand. "How many people do you have at your off-site location?"

Killian became as still as a statue, and his jaw twitched. *They could still be working against us.*

I was fairly sure he was saying the same thing to everyone he could link with. Although it could be true, my gut said otherwise. We could trust these people—every single person here had a good essence. Not even one of them was slightly soiled, which was unusual in a large group.

"More than we have here," Griffin answered. "I don't want to say specifics in case the wolves are close. The enemy might hear."

That was a good reason for not being overly forthcoming. The enemy could have a bird shifter working in their midst to relay information back to Tom.

"Draco, you and the other dragons shift," Egan said, his

attention locked on the tall man. "I'll half shift so someone on our side can communicate with the wolves and vampires."

"But sir, you won't be as strong that way." Draco cracked his knuckles as his forehead lined with worry.

The way Draco deferred to Jade and Egan made me think they were important to the dragon shifter community, but they were so young. They couldn't be the king and queen...surely?

"He's right. You should shift." Jade lifted her chin. "I can stay in human form."

"That's not what I was getting at, either." Draco glared. "I—"

Egan's golden eyes glowed. "I'm the only one who can half shift here, and that'll be enough protection." His attention softened as it landed on Jade. "And I need you to lead them."

Now that right there was exactly how I wanted Killian to view me—strong and capable. Though I didn't want to *lead* the wolves, having him trust me in battle would mean the world. My heart ached at the beauty of their relationship while also filling with shame at my jealousy over how they were together.

"Fine," Jade huffed. "Everyone in the thunder, come with me and shift." The ten largest individuals in the group raced toward the woods after Jade.

As they left, Killian linked, *What's wrong?* His irises darkened as he glanced at me.

This wasn't a conversation to have here. We'd agreed to work on things together, and I couldn't keep accusing him of anything when he hadn't had the chance to prove he was trying. That wouldn't be fair, and I wasn't that kind of person. *What isn't wrong at this point in time?*

Rosemary remained in the sky, keeping her sights on the enemy. "The wolves are closing in. You need to make your plans and *move*."

"I'll stay in human form as well," Sadie said, "so I can communicate with my pack and you."

The vehicles would be taking the last curve into view of the neighborhood soon, blocking our three Suburbans from leaving.

"I'll stay in human form, too." Griffin placed a hand at his hip where his gun was holstered. "I'm the best shot out of our group, and I can communicate with our two packs, the vampires, and the witches."

That was the best thing about the strange connection Killian had forged with them. Three packs could communicate with only a slight time delay. Too bad we couldn't also communicate directly with Sadie and Torak's pack.

Titan cleared his throat. "I think it makes the most sense if I stay in human form. I've learned not to be a horrible shot, and I'm not as strong in my animal form without one eye." There was sadness in his voice, and I swallowed hard.

"I'll stay in human form, too," PawPaw stated, and patted Birch's shoulder. "As will he."

Those two had gotten friendly, making their packs' adjustment to living in the same neighborhood easier.

"Everyone shift while you still can," Sadie commanded as she walked past Killian and me, facing the direction the five vehicles were coming from. Her eyes tightened as she lifted her hands.

As tires squealed, we dispersed into the woods, while Lillith and a few other noticeably pale people stayed behind with the shifters who'd decided to remain human. Killian and I went left, away from where most of the shifters from our side were running. Sierra and Luna veered off so they wouldn't be changing with us. Though most of us didn't mind nudity, we didn't want to destroy our clothes, so semi-hiding them was best for all parties involved.

How much longer until the rest of you get here? Killian linked as we found a spot behind two large red cedars.

I undressed as Lowe replied, *We're ten minutes away, trying to get there as quickly as possible.*

Ten minutes sounded like forever, but we'd purposely hidden them a little ways out. This was for the best; we just had to remain strong until everyone else arrived. Hopefully, the dragons would come in handy.

It'd be best if you parked a mile out and shifted. Circle them like they're circling us and attack from behind, Killian linked. *That's the very thing Sterlyn, Griffin, and I are discussing now.*

That was an excellent strategy, something Tom's pack likely wouldn't have accounted for. But there was one problem. *We don't have enough bodies to form a full circle.*

Once I was naked, I called my wolf forward. My skin tingled as my fur sprouted...and the wheels of five vehicles crunched to a halt.

They were here.

The panting of wolves and the scent of musk hung thick around us. Wolves were running through the woods to surround us and would be upon us in the next few minutes.

True, but Rosemary pointed out that their wolves are in groups of three, so there are gaps in their defenses as well. She's estimating they have one hundred fifty wolves, plus however many are in the vehicles. They have more than we do, but not by much, Killian replied.

On four legs, I turned to glance at Killian as his body changed from human to wolf. His back broke in two as fur covered his gorgeously defined body. Though my wolf approved of him in his animal form, my human side still treasured his furless body.

We'd always been outnumbered. Even though PawPaw's pack had been involved the first time, they'd been malnourished to the point they couldn't shift or fight, and I hadn't counted them in our first confrontation. We'd had to protect ourselves and an entire pack who couldn't defend themselves.

Doors slammed shut as men got out of the trucks. We needed to rush in case our friends needed us. *Are you ready?*

The last of Killian's shift settled over him, and he nodded. *Let's get this over with.* He then linked in the others, *They're here and getting out of their vehicles. Let us know when you're half a mile out.*

Us. The word warmed my heart, though dread still sat heavily in my stomach.

The two of us trotted back to the neighborhood, and Sterlyn, Luna, and Sierra joined us. The wolves behind us were closing in, but their pawsteps were slowing.

"Why am I not surprised that the angel and her flock are here?" Tom's voice echoed in my ears as Killian and I drew closer. "I see you've recruited new members, too. This is the girl who can shoot beams out of her hands, which means the dragons must be close by."

So he'd decided to be chatty again, chilling my blood further.

As our group stepped from the woods, Tom stood in front of Griffin, Rosemary, Egan, and Titan, his hands in his jeans pockets. His light hair was cut shorter, and his eyes seemed harder, as if he'd filled up on more hatred.

Twenty-four of his pack members stood behind him with large rifles. They smelled of musk, which screamed shifters. This was the first time he'd kept some in human form.

"Angels aren't birds. That's the equivalent of me making a dog joke at your expense." Rosemary placed her hands on her narrow waist. "Which we could make happen."

Levi hovered next to her in his shadow form, invisible to our enemies. At least we had that on our side.

Cutting his eyes to me, Tom sniffed. "There's the girl of the hour. Every time someone gets their nose in our business, Mila's daughter shows up."

He knew my scent. We all had a uniqueness to us, and my silver fur didn't help matters, but his acknowledgment that he *knew* me felt oddly personal and made me want to take a shower, pronto.

Growling, Killian stepped in front of me.

This time, it didn't bother me. Tom was singling me out and making sure the twenty-four wolves on his side knew who I was. *This* was personal.

Donovan, Roxy, and Axel appeared across from us in the other section of the woods. Sterlyn raced ahead toward her mate while keeping an eye on the threat in front of our friends.

When none of the guys or Sadie asked what he meant, Tom puffed out his chest. "Don't you want to know why she's the girl of the hour?"

Griffin shook his head. "We're more concerned about why you're working with humans to capture packs."

Laughing sinisterly, Tom placed a hand on his chest, wrinkling his royal purple shirt. "Aren't you the *alpha* of Shadow City and mated to the strongest wolf on the planet?" He glanced at Sadie and lifted his hand. "No offense. Your beams are impressive, but you aren't part angel."

He was going to tell them our secret. He wanted to divide us.

"Technically, all the wolves with the same shade of fur are part angel, but I'm sure you were aware of that." Tom waved a hand. "I had no clue about the silver wolves until I realized that was why Mila had left me. She and I were going to lead the strongest pack of the southeast region when Hal's and my pack merged, but no, a silver wolf stole her away. My dreams and the love of my life, gone at the same time. So I found a way to get her back and gain more power and influence than she stole from me."

Lillith took a few steps forward. "You're from Shadow City?" She turned to her group. "Isn't that where that bear was from? The one who was spying on us when the fae attacked?"

"Fae?" Rosemary glanced over her shoulder. "Fae don't come here."

Sadie narrowed her eyes at the vampire, and my stomach swirled with discomfort. Whatever they were hiding had to involve the fae.

Lillith bit her bottom lip and flicked her attention to Sterlyn, then to me. "And how can they be angels? They don't have wings."

She was changing the subject. Under normal circumstances, I wouldn't like it, but Tom would use anything he learned against us. If Sadie's secret had something to do with the fae—which made sense, considering her beams— we didn't need Tom to know. We had enough targets on our backs.

"My uncle, the guardian of the moon, was the angel who fathered the race," Rosemary gritted out. "Their magic is tied to the moon."

With the moon almost new, that wasn't evident; we

were essentially the same size and strength as the wolves around us.

"Mila didn't choose him over you because he was a silver wolf. He was her *fated mate*." Griffin's hand inched toward his gun, but he didn't grab it.

"Was?" Tom asked, his eyebrows arching. "What do you mean, *was*? Are they no longer together?"

Though Griffin hadn't meant to give anything away, he'd just done that, and unfortunately, Tom was smart enough to catch on.

Lifting his chin, Griffin didn't say another word.

"Interesting." Tom rubbed his hands together. "If they're fated, he wouldn't just leave her. That means he's dead." A sick smirk appeared. "If I take their daughter, everything she loves will be destroyed."

"You will *not* take my granddaughter." PawPaw clenched his hands as he stepped to Sadie's side. "I won't allow that to happen."

"Don't worry." Tom waved a hand. "I'll kill you, too. After all, the pack does *belong* to me."

Killian hunkered down and pawed at the cement. *He will never get to you.*

I had no plans of that happening, either, but now wasn't the time to make Killian feel as if I didn't need him, though reminding him that I could fight just fine on my own was at the tip of my snout.

"You won't take Jewel or any of these packs. It won't happen," Sadie said through clenched teeth.

Tom *tsk*ed and pursed his lips. "That's a shame. Even with them keeping their heritage secret, you still want to risk your life to protect her. All I want is her, and I'll leave without a fight. It's that simple. We have enough shifters now that I can spare the rest of you."

"I don't even know the girl, and I agree with her." Titan crossed his arms over his muscular chest. "That's not going to happen."

"The guy with one eye is acting all big and bad." Tom's shoulders shook. "Please, your threats are as useless as you are."

He was not only an asshole but a bigot, too. If I hadn't had enough reasons to enjoy killing him, he'd just added one more. I hated people who belittled others and underestimated them for their differences.

Titan didn't flinch. "The fact that you feel the need to insult me tells me a lot about you. No matter what you do, you'll never be happy or content with the things you have, and ultimately, you will lose it all."

"This is your last chance." Tom lifted a hand, getting ready to signal. "Give me the girl or die."

I thought about giving myself up, but that wouldn't accomplish anything. He'd continue to capture wolves and hunt Mom. Sacrificing myself would only make her angry and irrational and further Tom's plan.

Sierra and Luna, get ready to go for the guards, Killian linked. *We need to attack them before they can shoot us. At least fighting the wolves will put us on more solid ground.*

"That's where you're wrong." Rosemary spread her wings, preparing for battle. "No one on our side will be dying."

Run! Killian linked.

I pushed my legs, racing slightly in front of Killian, Sierra, and Luna, tapping into the little bit of moon magic I had on my side. The guards were maybe twenty feet away, but we were fast in our animal form.

Dropping his arm, Tom screamed, "Attack!"

I was already halfway to the fourth man closest to us

while Killian took out the woman on his right and Luna and Sierra went for the other men nearest to the edge. As Tom's people reached for their guns, the two of us lunged. My teeth sank into my target's arm.

He grunted and jerked back, pulling me on top of him. I extended my claws and dug through his bulletproof vest as I jerked my head from side to side.

The stench of blood assaulted my senses, and my already queasy stomach roiled. The warmth of the liquid in my mouth had bile inching upward.

Wolves howled their battle cries as the fight in the woods began. Bullets sprayed, and I could only pray they were coming from Griffin and Titan.

Chaos had descended.

The man yanked his arm from my mouth, shredding his skin. It didn't seem to faze him as he switched the rifle to his other hand. Adrenaline had to be masking some of the pain.

Jumping on my back legs, I sank my teeth into his throat and ripped it out. Blood coated my chest and chin. I launched off his chest and landed on my paws as he crashed to the ground.

I spun, ready to take on my next target, and surveyed the scene around me.

Killian, Sierra, and Luna were battling their enemies and seemed to be winning. Sterlyn had just taken down one person and was getting ready to take on another.

Soulless dark gray eyes and the glint of gunmetal forced me to focus in that direction. My stomach dropped. It was Tom, and he had his gun aimed right at me.

There was no getting out of this. I couldn't reach him before he fired.

His finger pulled the trigger, and I sucked in a breath. This was it. I was going to die.

CHAPTER TWENTY-SIX

I'D ALWAYS EXPECTED that when I faced death, time would stand still. That was what the books I'd read and the movies I'd watched had promised—enough time for my life to flash before my eyes—but they were wrong.

So wrong.

In fact, time sped up, and the sound of the bullet zipping toward me was all I could focus on.

Death surrounded me even before I was injured.

I closed my eyes, not wanting the last image I saw to be a bullet lodging into me. *Killian, I lo—*

A sharp breeze hit my body, and the sound of thunder crashed over me.

My eyes opened to find frosted, pale yellow feathers wrapped around someone standing in front of me. Golden hair cascaded from the small opening at the top, and a faint daisy scent wafted through my nose.

Eleanor.

The bullet bounced off her wings.

Jewel! Thank gods, Killian linked, and raced over, scanning me.

Eleanor took off, soaring toward Tom. I took a moment to brush my head against Killian's neck. After my close call with death, I needed to feel him for a second.

The buzzing of our connection calmed me, but then my eyes focused on a man with his weapon aimed at Sterlyn. I linked, *I have to help.*

I took off running toward the enemy. Out of the corner of my eye, I saw another woman swing a gun at us. Killian raced toward her, focusing on the closer of the two threats.

The fact that he hadn't tried talking me out of fighting meant something to me. Only a week ago, he'd have been telling me to take cover. Maybe things were getting better between us.

I focused on the man aiming for Sterlyn and tapped into my angel magic. Enough hummed in my blood to make me slightly faster. Moments before I reached him, a pink beam zapped into the space between us and hit the man's hand.

"*Ow,*" he grunted, and dropped the weapon.

I glanced at Sadie, who nodded and turned her attention to another guard aiming his gun.

Instead of actively attacking, she was preventing the enemy from shooting anyone. That was a smart strategy.

I lunged at my target and bit into his wrist where his artery was located. I hated to kill, but Tom had made it clear that he'd do whatever was necessary to eliminate us, and there wasn't a better option. This man didn't have a pure essence, and being close to him made my skin crawl.

He jerked away and grunted. "You'll pay for that."

Oh, goody. I'd found a chatty one. Dad had told us that the chattier someone was, the less in control they were in battle. This guy didn't even realize I'd already dealt him a fatal blow, but it would take time for him to bleed out unless I sped up the process.

Wings flapped, and I glanced skyward as five dragons flew overhead. They had to be moving to help the wolves fighting in the woods against our enemy. We were greatly outnumbered and needed our allies to get here quickly.

Refocusing on my enemy, I tensed as he swung his free hand at my head. I slackened my jaw and used his momentum to move backward, digging my claws into his vest and then landing on all four legs.

His hand hit the air where my head had been a split second before.

Blood trickled down his wrist and pooled underneath him. His pale green eyes widened.

At least he wasn't stupid.

"You *bitch*," he growled. He glared at me and reached for something at his side. As he removed the item, a sharp edge glinted in the sunlight.

A knife.

They have knives, too, I linked with our pack. *A rifle and a knife.*

I'll inform the others, Killian replied.

With a loud groan, Knife Man swung at my chest. His musky scent was tainted with the spicy scent of fear, causing my lungs to burn.

As I jumped back, the knife sliced uncomfortably close to my head—so close that the rush of air blew my fur into my eyes, causing them to sting.

He jerked his arm up and swung at my side, flicking his wrist as if he might throw the blade. I rolled to my opposite side. Pain seared into me, but nothing intolerable.

I leaped up on all fours and glanced at the cut. The knife clanked to the cement beside me.

"Shit," the man growled as he reached around his body

for the rifle. He had his injured wrist pressed against his chest, and sweat dotted his forehead.

I must have gotten my teeth deep enough to tear the ligaments in his hand. That made things easier for me, as he couldn't easily reach his gun.

Lowering my head, I steamrolled him in the stomach. He gasped as he stumbled back, trying to secure his footing.

Gunfire cracked around me, and my pulse pounded, but all the pack links were still warm, giving me comfort. No one I was tied to had died, and I hoped everyone on our side was faring well.

Knife Man landed hard on his back. The edge of the rifle smacked his head, and I bit into the strap holding it to his back and ripped the weapon away. I dropped it and hovered over him.

"Please, don't," he begged, and his voice quivered. "I have a mate and a little girl who needs her daddy."

Daddy.

That was what I'd called Dad growing up, and I'd proudly told everyone I was a daddy's girl. Dad had beamed when I'd said those words and run to him, wrapping my arms around his neck as he lifted me in the air and spun me around.

I couldn't take that away from a child, and I smelled no lie.

Relaxing my jaws, I desperately debated what to do. If I didn't kill him, he'd continue down this path, but if I did kill him, I'd be taking away a girl's father. That cut too close to home.

He took in a ragged breath, and his bottom lip quivered.

Maybe this would be his wakeup call. I nodded and took the rifle by its strap, moving away to find an enemy who was actively attacking.

Something grabbed the rifle, yanking my neck back toward Knife Man.

I spun around just as Knife Man leveled the gun at my head and cackled, "I'll see you in hell, bitch."

I'd allowed this man to manipulate me. *Killian!* I linked. *I might need help.* Part of us trusting each other involved me letting him know when I was in over my head.

The man's hand shook as he took aim. I could have a chance at getting out of this alive.

On my way, Killian replied, and his fear raged through our bond, chilling the heat inside me.

Knife Man pulled the trigger, but his shaking hand caused the barrel to point toward my left. I jerked right, hoping I had moved enough out of the way.

The bullet missed me by a millimeter, and I pounced on the guy's chest and slashed his uninjured arm with my claws. The rifle dropped from his hand, and the skin around his eyes tightened with pain.

I held up my paw, ready to claw his neck. That would sever another artery and kill him faster. I couldn't bring myself to rip out another throat. My stomach was still upset from the taste of the first person I'd killed.

"I'm...I'm..." the guy stuttered, but I wouldn't fall for it again. He'd already used my humanity against me, and I wouldn't make that mistake again.

Not willing to hear another word, I did the only thing possible—begged Fate to find solace for that innocent little girl.

Heart shattering, I dug my nails deep into the man's throat. His eyes bulged as he realized that death was moments away. His body lurched, and I placed my front paws back on the cement, not wanting to feel his heart stop beating under my touch.

Thank gods, you're okay, Killian linked as he brushed up against me. *I didn't think you were going to...* He trailed off, unable to finish the sentence.

I'm fine. The threat, though, wasn't gone.

I scanned our surroundings...and couldn't believe what I saw. All the enemies with rifles were lying dead around us. All except...

Where's Tom? I asked my pack. Every person who'd been here was still standing. The two older vampires stood next to Lillith, the three of them breathing raggedly with blood splattered on their shirts. Sadie was mostly clean but pale from whatever magic she'd conjured, and Titan had his gun aimed at the tree line, panning for another threat.

Egan was bare-chested again, with his large, scaly, dark olive wings protruding from his back. I'd have thought he hadn't fought at all, except his hair was in complete disarray.

PawPaw hadn't been so lucky. He had a deep cut on his cheek that oozed blood down his face. Birch stood next to PawPaw, his normally composed face spotted with blood. And Griffin had both hands raised, his gun in one and an enemy's rifle in the other.

Rosemary and Eleanor stood where the enemies had been, Levi and Zagan hovering in shadow form nearby. Every single wolf had blood on their mouth and coating their bodies, but it was most obvious on Sterlyn and me because of our light fur.

Silence greeted my question, and I tensed. I linked with Killian, *What's wrong?*

I don't know. I'm asking Griffin and Sterlyn, he answered. *I was focused on my fight.*

The gold in Griffin's eyes lightened, informing me that

someone was talking to the alpha telepathically. Griffin's attention went to Killian, confirming what I suspected.

"Does anyone know where Tom went?" Griffin's head turned as he took inventory of the corpses around us.

Eleanor had attacked him after he'd taken that shot at me, so if anyone would know, it would be her.

"He ran into the woods while a few of his warriors distracted me." Eleanor's hands clenched at her sides. "But I plan to find him and kill him."

I'd hoped she'd already handled him. Mom was out there, and if he ran across her, there was no telling how much more vindictive he'd become. I had to find her.

"I've got to go help my pack," PawPaw said gruffly. "Something's wrong."

I'd never heard him sound like that before, and the edge of hysteria sank its nails into me, causing me to shift from paw to paw.

"What do you mean?" Birch furrowed his brows.

PawPaw exhaled. "I don't know. But I need to find them *now*." He turned in the direction our group had gone to shift not too long ago. "They're struggling."

"My dragons have stepped in to help while they try to figure out what's inhibiting them." Egan lifted toward the sky. "I'm going to help them." He soared across the lot toward the trees.

"Sterlyn and I will help Sadie's pack and their friends," Griffin informed us. "Rosemary and Zagan, why don't you come with us so Levi and Rosemary can communicate quickly with each other? The more we split up and keep information flowing as quickly as possible, the better it will be for all of us."

"That makes sense." Rosemary nodded. "Though for some reason, I'm reluctant to agree with you."

"That's because you want to stay near me, love, as I do you," Levi answered.

Titan and the older two vampires started. Wide-eyed, the three of them looked around Rosemary.

The older vampire, a male whose dark hair matched Lillith's, leaned forward and said, "That has to be the demon." He narrowed his brown eyes as if that would help him. "Dawn, are you seeing this?"

"Cassius, I'm fairly certain you *don't* see him." The older woman's face was angular like Lillith's, but her hair was a dark blonde.

They had to be her parents.

A howl rose from the woods. We had to get moving. PawPaw's pack needed help.

"Let's go," Eleanor said as she pushed Levi's shadow form forward. "We don't have time to deal with Rosemary's irrationality."

A deep, threatening noise came from Rosemary, one I hadn't heard before. The sound was a cross between a growl, a hiss, and spitting.

Another howl rang through the woods, and our group split up, racing to help our friends, family, and allies.

I'm going with Sterlyn and Griffin, Sierra linked as she dashed across the driveway toward Torak, not bothering to wait for Killian's blessing.

Killian inched forward, but I stepped slightly in front of him. I suspected that something was going on between Sierra and Torak, and she'd be distracted if she wasn't near him. *Let her go. She can communicate with the rest of us more quickly.*

Lillith, Cassius, Dawn, PawPaw, Birch, and Egan headed in the same direction as Luna, Killian, and me.

How much longer? Killian linked with Lowe and the

others. We needed backup, and fast. If PawPaw's pack couldn't fight, we'd be more outnumbered than I wanted to admit.

We're parking and will be heading toward you shortly. We're a mile out, Lowe replied.

So that would be close to five minutes. We must have left them farther out than we'd thought.

The trees sped past us as we raced to the fight. The sounds of snarls and growls echoed all the way down to my soul. For a moment, I'd thought we might win without backup, but the sounds of battle sang a different tune.

"The groups came together this way," Egan said as he flew forward.

Eleanor and Levi were just behind the dragon but didn't try to take the lead.

The leafless branches allowed us to peek at the horror. Fifty wolves surrounded eight wolves from PawPaw's and Birch's packs. A man from PawPaw's pack lay dead in human form. His hands clutched his neck where a wolf had ripped out his throat.

I inhaled and nearly choked. A second body lay a few feet away in a weird state of transition, neither human nor wolf. I'd never seen that before. The scent belonged to a woman with whom I'd talked about books during my stay at PawPaw's. The two cries we'd heard must have been theirs, but how had the man sounded like a wolf when he was in human form?

The four dragons soared behind them, breathing flames and fighting, but they waited until they were attacked.

I realized they couldn't tell friend from foe. They didn't know us or the scents of everyone on our side.

My chest constricted, and my mouth dried. We

wouldn't have been in as bad a situation had we spent more time together, but we couldn't fix that now.

Even with the dragons, we were getting pummeled.

Egan, Eleanor, and Levi soared into the mix and engaged in battle, while PawPaw, Birch, Luna, Killian, and I raced toward our friends. The fifty wolves circled them, so we'd have to fight from the outside in.

The enemy wolves were so intent on their bloodlust that they seemed unaware that we'd arrived. A red merle wolf charged at the smallest of our wolves, and instinct kicked in. I lunged.

Please be safe, Killian linked as he ran past me and launched onto the back of a sandy-blond wolf with its teeth sunk into Ruby.

The same goes for you, I replied as I reached the red merle enemy. My attention locked on the wolf's side, where I would attack.

Bones cracked, and my paws slowed. Someone was shifting. I glanced around frantically to determine who.

Then I realized who it was—the small wolf I wanted to protect.

As the red merle lunged, the smaller wolf's body lengthened, and she shifted back into human form. She had no way to protect herself. She was just lying there, unable to move.

I had to do something.

CHAPTER TWENTY-SEVEN

UNABLE TO REACH the red merle wolf before he landed on the smaller struggling wolf from PawPaw's pack, I pushed myself harder than I ever had in my life.

The red merle landed on the half-shifted woman, his claws digging into her back.

An agonizing whimper left her as the enemy lowered its head. It was going for the woman's neck, and there was no way I could get there in time.

A dark shadow flashed past me and slammed into the red merle wolf. He tumbled off the woman and flew a good distance away.

Levi.

Those angels and demons sure came in handy in time of war. I hurried to the woman and wished like hell I could communicate with her. Throat tightening, I lowered my head and nudged her arm.

"Gods, no! Please," she cried.

My stomach lurched. She thought I was the enemy, and I had no way of reassuring her.

I turned, searching for PawPaw. His warm brown eyes found me, and he nodded.

Taking a moment to survey the fighting, I noticed that Luna was running toward the other member of PawPaw's pack, who was hunched over and didn't seem to be faring much better than the woman I'd helped.

Something was seriously wrong. *Why is PawPaw's pack struggling to fight? They've been shifting and running in the evenings, so they should be recovered.* There was absolutely no reason for them to be acting this way. It reminded me of how Chad hadn't shifted the last time we'd fought Tom, the day we'd met Sadie and the others. Maybe he was having issues and didn't want to tell us.

I don't know, Killian replied as he stood on his hind legs and attacked the enemy he was fighting.

A low snarl came from my left as the red merle enemy picked himself up and met my gaze.

Levi had moved on to another wolf who was outnumbered. He and Eleanor weren't fighting but rather soaring through the open area, helping every wolf on our side who was overwhelmed.

The dragons were attacking, taking a few wolves at one time, but we were still outnumbered.

I hunkered down, thankful that the red merle was targeting me and not the woman. Her bones continued to crack, the process taking too long. I wasn't sure if she was shifting into human or wolf form, but either way, she couldn't fight.

Another wolf ran into view, his mossy green irises locked on me. Maybe he knew I was the one Tom was after.

Baring my teeth, I kept my gaze on the red merle wolf, wanting him to think he held all my attention. I would take these two assholes down at one time.

Charging at me, the red merle lowered his head to slam into my chest. The idiot did it while too far away, giving me plenty of time to move.

But as I shifted my hips to jump out of the way, I realized I'd underestimated him.

To avoid him, I'd have to move away from the woman I was protecting. This would allow him to attack her right in front of me. If I moved toward her, I would trample her and hurt her. Either way, she'd suffer.

Refusing to give in, I crouched. Two could play this game.

The fur on my neck rose as I sensed Moss Eyes sneaking up behind me. They had to be pack and linking to discuss their strategy.

I wouldn't give them the pleasure of falling for their cowardly plan.

Taking a small step, I pretended to spin away from the woman. As soon as I heard Moss Eyes' paws pound the ground, I stopped and crouched. When the red merle was just two feet in front of me, I tapped into my moon magic and jumped as high as possible. The front half of my body landed on the red merle's back as my back paws hit him in the face. My claws dug in, and the red merle whimpered as he bucked, desperate to get me off him.

Moss Eyes snarled, and I turned my head to see him racing toward me.

I had to get off this bucking bronco, or Moss Eyes would rip into me. When Red Merle's back legs landed again, I pushed off his back and head and landed next to the woman I was protecting.

Moss Eyes slammed into Red Merle, and they stumbled over each other. Blood poured into Red Merle's eyes from where my claws had slashed his forehead, and crimson slicked down his back, into his fur, and onto the ground.

Our group has split up, and we hear fighting, Lowe linked. *We've caught the enemy's scent and are running toward it.*

Thank gods. The cavalry was finally arriving. We needed every ounce of help we could muster.

Is everyone okay? Killian asked.

Yeah. I was worried we might run into their backup, but nothing seems amiss, so hopefully, we're in the clear, he replied.

It's about damn time, Sierra said. *Sadie can't beam anymore and almost passed out. Her friends have surrounded her to protect her, and it's affecting our side.*

We needed to take out the threat and get to them. The dragons had taken down their two opponents and were taking on another. With the four of them and Egan, they'd reduced the fifty down to forty. Every person on our side was fighting against two, and the situation was far from ideal.

The vampires moved quickly but didn't use their weapons since we were on top of one another. They could easily injure someone on our side. The wolves could counter their moves, and though the vampires got a few blows in from time to time, punches weren't as effective as fatal injuries.

Two men from Birch's pack were injured and running out of steam as two enemy wolves waled on them, and Killian was protecting Ruby, who had a large gash in her side as if someone had bitten her.

Birch's pack wasn't as trained as I'd hoped, and PawPaw's pack couldn't stay in wolf form.

If you could hurry, that would be nice, Luna added as

she tried to counter a joint attack. Levi swooped in and knocked the enemy who was about to sink its teeth into her shoulder out of the way.

Maybe we weren't doing as well as I'd thought.

Moss Eyes shoved Red Merle aside, not caring that his pack member was injured. His attention was locked on me as he opened his mouth and...smiled?

The hairs on my scruff rose. I'd *never* seen a smiling wolf before, and I hated that it had the intended effect on me.

I had to remain calm.

Going back to my roots, I played Beethoven's "Für Elise" in my mind, remembering each stroke of the piano keys that only a master could bring to life. Some of my anxiety released, helping my body relax and my mind clear so I could focus on the memory of the beautiful notes and how a fight was similar to a dance in that you read your opponent and reacted accordingly.

Tongue hanging from his mouth, Moss Eyes raced toward me. His attention flicked around frantically to avoid giving me a hint of his final move.

Tom had been planning his revenge for a long time and had trained his pack accordingly.

I lowered my body, protecting the woman behind me. There was no way in hell I would run away and leave her to die. I would protect her. PawPaw's pack had gone through enough because of *them*.

His attention settled on my neck for a moment longer than anywhere else as he lunged at me. If I moved too far, he'd land on the woman.

As he sailed toward me, I pivoted to the side, ready to counterattack. I wouldn't just stand here and get injured. I'd go down with a fight.

Jewel! Killian linked, and his fear slammed inside me. *I'm coming.*

We both knew he wouldn't reach me in time.

Moss Eyes' nostrils flared as he realized my plan, but he was in midair and couldn't correct his trajectory to fix his miscalculation. Eyes bulging, he realized this was the end for him. I jerked my head forward and sank my teeth into his neck.

I could've released him and left him only wounded, but he'd just attack me or someone else again. Death was the only option.

I ripped out his throat. Fresh blood spilled down my snout and chest, mixing with the blood from the previous enemy. Bile inched up my gorge as I gagged from the metallic taste and the horrible stench in my nose.

I'm fine, I linked with Killian. *I'm not hurt.* Fine had been a lie, though I hadn't meant to fib.

Killing was never easy, but Dad had warned us it would be that way. We were meant to protect and not take life, but sometimes, killing was the only way to keep justice in the world. However, if we started to delight in it, we'd be no better than our enemies.

I had to be better. I wanted to be like *him.*

An agonized howl hurt my ears as a pearl-white wolf charged toward me. Pain blazed in her eyes as she stared at me with hatred.

Moss Eyes must have been her mate.

My heart fractured at the thought of the agony she was experiencing, but my hands had been tied. This was war.

The noise of our arriving backup sounded better than any musical composition I'd ever heard. Not even Beethoven or Bach had anything on the sound of my friends arriving in the midst of a devastating battle.

We're here, Lowe linked. *We see you.*

Help Jewel and Luna. They're protecting some of Hal's pack members, who are struggling to shift, Killian commanded. *How many are on the other side to help?*

Fifty, Lowe answered. *April went there. Eliza, Herne, and Lux are with us. We split every group evenly.*

Smart.

A few enemy wolves paused and watched as our friends ran toward us, but not Red Merle or Pearl Wolf. They were focused on one thing: revenge. Unfortunately, that was another way to say *me*.

Red Merle pawed at his eyes, trying to see through the blood running into them. With his shifter healing, the bleeding had slowed, which was problematic for me.

The dragons and vampires were still fighting their own battles. The enemy wolves were figuring out better ways to fight them, using their smaller size to their advantage. Eleanor and Levi flew around, helping whoever needed them most, which tended to be PawPaw, Birch, and their pack members.

We were stretched thin, but we needed to hold out a little longer.

Pearl Wolf homed in on my neck. She was going for the kill.

Red Merle picked up his pace, sprinting at me from my other side.

They were launching a joint attack, much like earlier, but I couldn't discount it. This time, it could work, so I had to keep focused.

The woman who'd been half-shifted finally stood on all fours. Her brindle-colored fur wasn't as long as normal, as if she might shift back to human at any time.

I nodded toward the gigantic red cedar tree, hoping she'd understand that I was telling her to go.

Without hesitation, she took off, running away from the battle, and I turned back to my attackers to see that her departure hadn't fazed them. They weren't after her.

The two of them ran hard at me, and I braced myself for the inevitable. If I moved, they'd follow, and I refused to cower.

I could use some help, I linked to Killian. The words hurt to say even telepathically, but I had to hold on to what Dad had told me time and time again: asking for help wasn't a sign of weakness.

Inhaling deeply, I braced myself. Both wolves were only a few feet away on either side. They were timing the attack perfectly.

As they reached me, my wolf took control and dropped to the ground.

The two wolves slammed into each other and crumpled on top of me, pounding my body harder into the dirt as their claws dug into my back. It hurt, but it was better than if they'd bitten my neck.

With their weight on top of me, my lungs struggled to fill. A wolf's hot breath hit my ear as they lowered their mouth to the back of my head. My move might have prevented me from having my throat ripped out at that moment, but I wondered for how long.

Suddenly, one of the wolves was torn from my body. Killian fought the wolf, giving me a slight reprieve, but the lack of oxygen from having both of them on me had weakened me.

"*Hostem rursus flare!*" Eliza shouted from close by, and a breeze whipped around me.

The heaviness vanished, and I gasped in a deep breath.

I raised my head to find the older witch about a hundred yards away, her magic working despite the distance. Her hands moved away from me, toward another person needing help, as Lowe and thirty other wolves reached our circle of war. The vampires stood in their all-black uniforms, guns raised in our direction, but they weren't firing.

As I glanced at our group, I understood why. With the way we were all fighting, they still could hit one of us by accident.

"Use your knives!" the tall vampire man in front called as he removed his weapon from its sheath and lifted it in the air. "We protect our king and queen's allies." The group blurred as they used their vampire speed to reach us.

Jewel, your side!

I jerked around. Killian was a few feet away, eyes wide in terror.

I tried to turn, but something sharp pierced my left side, and my legs almost gave out from the pain. Using my right front paw, I reached across my body and swatted at Pearl Wolf, who'd taken a huge bite out of me while I'd been distracted.

Though I'd felt worse pain, this was still miserable, and my right paw couldn't reach her at this angle.

She released her hold, only to slice through another section of my side before I could get away. Blood coated her mouth, and she snarled at me. She wanted to torture me before she killed me.

Killian reached me and didn't hesitate. He clawed at her face, causing her to release her hold on my side, and Pearl Wolf's jaw opened. Though angry, she wasn't suicidal.

Snarling, she leaped at Killian.

That bitch wouldn't hurt my mate. He hadn't come here to pick a fight with them—they had brought it to us.

Refusing to let her injure him, I bit into her neck. Now that she wasn't attached to my side, I could reach her. My body screaming, I pushed through the pain and ignored the warm liquid seeping from her. This was more throats than I'd ever wanted to slit.

Whimpers and howls of pain echoed around us. This war was a bloodbath.

I loosened my hold, and Pearl Wolf dropped in front of me.

That asshole isn't getting away, Killian linked. He growled and took off running toward Red Merle, who was fleeing the scene.

Just as I was about to link and tell him not to go after him, my body turned to ice. We couldn't let them leave, not with what they were doing to the supernaturals.

My only solace was that Killian was running away from the main fight, and he would be safer for a minute. With how injured Red Merle was, he wouldn't put up much of a fight.

As I turned to see who else needed help, my stomach soured. Every single wolf shifter of PawPaw's pack was either in human form and completely naked or in a transition between human and wolf. Each one looked to be in agony and unable to fight.

What the *hell* was going on?

Now that Lowe and the rest of our allies had joined us, and with the dragons on our side, we were coming out ahead. Levi and Eleanor were battling and killing their opponents effectively, and the vampires were as skilled with their knives as they had been with their guns.

We might win this war, but then we'd have to find the missing shifters.

A branch snapped, and I jerked my head toward the

woods. Between the sounds of fighting and the blood overpowering my senses, I hadn't sensed a person sneaking up on me.

From behind a thick oak tree twenty feet away, light blond hair appeared, followed by soulless, cold eyes.

Tom.

And he had a rifle pointed right at me.

CHAPTER TWENTY-EIGHT

THE SOUNDS of battle faded into the background as Tom and I stared at each other. He smirked as his finger tensed on the trigger, but not enough to release the bullet.

He wanted me to cry for help...to show weakness.

I refused to give him that kind of power.

I hunkered low and growled. With his attention locked on me, there was no way he'd miss. He wanted to hurt Mom in the worst way possible.

Tom snickered. "I won't *kill* you. That'd make things too easy for you and Mila. I have bigger plans for you that coincide with the issues Hal and his minions are having. But that doesn't mean I can't hurt you."

He wasn't surprised they were struggling with their wolf form, confirming my worst fears. The humans had done something to them...but what? They could still shift into wolves, but they had problems holding that form when in battle.

If he thought I was going with him willingly, he'd learn otherwise. If I was going to get shot, I might as well get a swipe in.

Tapping into my angel power, I sprinted toward him. My side throbbed from where Pearl Wolf had bitten me, and I couldn't run as quickly as I wanted.

Tom's here, I linked with Killian. I hated to inform him of that and potentially distract him from his fight with the red merle wolf, but if I were in his place, I'd want to know what my mate was facing. I'd promised him that I wouldn't try to take on the weight of the world without letting him know.

Where? he linked, the cold tendrils of his panic surging through our bond and freezing my chest.

The discomfort took the edge off the agony in my side, but it made breathing harder as I panted toward Tom.

In front of me, aiming his gun, I linked just as Tom chuckled darkly and pulled the trigger.

There was no time to dodge the weapon. The bullet lodged in my right shoulder. Sharp pangs of torture shot through my body, and I crumpled hard on my stomach.

A whimper stuck in my chest, but I refused to let it out. If he was going to torture me, I wouldn't allow him to get more pleasure than he already was.

Baby! Killian connected. *I'm on my way.* A faraway snarl sounded just like Killian, and a second later, a sharp yelp pierced my ears and cut off abruptly.

I turned my head to make sure Killian was okay, but he and the wolf he attacked had run far enough away that the oaks and red cedars kept them from sight.

The stench of musky bitterness damn near made me gag, and I turned my attention back to Tom.

That scent fit him perfectly and made my stomach churn more violently.

"Oh, how a *mighty* silver wolf has fallen," he sneered as

he crouched in front of me. "If Mila and her scumbag mate could see you now."

Hot rage warmed my body, overcoming the frigid fear wafting through Killian's and my bond. I jumped to my feet, ignoring the piercing pain that made me want to curl into a ball and cry. This asshole had to die.

He jumped back as I snapped at him.

I latched onto his wrist, the closest body part to me, and bit down as hard as I could.

Growling menacingly, Tom swung the hand holding the rifle and slammed the end of the weapon into the top of my skull.

The world spun as my legs wobbled. My jaw opened, and I crashed, unable to hold up my head.

My attack hadn't been smart, but at least I'd made him bleed. Hopefully, the scar would remind him that I'd injured him when he'd thought he had me on my knees.

The edges of my vision darkened, and the sick bastard chuckled even louder. The sounds and scents merged until I couldn't discern anything.

"It's a shame your *dad* died," Tom said as he stepped on my back, putting pressure on my spine on top of everything else inside me. "I'd love to make him watch humans torture you and Mila."

Stay with me, Killian linked, but even the communication of our fated-mate bond echoed as if through a tunnel. *I'm coming.*

Something tickled the edge of my consciousness as if someone had appeared beside me. But with Tom continuing to dig his heel into my back, I could only fathom it was wishful thinking that someone was here to help me.

The weight vanished from my back, and I'd have bet anything I was fading into darkness. But when the combination of rose and sweet peony replaced some of the musky bitterness, I knew who I'd sensed.

Levi.

Bones crunched, and I forced my head to turn toward the fight. If something happened to Levi, I'd need to find a way to help him. No one could die trying to protect me.

The world spun, and I saw three of everything. The images were distinct enough that I could tell what was going on.

I needed Killian to know that I wasn't alone. *Levi is helping me.*

Levi's mocha irises were dark as he lifted Tom by his shirt and punched him in the nose over and over. Tom swung right in front of him and hit Levi.

Groaning, Levi dropped Tom, who landed on his feet and aimed his rifle at where Levi had attacked him.

Unfortunately, Levi was standing right there.

No, I wanted to shout, but all that came out was a noise between a bark and a whimper.

I tried to stand, but as soon as I put weight on my front legs, I lost my balance. My shoulders and head screamed, and the world spun faster.

I couldn't help him.

Tom struggled to aim because of his injured wrist. Levi slammed into him. With a loud thud, Tom fell on his back, dropping the rifle beside him. As he reached for the weapon, Levi kicked him in the side.

"You will tell us where the packs are located and how we can end this," Levi commanded, and kicked Tom again.

"There's no ending this." Tom smiled, despite the blood pouring from his nose and oozing into his mouth. He glanced around, expecting Levi to appear at any second. "Too much is already in motion."

Levi reached down and snatched the rifle. "Then I guess there's no point in keeping you alive."

"No one else in my pack knows how to get in touch with the people in charge." Tom patted his chest. "If you want a chance of knowing anything, I'm the only person who can help you."

My stomach roiled. He was going to use that as leverage so we didn't kill him, and the worst part was it would work.

"And why should I even pretend to consider what you're saying?" Levi asked as he leveled the rifle at Tom's head. "You won't tell us anything."

"I can tell you what's wrong with Hal's pack." Tom wiped the blood from his nose and his sleeve. "My contact is supposed to call me soon, and I can wrangle some answers."

Head pounding, I didn't want to think about the ramifications. He could be bluffing, but what if he wasn't?

Levi held the gun steady, and I knew he was thinking over the options. Something was clearly wrong with PawPaw and his pack. We had no good option, and I hated that it wasn't simple.

Levi lowered the gun, confirming his decision was made.

Tom would get out of this with his life.

It's almost over, baby, Killian linked, and the tug of our connection proved he was close.

Having him near me would make the pain more manageable. I took a deep breath, trying to get my bearings. If I didn't get the swirling sensation to stop, I'd likely barf, even in wolf form.

Killian's dark wolf ran past me and lunged.

My heart stopped as he landed on Tom and sank his teeth into the enemy's neck.

"Kill! No!" Levi yelled, and flung himself into Killian's side.

All his action accomplished was to help Killian rip out Tom's throat. Killian stumbled but remained on his feet. He breathed heavily as he watched the life ebb from Tom's body.

Tom grasped his throat with his uninjured hand. He'd killed enough people to know the action was in vain, but he was trying to stop the bleeding.

"You...don't...know..." he rasped. "What...you're...up... against." His eyes rolled back, and his head turned toward me. His lifeless eyes locked on me as death overtook him.

Killian lurched to his feet and spun to me. He lay in front of me, examining me.

He didn't have time to let his guard down. *Go help the others.*

It's over. Killian nodded at something behind me. *The battle is done. Once backup came, we got the edge.*

Jewel! Luna linked to Killian and me. *What happened?* Paws pounded toward me, and from what I could tell, it was more than just her.

Tom was hiding in the trees and attacked her with a rifle, Killian answered for me.

Now that battle wasn't imminent, the pain I'd already thought was unbearable crashed over me. Adrenaline no longer kept it at bay.

If I'd thought the world was spinning earlier, I stood corrected. I wouldn't even have been sure I was lying on the ground, but not falling over or tumbling sideways clued me in that it was just my head.

Griffin asked, "How badly is she hurt?"

I couldn't gauge the distance, but when a hand touched my head, his leather scent gave him away. I whimpered, the pain from just the brush of his fingers bringing tears to my eyes.

"Eleanor!" Griffin yelled. "We could use your help over here!"

Chaos descended, adding to my misery.

"Do you really think *she* is going to help Jewel?" Levi snorted. "I've asked Rosemary to come. Their battles are wrapping up over on that side, too."

Is PawPaw okay? He'd been distraught earlier and trying to keep the wolves away from the one man with Luna.

Yes, he's heading here now. I can see him, Killian said.

Some weight lifted from my shoulders. I linked with my entire pack, including the ones on the other side, *Are you all okay? Is anyone hurt?*

We've got some battle scars, but that's about it, April answered.

That was odd. Lowe was normally the spokesperson for that side. He was next in command after Billy.

What's wrong with Lowe? Killian asked, thinking the same thing as me. *He feels as if he's asleep.*

He got slammed into a tree while protecting one of the other pack members, April replied. *He's fine, just resting.*

I wished I were passed out instead of dealing with the never-ending tilt-a-whirl. At least then I wouldn't be trying not to throw up in front of everyone.

Eleanor landed in front of me, her golden hair reflecting like a halo in the sun...or it could have been the result of my vision blurring. I couldn't tell.

"Tell Rosemary to stay and help over there." Eleanor sighed. "I'll heal her."

Shock numbed my pain ever so slightly, enough to give me a reprieve. The angel had refused to save one of our pack members not even two weeks ago, so her willingness to help me was very unexpected.

Her hands glowed, though not nearly as brightly as Rosemary's, and she placed them on the top and back of my shoulder. She said, "She's lucky the bullet went through her."

Under normal circumstances, I would've disagreed, but I remembered the agony when Sterlyn had held me down and Rosemary had removed bullets from my wounds the night PawPaw's pack cabins burned down. That agony had been far worse than this.

PawPaw ran around Killian, dodging Eleanor's wings, and squatted next to her. His face was lined with worry, and he looked like he'd aged twenty years. He didn't touch me, but his presence was enough—and that was all I needed.

Warmth surged into me, her magic feeling foreign. Though it didn't hurt, it wasn't comforting like Rosemary's. It buzzed through my skin, causing friction in my blood. I held back a wince, not wanting to move and cause my injuries to flare up again.

After a few seconds, the pain ebbed, and the world slowed its spin. Her magic almost felt like sandpaper against me, but if it healed me, I could deal with the discomfort.

Is it working? Killian asked, and nuzzled my uninjured shoulder, careful not to hit the wound on that side. *You seem to be healing.*

It's working. The pain isn't as bad. I closed my eyes, not wanting PawPaw to read my distress. He was one of the few who could tell my mood by looking into my eyes. I wanted her to continue healing me for as long as she was willing.

Eleanor groaned. "Rosemary makes it look so easy." Then more of her power surged into me, making my skin crawl.

After what felt like forever, her magic weakened inside me, and she removed her hands from my fur. The strange, raw sensation within me made me feel vulnerable and naked, but when I opened my eyes, the world didn't spin. I glanced at my shoulder and saw that the opening was now a scab under the thick blood drying in my silver fur. Slowly, I climbed to my paws, and though my side ached, it was nothing like before.

"That'll have to be good enough." Eleanor pulled her pale yellow shirt down over her jeans. "I'm almost depleted. That was rather uncomfortable, but the job is done."

I couldn't disagree with her there, but I knew better than to express it. I wanted to thank her, but that wasn't possible in wolf form.

PawPaw stood, a faint smile on his face, though stress was still visible in the tightness around his eyes. "I need to check on the rest of the pack."

My body stiffened. There was no telling how many of his pack members had died. I nodded, not wanting him to feel as if he had to stay with me. I had my mate and my friends by my side.

"Why don't you two shift back?" Griffin gestured to the trees where we'd shifted to our wolf forms earlier. "It'll be best if we can all communicate. The others shifted while Eleanor was healing Jewel. They're heading out here to help clean up the mess. All of us should hurry. We don't want to be here if anyone else shows up...ally or foe."

If Tom's contact didn't hear from him, more people would likely come to check on the area, and I had a feeling they'd bring serious backup.

Come on, Killian linked, and nudged me gently.

As we headed toward our clothes, I tried to ignore the bodies littering the ground and focused on changing back into human form. At least that way, the blood would be off me, though I'd want a shower as soon as we got home.

When we reached our clothes, I tugged my wolf back. I was desperate to get out of my animal form, and the wounds should be completely healed during the shift, so I'd be whole when I was human once more. My bones cracked, my body changed, and soon, I was standing on two legs. I snatched my clothes off the ground and dressed quickly, wanting to get back out and help the others clean up the area.

When I spun around, I got to see one of my favorite things in the entire world. Killian's abs rippled as he put his shirt on. Even when I'd been on the brink of death, my fated mate had my hormones going wild. When he pulled the shirt into place, his warm brown irises met mine. He closed the distance between us and wrapped me in the safety of his arms.

I breathed in his sandalwood scent, needing a moment to get my bearings. I'd honestly expected not to make it out of this alive. Placing my head on his chest, I listened to his heartbeat—the one sound that could comfort me even at my darkest point.

He kissed the top of my head as he crushed me. *I was so damn scared I would lose you.*

You can thank Levi for saving me. If it hadn't been for the demon, there was no telling what state I'd be in right now.

Tensing, Killian growled. *He was going to let that asshole live.*

Because he thought we could get some answers. I didn't blame Levi for taking that option— killing Tom might not have been for the best—but I remembered my rage when someone had hurt Killian, and I couldn't blame him for killing Tom. If Killian had been in that situation, I would've made the same decision.

If it had been Rosemary— he started, but I cut him off with a kiss.

We didn't need to get angry with each other.

He moaned as his tongue slipped inside my mouth, tantalizing my senses with his scent and citrus taste. He was the anchor I desperately needed to hold on to and the one thing I enjoyed most in the entire world.

Killian tensed and pulled away.

I tried following his lips, not ready for our moment to be over.

He chuckled warmly. *I'm sorry, but Griffin was checking in on us, worried that something else had happened. I hate to interrupt our moment, but...*

The words chilled me, bringing me back to the present. *We should go. We don't need to be an undue burden.*

We hurried back toward the sizable clearing where the fight had taken place. As we approached, a cell phone rang, then stopped.

We stepped through the last few trees and saw Eliza, Herne, and Lux standing in a large triangle with their hands extended. The ground between them was splitting open as wolves, dragons, and vampires dragged bodies toward them.

They were working on burying the dead.

Nearby, Egan, Levi in human form, and Griffin had surrounded Tom's body. Griffin held a cell phone in his hand, and all three of them were staring at it, unsure about what to do.

"What's going on?" Killian asked as he took my hand and tugged me toward the three men.

"His phone rang." Griffin lifted it like it was the most perplexing situation he'd ever been involved in.

I was missing something. There had to be a punchline. "Why didn't you answer it?"

"We were helping with the dead, and it only rang three times." Griffin lifted the phone and pointed at it. "It's a restricted number."

So we couldn't call back. We could have missed our only lead.

"If Killian hadn't killed the dickhead, we might have gotten some information out of him," Levi said through clenched teeth, and glared at him.

Releasing my hand, Killian snarled and stuck his chest out as he bellowed, "He wouldn't have stopped until he had captured or killed my mate. There was no fucking *way* I was letting him live."

Whoa. Things had escalated quickly. "There was *no right answer.*" I placed a hand on Killian's chest to calm him and hold him back. "We were all doing what we thought was best." Even me, though I'd been trying not to vomit everywhere.

Griffin lifted his hands. "Jewel's right. Tom's dead, so arguing over it now is pointless."

That had to be one thing we all could agree on.

"We need to decide our next steps," Egan said, watching Levi and Killian warily. "Someone was *protecting* their mate. I'll be honest, if that had been Jade, I would've done worse than Killian. What if it had been yours?"

Levi's head tilted back, and he shrank as his anger deflated. He opened his mouth, but before he could say anything, the phone rang again.

CHAPTER TWENTY-NINE

THE FIVE OF US FROZE, but when *Restricted Number* flashed across the screen, it brought us all back to life.

"Sterlyn says we should answer it," Griffin informed us even as he moved to tap the screen.

"Wait!" I half shouted. "We need the person who sounds most like Tom to answer it. They'll be expecting him." My nausea returned. If we didn't handle this correctly, it could be over as soon as the person said hello. "If it's whoever he's working with, they may not talk to anyone else. They won't trust anyone. Whoever answers has to play the part, and well."

The phone rang a third time.

Levi snatched the phone. "Let me handle it. After all, I'm the only one who grew up in Hell. Pretending to be a pompous ass is something I've had centuries of experience with." He swiped the phone before any of us could disagree.

"Hello," Levi said, sounding almost identical to Tom. He'd raised his tone and added a slight southern accent.

"Why didn't you answer the phone the last time I called?" a nasal voice demanded.

I leaned into Killian, needing his support. One wrong word could ruin this charade, and who knew what else might happen? My mate wrapped his arm around my waist, anchoring us to each other. The buzz of our connection calmed me marginally.

Levi rolled his eyes. "Let's see. I'm fighting a pack that's way too damn nosy with someone insistently calling me during the fight so I can't shift. Maybe *that's* why." His tone sounded so similar to Tom's that it was eerie. He'd even nailed Tom's condescending edge.

That was a gamble. I wasn't sure Tom would talk to whoever it was like that.

"I've told you before: do *not* take that tone with me. I may not be supernatural, but we can decide to forfeit our agreement," the nasal voice warned. "Now, did you retain control of at least some of the wolf shifters we performed the tests on, or did you mess up again?"

This time, Levi didn't seem comfortable answering. He scratched the back of his neck as Griffin mouthed the word *no*.

If he said yes, we'd have to hand over someone from our side. That wasn't an option.

He narrowed his eyes. "I'm *in a battle* and on the *phone*. Capturing them would be much more likely if I were engaged in the fight."

"Well, you have somewhere else you need to be." The man on the other end huffed. "Your contact is heading to the meeting location. She needs you to bring the clothes of the pack member you want her help locating. Again, I'm working with a supernatural, but witchy magic has come in handy. Remember, she can't be away too long."

This situation continued to worsen. Maybe we shouldn't have answered the phone. We couldn't show up there without Tom, and what kind of material did this "she" want us to bring? She'd immediately know something was wrong.

"I'll send someone there to meet her," Levi snapped. "I can't leave my pack like this. I need to be here to ensure enough wolves are captured."

"I can agree with that." The man sounded relieved. "Send your most trusted person. I'll text you the meeting location, but whoever it is needs to get moving."

I sagged into Killian. Thank gods Levi thought quickly on his feet, and I was relieved that Tom didn't already have the meeting location. That would've been another issue we would've had to resolve somehow.

"Already working on it." Levi had lowered the phone to hang up when the nasal voice said, "Oh, and Tom?"

Griffin hung his head as Egan ran a hand through his hair.

We all thought we'd come out of this unscathed, but of course, the conversation wasn't over.

"What?" Levi said exasperatedly. "I need to get back to my pack."

"Don't *fail* me *again*," the man replied, and the phone went dead.

"That was risky," Killian rasped as his hand tightened on my side. "You were being a complete ass."

Levi gestured to Tom, who lay in the center of us. "And you think he would've been nice and respectful? Please. He had almost as big of a vendetta and ego as Lucifer. I just channeled him."

One of the princes of Hell. Mom had informed me he was the prince of pride. That sounded about right.

Wings flapped overhead, the smooth sound identifying an angel.

Rosemary.

She landed behind her mate and scanned the surroundings. "Has he sent you the text yet?"

Obviously, Levi had clued her in on everything. I'd like to believe that Killian would have done the same for me if we'd been separated.

"Not yet." Levi stared at the phone. "But we need a plan."

Faint footsteps trucked toward us, and I turned toward the sound. Someone was coming from the pack neighborhood.

It's Sterlyn and Jade, Killian linked. *Since Hal went to their side to check on his pack, they decided to come here. If anything happens, they'll alert us.*

My stomach dropped. *Did Chad and Mom struggle to shift, too?* I tended to forget that he could communicate with him at times.

He nodded. *Just like the others, but they didn't get hurt. They were able to fight in human form.*

That was because Dad had trained us in both forms. PawPaw's pack never trained like we did. They were content with what they had and didn't anticipate a threat to their pack. Clearly, they'd been wrong.

Stomach easing, I held on to the fact that my foster brother and Mom hadn't been harmed, but I also shared the sting of the losses PawPaw was experiencing. They'd welcomed me and helped me through my time of grief. *I should go check on them.*

Both Sterlyn and Jade hurried to their mates.

We need to deal with this first. Killian lowered his head. *Sterlyn is saying they aren't in the best frame of mind and are trying to overcompensate by tending to the injured and helping with the dead.*

My heart hurt. Chad didn't like appearing weak, and Mom's anger was getting the best of her. When either of them was in this mood, I tended to bring out the worst in them. They needed space and time.

Jade stopped short when she noticed the body we'd surrounded. "It is not *normal* to be standing around a dead guy. I mean, I get that I was human for most of my life, but I've been part of the supernatural world for years, now, and I've never seen this before. Why don't you move?"

"Because his phone was ringing, and we gathered here to determine what to do," Levi said and winced. "Though I'm not sure why we're still standing here."

"You were human? Did your mate bite you or something?" I asked. In all the books I'd read, if a supernatural's mate was human, they remained that way.

"The mates of born dragons are always human," Egan explained as he walked toward Jade. "Once the bond is cemented, the mate transforms into a dragon. That's why our coloring is similar."

Interesting. Another thing the stories had gotten wrong.

The phone dinged, and Levi's brows furrowed. "It's a gas station in Lenoir City. Isn't that near the government building where the first pack was held?"

"I don't know about that, but it's an hour and a half away from here," Jade answered. "It's not too far from Kortright University, where I met Egan."

Maybe the other packs were taken to the same place, I linked with Killian. Though that might not be a good thing. They'd have backup security measures, and who knew what that would involve?

"Well, a group of us needs to go while the others stay here and clear things out." Sterlyn avoided glancing at Tom.

"Levi, Zagan, Eleanor, and I can go." Rosemary lowered her wings. "That way, if something goes wrong, we can notify everyone here of the incoming threat."

My pulse sped up, and I sent Killian a quick, rather scrambled message.

He nodded. "Jewel and I would like to go meet the contact. We thought that after the meeting, we might run by and check on the government building to see if there's any sign that the other packs are being held there. Even if it's just a quick run to the location where we kept watch. We don't want to risk the demons entering the building in case the humans have planned for something like that, now that they're aware of them."

My heart warmed. He hadn't dismissed my thoughts. He'd listened. That was rare for a man, but not when it came to him.

Griffin stared at the sky. "I'm not sure if that would be the best scenario or the worst one."

No one had an answer for that.

"Griffin and I will go with you. There's no point in us separating since we'll be too far away for our pack links to work." Sterlyn rubbed her hands. "But we'd better get moving."

Lifting the phone, Levi frowned. "I guess I'm stuck with this thing, seeing as I'm the new Tom."

"Jade and I would go with you to survey the meeting, but if you needed backup, two dragons landing in a populated area would cause more press than Killian has." Egan frowned. "What kind of fabric will you take, since the contact is expecting something?"

Guys, Killian linked with our pack. *Jewel and I are*

leaving with Sterlyn and Griffin to meet Tom's contact over an hour away. I hate to leave you here, but there's a lot to clean up, and we don't need humans stumbling over our dead. The vampires, the witches, Rosemary, Levi, Zagan, and Eleanor are staying with you. As long as we show up to meet the contact, the humans know what happened here, since Tom let it slip that he was the only one talking with the humans. Do you mind informing Sadie of what's going on?

Got it, Sierra quipped. *We'll let Sadie and the others know.*

"We have to figure out what to take." Sterlyn licked her lips. "We have to be careful. Whatever we take can't lead this contact here or to the Shadow City area, or it'll look suspicious."

This made things harder. "So we need to get a piece of clothing from someone who will leave this location, so they can't be tracked."

"Now that's something Jade and I can do." Egan removed his shirt, tossed it at Killian, and said, "You can use this. Jade and I can fly somewhere a decent distance away, so when the spell is performed, it won't seem strange."

Flying friends were the best.

Jade's pupils elongated. "You could've just ripped off a piece of your shirt. You didn't have to remove it from your body."

Beaming, Egan took her hand and replied, "You're the only one I have eyes for. Besides, all these women are mated. They aren't looking."

Thank gods Sierra wasn't here. I didn't need her riling up Jade.

"I'm enjoying the view," Lillith called from across the clearing as she dropped a wolf body into the grave.

"Watch it," Jade sneered. "You may be one of my best friends, but I don't have a problem hurting you."

Eliza shook her head and murmured, "She reminds me of Sierra." She then chanted to open up another grave for the shifters who were being carried over.

Lux smirked, enjoying the shenanigans.

"Let's shift and get some distance." Egan led Jade toward the woods, and surprisingly, she relented—probably because she wanted Egan to be hidden from everyone's view.

Tugging me toward the neighborhood, Killian shook his head. "Call us if you need anything."

"The same goes for you." Rosemary fluffed her wings. "We can be there quicker than anyone else, but there is a risk here of more enemies arriving."

"We'll keep everyone updated," Sterlyn vowed, and fell into step with Killian, Griffin, and me.

The four of us trudged toward the vehicles. The forest creatures seemed to be hiding, so the only noise was from the people in the clearing and the cool December breeze rustling the bare branches. The sun was already descending, the winter days short. It was likely only two in the afternoon, but after the injuries and the battle, it felt like midnight.

As the roofs came into view, my steps grew more urgent. I wanted to get out of here and away from all this craziness. Granted, we were heading into potentially more danger.

The vehicles appeared, and I noticed Torak and Sierra leaning against the hood of the Suburban closest to us. Torak kicked at the ground as Sierra glared at him.

She must still be upset with him for shooting at us earlier. I'd hoped that fighting as a team would bring her around, but clearly, it hadn't.

Griffin pursed his lips. "What's going on?"

Sierra pounded her chest. "I'm coming with you."

"No, *we're* coming with them." Torak stood straight and lifted his chin. "Sadie wants me to tag along in case something is said about the pack that lives here. Tom or the humans must have known something about them before they captured the pack. If the person we're meeting alludes to whatever Tom or the humans held against this pack, I might be able to figure out an appropriate answer so it's clear that I'm in Tom's inner circle."

Sterlyn opened the passenger door. "We can bring you back here afterward."

Torak shook his head. "Dad and Winter can pick me up halfway."

"Oh, are Daddy and Stepmommy gonna take care of you?" Sierra did some weird puckering movement with her lips.

Are you okay? Killian linked to her. *Or are you having a spasm?*

What? No. Sierra cut her gaze to him. *I was pretending to have a pacifier because he's acting like a baby.*

I had no words.

Killian's eyes glowed, indicating he was going to respond, but I touched his arm and linked to just him, *Let it go.*

Griffin's face twisted into a look of consternation, and he glanced at Killian. "I'm not sitting in the back with *that.*" He waved his hand between Sierra and Torak. "Toss me the keys."

Killian underhanded them. "And I don't want to hear you scream like a girl when I'm only turning onto a road. So yes, please drive."

For a second, things felt normal.

"I call sitting way in the back with Jewel," Sierra shouted, and ran to the back passenger door.

"*Not* happening." Killian's lips mashed into a line. "And I'll use my alpha will if you push the issue. Jewel will be back there with me."

Sierra rolled her eyes.

Placing his hands into his pockets, Torak quietly walked to the driver's-side back door. He was not engaging with Sierra, proving he was intelligent.

We all climbed in, and as promised, Killian and I sat at the very back. I laid my head on his shoulder, and Griffin turned the vehicle around.

"Hold on. I have to go over the curb to get around Tom's vehicles," Griffin called seconds before my body was jostled.

I didn't mind. All it did was push me more into Killian's arms. The buzzing between us ebbed the tension in my body, and I was finally able to relax. Somehow, we'd come out on top, even though we hadn't yet won.

WE RODE IN SILENCE, and the sign stating that our exit was just one mile away appeared.

Even Sierra was abnormally quiet, not singing random songs at the top of her lungs. Instead, she glared at Torak, who didn't seem to have a care in the world.

Hugging me more tightly, Killian asked, "What's the plan? We can't all show up there. Levi said only his most trusted pack member would show up."

"I looked at the satellite map. Griffin can drop us off at a vape store two blocks down from the gas station." Sterlyn glanced at us over her shoulder. "That way, we can do a quick survey before he heads there unprotected."

"Why Griffin?" Torak asked, leaning forward.

Glancing in the rearview mirror, Griffin answered, "Killian is all over the news, and they wouldn't expect a man like Tom to send a woman. And I'm already driving."

"Whatever." Torak shrugged. "I was just curious. I figured it wouldn't be me since I'm the only outsider here."

"If Griffin needs answers, he can link with me so we can get them from you." Sterlyn rubbed her hands down her thighs. "I hate that you're the one who's going to the meeting, though."

"Now you know how I feel every time I have to stay back and watch you." Griffin lifted a brow and turned his attention to the road.

I wished none of us had to do this. If people would just mind their own business, none of this would be happening. Rage and vendettas were the two reasons we were in this situation.

As Griffin turned onto the road, we drove past the Shell station. I begrudgingly pulled away from Killian so I could get a view of the gas station as well.

Scarlet red hair with black streaks caught my attention. My lungs stopped working.

"Oh, my god!" Sierra gasped. "There's no fucking way. Seriously, that bitch Erin is here."

With the lack of oxygen, I couldn't verbally agree, but there was one thing I knew for certain.

That *bitch* was going to die.

ABOUT THE AUTHOR

Jen L. Grey is a *USA Today* Bestselling Author who writes Paranormal Romance, Urban Fantasy, and Fantasy genres.

Jen lives in Tennessee with her husband, two daughters, and two miniature Australian Shepherds. Before she began writing, she was an avid reader and enjoyed being involved in the indie community. Her love for books eventually led her to writing. For more information, please visit her website and sign up for her newsletter.

Check out her future projects and book signing events at her website.
www.jenlgrey.com

Ruthless Moon

The Wolf Born Trilogy

Hidden Mate

Blood Secrets

Awakened Magic

The Hidden King Trilogy

Dragon Mate

Dragon Heir

Dragon Queen

The Marked Wolf Trilogy

Moon Kissed

Chosen Wolf

Broken Curse

Wolf Moon Academy Trilogy

Shadow Mate

Blood Legacy

Rising Fate

The Royal Heir Trilogy

Wolves' Queen

Wolf Unleashed

Wolf's Claim

Bloodshed Academy Trilogy

Year One

Year Two

Year Three

The Half-Breed Prison Duology (Same World As Bloodshed Academy)

Hunted

Cursed

The Artifact Reaper Series

Reaper: The Beginning

Reaper of Earth

Reaper of Wings

Reaper of Flames

Reaper of Water

Stones of Amaria (Shared World)

Kingdom of Storms

Kingdom of Shadows

Kingdom of Ruins

Kingdom of Fire

The Pearson Prophecy

Dawning Ascent

Enlightened Ascent

Reigning Ascent

Stand Alones

Death's Angel

Rising Alpha